POACHING IS PUZZLING

A Cookbook Nook Mystery

Daryl Wood Gerber

BEYOND THE PAGE
PUBLISHING

Poaching Is Puzzling
Daryl Wood Gerber
Copyright © 2023 by Daryl Wood Gerber
Cover design and illustration by Dar Albert, Wicked Smart Designs

Beyond the Page Books
are published by
Beyond the Page Publishing
www.beyondthepagepub.com

ISBN: 978-1-960511-14-0

Praise for Daryl Wood Gerber's
Cookbook Nook Mysteries

"There's a feisty new amateur sleuth in town and her name is Jenna Hart. With a bodacious cast of characters, a wrenching murder, and a collection of cookbooks to die for, Daryl Wood Gerber's *Final Sentence* is a page-turning puzzler of a mystery that I could not put down."

— Jenn McKinlay, *New York Times* bestselling author of
the Cupcake Mysteries and Library Lovers Mysteries

"In *Final Sentence*, the author smartly blends crime, recipes, and an array of cookbooks that all should covet in a witty, well-plotted whodunit."

— Kate Carlisle, *New York Times* bestselling
author of the Bibliophile Mysteries

"Readers will relish the extensive cookbook suggestions, the cooking primer, and the whole foodie phenomenon. Gerber's perky tone with a multigenerational cast makes this series a good match for Lorna Barrett's Booktown Mystery series . . ."

— *Library Journal*

"So pull out your cowboy boots and settle in for a delightful read. *Grilling the Subject* is a delicious new mystery that will leave you hungry for more."

— Carstairs Considers Blog

Books by Daryl Wood Gerber

The Cookbook Nook Mysteries

Final Sentence
Inherit the Word
Stirring the Plot
Fudging the Books
Grilling the Subject
Pressing the Issue
Wreath Between the Lines
Sifting Through Clues
Shredding the Evidence
Wining and Dying
Simmering with Resentment
Poaching Is Puzzling

The French Bistro Mysteries

A Deadly Éclair
A Soufflé of Suspicion

The Fairy Garden Mysteries

A Sprinkling of Murder
A Glimmer of a Clue
A Hint of Mischief

More Books by Daryl Wood Gerber

Suspense

Girl on the Run
Day of Secrets
Desolate Shores
Fan Mail
Cold Conviction

Writing as Avery Aames

The Long Quiche Goodbye
Lost and Fondue
Clobbered by Camembert
To Brie or Not to Brie
Days of Wine and Roquefort
As Gouda as Dead
For Cheddar or Worse

To my father, who introduced me to the wonderful world of crosswords,
and to my adorable husband, who enjoyed doing them with me.
What fun we had!

Cast of Characters

Bailey Bird Martinez, Jenna's best friend
Brianna Martinez, Baily's daughter
Bucky Winston, Cinnamon's husband
Cary Hart, Jenna's father
Charlene Grater, owner of Say Cheese Shoppe
Cinnamon Pritchett, chief of police
Eva Wainwright, publisher
Faith Fairchild, Flora's twin sister
Flora Fairchild, shop owner
Ginny, concierge at Crystal Cove Inn
Gran, Gracie Goldsmith, works at Cookbook Nook
Jake (Old Jake) Chapman, friend
Jenna Hart, owner of the Cookbook Nook
Katie Casey Landry, aka Chef Katie
Keller Landry, Katie's husband
Lola Bird, Bailey's mother and owner of Pelican Brief
Marlon Appleby, police deputy
Noam Dixon, professor
Pepper Pritchett, Cinnamon's mother and owner of
    Beaders of Paradise
Rhett Jackson, Jenna's husband and owner of Intime
Sunny Shore, crossword researcher
Tina Gump, sous chef at Pelican Brief
Tito Martinez, reporter and Bailey's husband
Ulysses Huxley, tournament participant
Vera Hart, Jenna's aunt
Wesley Preston, renowned cruciverbalist
Yvette Simms, Wesley's former fiancée
Z.Z. Zoey Zeller, mayor and realtor

Chapter 1

Cruciverbalist: crossword puzzle designer

"What's wrong?" I glanced at my aunt, the brightest woman I knew and the person who'd given me a new lease on life at the Cookbook Nook when my career at an advertising agency wasn't putting a smile on my face.

"Nothing," she murmured.

"Liar." I couldn't read tea leaves, but I could read her.

"*Pfft,*" she said dismissively.

"Talk to me," I said. She was the closest thing I had to a mother. Mine had passed away a number of years ago.

"I'm fine."

She and I were sitting at a table and sipping tea in our modest café that abutted the bookshop. The tables were set with white linens and vases of flowers. The view of the ocean through the windows was spectacular—not a cloud in the sky. The garlicky aroma of the prix fixe entrée shrimp risotto graced the air. The place was brimming with satisfied customers who were listening intently to the guest speaker, Wesley Preston. At the same time, the waitstaff was either refilling beverage requests, clearing tables of plates, or delivering a delicious array of petit fours.

"Is it the chatter or the clatter?" I asked.

"I might be twice your age, young lady, but my hearing is A-OK."

"I wasn't implying—"

"*Shh.*" She smoothed the lap of her silver Moroccan caftan and returned her attention to Wesley. When not running our culinary bookshop, she liked to do tarot card and palm readings and believed she should dress exotically for her customers.

"Is it Wesley?" I asked, tucking my chin-length hair behind my ears.

"No."

Wesley wasn't a handsome man, but he wasn't un-handsome, either. Though his face was narrow and his retro round wire-rimmed glasses were reminiscent of John Lennon's specs, he had a winsome, toothy smile, and his posture was impeccable—probably because he was vertically challenged, and the more erect he stood, the taller he appeared. His ensemble of pinstripe suit with a pen-and-pencil set poking from the handkerchief pocket made him look scholarly. His salt-and-pepper mustache added to the image.

"He's very cocky," I said. When Wesley had introduced himself as a crossword designer extraordinaire, he'd seemed smug. My aunt didn't like people who were full of themselves.

"With good reason. Stop pestering me."

Wesley motioned to the blackboard that I'd wheeled in for today's chat. Seven strips of colored paper were taped to the board in even horizontal lines. "If I might draw your focus to the front of the room . . ."

"Is it the crowd gathering in the parking lot that's got you flummoxed?" I asked, knowing I was crossing the line, bordering on pesky underling, but her lips were pressed into a thin line and her jaw was taut.

She didn't respond.

The attendees for the seminar had paid an admittance fee. Outside the restaurant, sunlight highlighted the growing throng of Wesley's fans waiting for him to emerge so he could autograph their crossword puzzle books.

"I can't believe the two of you haven't seen each other in nearly twenty years," I whispered. Earlier in the day my aunt had told me their history. They'd met in grade school and had gone to high school and college together. Over the years, they'd lost touch. "Especially since you're a cruciverbalist yourself," I added, loving how the word *cruciverbalist* — from *cruci*, meaning cross, and *verbalist*, meaning wordsmith — rolled off my tongue.

"Amateur," she murmured. "I'm an amateur cruciverbalist."

"Why haven't you reached out to him until now?"

"Because."

Wesley was in town to serve as emcee for Crystal Cove's popular Crossword Puzzle Tournament, held annually between Halloween and Thanksgiving at the Center, a convention-sized site located on the grounds of the community college. On Friday and Saturday, fifty solvers would participate in the competition. The fifty would be winnowed down to twenty-five based on their solving success, and on Sunday those twenty-five would vie for the trophy and a cash prize of twenty thousand dollars. Also on Sunday, the twenty-five finalists would have a chance to prove their mettle as cruciverbalists by creating an original puzzle, based on a given theme, to be announced that day. One of the would-be constructors could win a ten-thousand-dollar prize my aunt was putting up for the most imaginative puzzle. He or she would also score the chance to have that puzzle published in the *San Francisco Gazette*. Tomorrow night, Intime, my husband's French restaurant—how I enjoyed calling Rhett my husband; we'd married in June and had been living in wedded bliss ever since—would host a cocktail reception for the tournament participants and their guests.

For additional puzzling fun, Wesley had created daily puzzles that the puzzlers, audience, and us regular folk could try to solve starting tomorrow, Wednesday, and running through Saturday. Eight restaurants in town would be offering freebie appetizers or sweet treats—two establishments a day—to whomever solved the puzzles without erasures. The Nook Café and Latte Luck were on board for tomorrow. Brick's Barbecue and Taste of Heaven would host Thursday. Shredding and Mum's the Word would take Friday, and California Catch and Pelican Brief Saturday. All the shops in town, including ours, had copies of the puzzles, sorted by days, to hand out to participants.

This year's tournament theme was food, which was right up my alley. Not to create a foodie puzzle—I had no lofty dreams of becoming a puzzle constructor—but I couldn't wait to try my hand at deciphering the daily clues. For the event, I'd stocked a variety of crossword puzzle books as well as crossword solver's dictionaries at the shop. I was eager to return to see how they were selling.

"If you must know," my aunt began, "I meant to reach out to Wesley over the years, but I never mustered the courage."

"Why would you need courage?"

"The last time I saw him, I told him to get a life."

"Ooh. Why? What did he do?"

Aunt Vera didn't answer because she'd become transfixed with something across the room.

I followed her gaze and saw Noam Dixon, another of her grade school buddies, sitting at a table by himself. He'd come into the Cookbook Nook earlier, tripping over the carpet as he'd made his entrance.

At first glance, Noam, with his swoop of gray hair covering one eye, the knot of his paisley tie loosened, and the rumpled state of his plaid shirt, reminded me of an absentminded professor. Now, he was twisting and turning the top of his ballpoint pen repeatedly. The movement must have been making a sound because the woman to his right was giving him an annoyed look.

"C'mon, Aunt Vera, something else is bugging you," I said. "Spill. Is it Noam?"

"It's nothing." She toyed with her napkin and set it aside, turning her distracted attention to the single daisy in the petite vase. She ran her finger along the petals. "A memory best forgotten."

A memory? What memory? Why couldn't she confide in me?

My aunt patted my hand. "Quiet now."

"As any cruciverbalist knows," Wesley continued, his chest swelling with pride, "there are basic tips to creating a crossword puzzle. Number one . . ."

Everyone in the café was on tenterhooks, hoping to pick up a clue as to how he or she could come up with this year's winning puzzle. Wesley, my aunt, and our mayor would be the judges.

"First, think of the theme." Wesley removed the topmost strip of paper from the blackboard to reveal the advice he'd uttered.

A puzzle theme for foodies could be anything, my aunt had told me. Types of food, types of cooking styles, movies or books featuring food, and more.

"Write a long list of words" — Wesley peeled away another strip of paper to reveal his advice — "but then that's obvious, isn't it?" He amused himself so much that his mustache twitched with pleasure. "Remember to include words of varied length," he continued. "No two-letter words, of course, but you'll need plenty of three-letter words. They are the basic connectors for your longer answers." He rattled off a list. "Ale, are, era, eta, one, ore. The list is extensive."

"I remember the two of us going over a list of three-letter words in sixth grade," my aunt said to me. "How we delighted in coming up with clues for each. *One*, the last digit in a countdown. *One*, a digit in binary code. *One*, no longer divided. *One*, wedded." Her eyes glittered with enthusiasm. "Wesley eventually published a book of three-letter words."

"Were you two ever an item?" I asked.

"Heavens, no."

"Truth?"

Her cheeks tinged red. "Wesley was in love with another girl, Elyse. He had been since sixth grade. I didn't stand a chance. They became engaged in high school, and they married in their sophomore year of college, but it didn't last. They divorced a year later."

"Did you try to win his heart then?"

"Nope." She clucked her tongue. "By then, I'd fallen for another guy."

"The guy who left you at the altar?"

"No, not him. Way before him."

After the altar fiasco, she'd marched through life solo until she fell for Deputy Marlon Appleby.

"Did Wesley remarry?" I asked.

"Hush now." She patted my arm. "I want to listen."

While we'd been chatting, Wesley had removed two more strips from the blackboard. "Make sure you link words together in the center so they become one long word. They're the anchors for your puzzle. Next, create clues. Don't make them too verbose. Here's a clue for the answer *Rudy*. A man's name that rhymes with *foodie*."

The audience chuckled politely.

"If you need help coming up with possibilities, remember that the Internet is your best friend. On it, you'll find loads of word-themed sites." Wesley uncovered his final tip. "Do you want to write a museum-themed puzzle? You'll find a healthy list of related words online like *halls*, *art*, and *diorama*. How about animals? *Four-footed*, *hooved*, and *fauna*. History-themed? *Ancient*, *medieval*, and *illustrious past*."

Someone in the crowd *ooh*ed.

Wesley hoisted a finger. "Lastly, remember to get your facts right. For example, who wrote 'The pen is mightier than the sword'?"

A few hands rose.

"If you think William Shakespeare, you're wrong," he said.

Hands dropped. A few in the audience looked perplexed.

Wesley smirked. "Edward Bulwer-Lytton created the metonymic adage in 1839."

"Who?" the woman Noam had irritated chirped.

"He's the author who wrote the play *Richelieu; Or the Conspiracy*, and believed the written word was far more effective than violence for getting a point across."

"What's a metonymic adage?" a man in a bow tie asked.

"Ah, the better question is what is a metonym?" Wesley grinned. "It is a figure of speech in which a thing or concept is referred to by the name of the said thing or concept. The Pentagon is a perfect model of a metonym, referring to the U.S. military and its leadership, as well as to the building itself."

My aunt leaned into me. "He does like to flaunt his cleverness."

I detected a trace of bitterness in her tone and elbowed her. "C'mon, now, you've forgiven him for falling for someone else, haven't you?"

"Most definitely." She pulled a face. "Had we ended up together, we would have torn each other to shreds."

Chapter 2

Puzzle: enigma, riddle, conundrum, poser, dilemma

When the event disbanded and the majority of the fans exited the café, my aunt clasped my elbow and approached Wesley.

"Vera! So good to see you." He air-kissed her on both cheeks. "You look radiant."

My aunt murmured her thanks. "This is my niece, Jenna. She and I own the Cookbook Nook and this charming café."

"Yes, we met earlier when I asked her to prepare the display board. A pleasure." Wesley took hold of my hand and in a courtly gesture kissed the back of it. I was towering over him but he didn't seem flummoxed by my height.

"Wesley." An athletic and leggy sixty-something woman with a stylish silver haircut approached him, arms outstretched. Her gaze flickered with feistiness.

I stepped back to allow them space.

"How nice to see you in person after all this time. It's been too long." The woman clutched Wesley's shoulders and held him at arms' length. Like me, she was about a head taller than he was.

"Eva." Wesley air-kissed her as he had my aunt. "You look lovely, as always."

She released him and fingered the lapels of her mocha, drape-collared jacket. "Thank you. It's Valentino."

I gulped. The cost of an outfit like hers would use up my entire yearly budget for clothes.

"You, on the other hand, look too thin, my love," Eva said. "Are you eating well?"

"Well enough." He cocked his head. "How long are you in town?"

"For the whole event."

My aunt cleared her throat.

"I'm sorry," Wesley said. "Eva Wainwright, this is an old friend of mine, Vera Hart, and her niece, Jenna. Eva is the brilliant editor of the puzzles and entertainment section of the *San Francisco Gazette*."

"I'm impressed, Miss Wainwright," my aunt said. "Your eye for great puzzles knows no bounds."

"I appreciate the compliment." Eva's dulcet Southern accent

could win over the coldest heart.

"I read the news online, but I print out the puzzles daily," my aunt went on. "The Sunday puzzles are harder to do, purely because the boxes are so small. I need a magnifying glass."

"I've pressed my boss to enlarge them, to no avail," Eva said. "Um, forgive me for intruding, but"—she stepped forward and clutched Wesley's elbow—"we need to talk. Urgent business."

"My fans are waiting." He motioned to the throng outside.

"They'll have to kill time a bit longer." She guided him to a far corner of the café.

I noticed Noam Dixon watching the two of them circumspectly over the rim of his teacup and tamped down a giggle. Dress the guy in a black suit and fedora and he could have been mistaken for a covert spy.

Katie, the chef at the café and a dear friend of mine, hustled up to my aunt and me. Her curls were tucked beneath her toque. Her white chef's coat was splattered with something as yellow as the flowers of her skirt. Katie never cared about being a fashion plate. She was devoted to focusing on flavors and textures that stimulated one's palate. "Are you ready for the taste testing, Jenna? I can be prepared to go in ten minutes."

The Nook Café, as one of the eight participating restaurants, would reward puzzle solvers by offering finger food appetizers. As an added bonus, later in the week, Katie would give a class at the Cookbook Nook about how to proof bread and make hot cross buns, which she said was an inspired idea, given the crossword puzzle theme—*cross* and *crossword*. I'd cautioned her that teaching folks how to make a proper dough might be too adventuresome in the time allotted for her sessions, but she wouldn't be dissuaded. She'd make it work. Katie was nothing if not enthusiastic.

"How about I come over in thirty minutes?" I said. "I have to wind up a few things at the shop. Two shipments just came in."

"Okay. FYI, later I have to pick up Min-yi at day care." Katie and her husband had adopted their daughter Min-yi when she was three months old. Whenever she was with the girl, she beamed with pure love. "Reynaldo will man the kitchen."

"I'm so glad you trust him," I said. He was the executive chef who reported to Katie.

"He's a gem."

"Which appetizers will you be serving?" I asked.

"We're trying out fiery chicken empanadas, salmon-prosciutto bites, and one other."

"Yum." I adored anything made with salmon. "Can't wait."

I walked through the enclosed breezeway connecting the café to the Cookbook Nook and greeted Bailey Bird, my best friend, an inspired salesclerk, and limited partner in the shop. I was so thankful she'd decided to work for me and my aunt. She had an outgoing personality and a steel-trap memory. She didn't seem upset to have been asked to work on her day off. As always, she was smiling as she chatted with a pair of women by the front display table, where I'd set out two of my favorite cookbooks, *Beautiful Boards: 50 Amazing Snack Boards for Any Occasion*, and *Small Bites: Skewers, Sliders, and Other Party Eats*. Because the town restaurants were offering free appetizers or desserts to crossword puzzle solvers, I'd decided that the featured cookbooks in the shop should focus on those, too.

"Meow!" Tigger, my rescue ginger cat, scampered to me and rubbed against my ankles while peering up at me with his gorgeous eyes.

I bent to pet him. "Yes, I missed you, too." I'd barely been gone an hour, but Tigger, who at times acted more like a dog than a cat, loved to connect with me. When he'd had his fill of petting, he leaped onto the three-story kitty condo my father had made him and promptly fell asleep.

"Jenna." Gran, aka Gracie Goldsmith, waved to me from the sales counter. When I'd first met her, she'd been accompanied by her granddaughters and said everyone called her Gran; it wasn't until I'd hired her part-time that I'd discovered her first name was Gracie. Like Bailey and me, she had donned a light knit sweater, but hers had probably cost five times what ours had. "The delivery guy stowed the boxes of books in the stockroom."

"Excellent."

To the left of the sales counter, beyond Tigger's kitty condo, was the stockroom. In the middle of the Cookbook Nook there were a half dozen moveable bookshelves, each featuring cookbooks arranged by theme. On the far wall we'd set shelving to hold all sorts of culinary items, like one-of-a-kind colorful spatulas and arty cookie jars. In keeping with this week's theme, I'd found two cute jars featuring a *New York Times* crossword puzzle—one in red and one in white. On eBay, I'd also found puzzle-themed salt and pepper shakers and a cream and sugar set. Why not go all out if I could? Our customers loved kitsch. Beyond the salt and pepper shakers hung a variety of aprons on hooks. Of course, the most popular this week was the white linen one with a blank crossword grid on it. So cute! By the front door stood a vintage kitchen table where we typically set out food-themed jigsaw puzzles for customers to fiddle with. This week's puzzle, however, was a colorful one featuring all sorts of games, cards, and dominos.

"Also," Gran said, "I'm afraid one of the customers raided the display window. She absolutely had to have the crossword solver's dictionary."

"Oh, no." It had taken all day yesterday for me to put the window display together. I'd installed a crossword cookie jar, an apron, a couple of crossword puzzle books, an array of pencils and pens with erasers, and a spray of white and black flowers. "Didn't she see the ones on the display table?"

I'd added a specialty table temporarily for the extra books we'd needed to order. Alongside the dictionaries, I'd slyly positioned copies of *Hungry Games*, in which former food editor Kate Heddings toyed with her audience and purposely made her recipes have errors, forcing the reader to fix what was wrong. She paired those with crossword puzzles and word search games. I'd bought a copy for myself.

"I pointed it out to her," Gran said, "but by then, it was too late. She'd pulled it free and had toppled the vase of flowers."

Luckily, the flowers were silk so the vase hadn't held any water.

"I'll spruce it up in a minute," I said.

Tourists that came to Crystal Cove adored window shopping. Creating beautiful displays to lure them inside was vital to our business.

"How was the seminar?" Bailey asked, tugging the hem of her aqua-blue sweater over the waistband of her trousers.

"Smooth. Effortless. Painless."

She wrinkled her nose. "What are you, a walking *Roget's*

Thesaurus now? Keep it to fifty-cent words or less for my benefit, okay?"

"Ha-ha!"

"Nice sweater," she noted.

"Thanks." My outfit consisted of a crochet-knit burgundy sweater over a tank top, skinny jeans, and sandals. Something about the November season made me want to stick with fall colors. I'd wear plenty of red come the Christmas holiday. "It's the ideal texture for a day like today."

In Crystal Cove, we rarely had to dress warmly. Located on the coast of California and bordered by the Santa Cruz Mountains, our town was blessed with a moderate, Mediterranean-type climate. In fact, there was no rain in the forecast for at least a week.

"Ladies!" Flora Fairchild strode into the shop, her single long braid bouncing on her shoulder. "I finished the first puzzle!"

"Already?" I asked. "It's not official until tomorrow."

"You know me. I like to get a jump on things."

Flora, the owner of Home Sweet Home, a charming home goods shop on Buena Vista Boulevard, was a regular at the Cookbook Nook. She hoisted a number 2 pencil with a pristine eraser into the air. "I usually do my crosswords in pen because I don't mind making mistakes, but I'll use a pencil from now on. It's so lovely to see a puzzle with no scratch outs, don't you think?" She flaunted her puzzle but quickly turned it around to face her and pressed it against her bejeweled hand-knit sweater. "No peeking. You'll have to solve yours yourself." She chortled. "By the by, I saw Wesley Preston outside." She hooked her thumb over her shoulder.

As I was chatting with Gran, I'd noted Wesley moving outside to greet his fans and sign their crossword puzzle books. Now, I couldn't see him through the throng. I didn't see his editor, Eva, either. They must have concluded their business.

"He's dreamy," Flora said.

"Don't let your fiancé hear you say that," I teased. She'd recently become engaged to the assistant pastor at her church.

"Stop." Flora swatted my arm. "I'm allowed to appreciate other men. Admiring is harmless." She giggled as if she'd said one of the funniest things in the world.

Her laughter was topped by laughter in the breezeway. Wesley had abandoned his admirers and had reconnected with my aunt. The two of them passed into the shop through the archway.

"Here we are." My aunt released Wesley's arm and flourished a hand. "My shop. I mean *our* shop," she revised. "Jenna's and mine."

"It's just as I pictured it." Wesley moseyed to the display table and ran a finger along the top rim of one of the books. "Orderly, well laid out, and sensible."

"Sensible? Yes, that's me now," Aunt Vera said. "But I wasn't years ago. Remember when we were at summer camp, and I adopted a squirrel?"

"It ate your trail mix."

"And nearly gnawed through my sleeping bag."

Wesley sniggered. "Do you recall when we were eleven, and I started collecting pencil nubs, and I boasted about how cool I was during lunch?"

"Oh, my, yes. Harold Marsh made such fun of you."

"Good old Marshmallow." He laughed.

"He dubbed you Lead Head for a full month. If I recollect, your mother, when she was making us mayonnaise and olive sandwiches, said" — she raised a finger and intoned — "braggarts never prosper."

"Good old Mom. Mixing her metaphors, per usual." Wesley moved to inspect the crossword puzzle cookie jars and paused. He spun to face my aunt, his brow puckered. "You know, Vera, I'm wondering why you didn't do more with your life than purchasing this shopping mall and opening this shop and the café."

Flora gulped so loudly I heard it. I eyed my aunt. She'd turned ashen. Wesley's insult had clearly caught her off guard. Most likely, she'd expected a compliment from him for all her accomplishments, not a dig.

Aunt Vera arched an eyebrow. "Do more?"

"You have an incredible brain. I expected you to become a scientist. A doctor. Someone who would save the world. Not . . . a proprietor of a bookshop and diner."

"We have enough saints," she said acidly. "I wanted to provide the world with a place to savor books, and I wanted to give them a *café*" — she stressed the word — "with food that would tantalize their taste buds."

"Admit it, though," Wesley said, seemingly oblivious to her

12

pique, "if you'd applied yourself, you could have been someone important."

"I'll have you know I am important. Fisherman's Village is a sought-after location and earns a steady income. The shop and café do nicely, too."

"Yes, of course. I meant important in the crossword world."

"Is that your measuring stick?" Aunt Vera snorted. "Well, if you hadn't stolen my mythology-themed puzzle and published it as your own, perhaps I would have excelled."

Wesley sputtered. "Me? A thief? Why, I never!"

"Uh-oh," Flora said under her breath.

I flicked her arm with a fingertip. *Shh.*

"I came up with the one for mythology," Wesley said.

"No siree." My aunt shot a finger at him.

The way she was glowering made me shudder. Was that what she'd been referring to earlier? Was the stolen puzzle the memory best forgotten?

"You didn't know the difference between the Greeks and Romans," my aunt went on. "You barely knew who Aesop was, let alone Persephone, goddess of the underworld, or Zeus, the god who rules Mount Olympus, or Prometheus, the only Titan that sided with Zeus against Cronus."

"I knew all of those things." Wesley guffawed. "Give credit where credit's due, Vera. You know I came up with that puzzle."

"It was mine from the first clue."

"Over my dead body."

"Hack," my aunt hissed. "Plodder, lackey."

"Flunky, grind, drudge."

"Poser, imposter, fraud."

"Oh, yeah?" Wesley worked his tongue between his teeth. "Well, I'm rubber, and you're glue—"

"Whatever you say bounces off me and sticks to you," my aunt finished.

Flora and I exchanged a worried look. Were my aunt and Wesley serious? They sounded like they were back in grade school. I caught Bailey staring at them. Gran, too.

Wesley fixed his gaze on my aunt. His hands fisted and unfurled. And then, after a long moment, he burst into laughter.

13

"You jokester." My aunt slugged his arm and giggled.

Wesley laughed harder.

Aunt Vera said to me and the others, "Wesley and I have always enjoyed sparring. We've had some legendary matches, haven't we?" Her smartwatch buzzed. "Oh, my, we're late. Wesley, I've got to get you to the Theater on the Pier. We need to do a tech rehearsal before the chat." She rushed to the sales counter, fetched her purse, and nabbed Wesley's arm. He didn't resist. "Jenna, Flora, we'll see you there."

"I wouldn't miss it," Flora said, smashing her lips together as if she couldn't wait to tell everyone in town about the fracas she'd just witnessed.

Chapter 3

Poach: (verb) boil, steam, simmer; (verb) thieve, pilfer, plunder

Relieved that the exchange between my aunt and Wesley was nothing more than a silly rehashing of their childhood feuds, I spent the next few minutes refreshing the window display, and then went to the Nook Café to sample Katie's appetizers. The kitchen was abuzz with activity. Katie was supervising the sous chef, who was assembling salads.

I crossed to them and said, "It smells divine in here, as always."

"What's not to love about fried fish?" Katie said and smiled. "The café is so busy after this morning's seminar that we had to add two salads and three additional sandwiches to the menu. Otherwise, we'd run out of supplies for the daily specials."

I loved how she could adjust to a situation in a flash.

"Follow me." She beckoned me and made her way to the chef's corner at the rear of the kitchen. "Feast your eyes." She brandished a hand.

On the table were three trays of appetizers. The salmon-prosciutto bites were topped with a healthy dollop of a cream cheese–chive mixture. The empanadas looked crisp and inviting.

"Oh, yum!" I said. "They're beautiful. What are those?" I pointed to small fried disks surrounding a bowl of pale green dip. "Are they crab cakes?"

"Nope. Zucchini patties with dill sauce. Sit. Taste. I found the recipe in a book from the shop. *Salsas and Dips: Over 100 Recipes for the Perfect Appetizers, Dippables, and Crudités.*"

She fetched a simple white plate and napkin and handed them to me along with a pair of tongs. I selected two of each appetizer and sat on a nearby stool. First, I dunked a zucchini patty into the dip and popped it into my mouth. "Oh, man. So good." I bit into a salmon-prosciutto bite, which was still warm, and I gushed with praise. "You have outdone yourself with these selections, my friend. The empanadas are zesty and fun, too," I said around a mouthful of one. They were packed with beans and jalapeños. "I'm so glad you didn't put cilantro in them. You know me and cilantro."

"You're one of the rare few who thinks it tastes like soap."

"With this assortment"—I waved a hand over the tray of goodies—"the Nook is certain to be a hit with successful crossword puzzlers."

Katie curtsied.

"Please give me the recipe for each."

"Better yet, I'll show you how to make them."

"Aren't you due to pick up Min-yi?"

"In an hour and a half."

I checked my watch. "Let's do it. I've got time until I have to be at the theater."

"Slap on an apron."

I'd always had a good palate, but I wasn't a stellar cook, although I was better than I used to be because both Rhett and Katie were teaching me how to improve, one meal at a time.

With Katie as my guide, I learned how to roll out phyllo dough for the empanadas and how to finely chop zucchini so it would smoosh well with panko. I also learned how to snip dill with scissors and how to fry salmon-prosciutto bites without splattering myself with sizzling hot butter.

When I'd completed making a round of appetizers, Katie bumped my hip with hers. "Not bad."

"Who are you kidding? I did an excellent job." I swept a hand over my masterpieces. They weren't remotely good enough to serve to our customers, but they would do in a pinch for Rhett and me.

"Your mom would be so proud of you."

"Yes, she would." My mother had done all of the cooking when I was growing up and had never brought me into the equation. My sister had picked up the skill because she was crafty.

"By the way," Katie said, "did you notice that none of the recipes had more than ten ingredients?"

"I did."

A couple of years ago when she'd given me five-ingredient recipes to tackle and then ten-ingredient recipes, saying that they were merely two five-ingredient ones, I'd found my confidence.

I gave my friend a hug, thanked her for the lesson, and headed back to the shop. A half hour later, I nabbed Bailey, and we went to the Pier to watch my aunt interview Wesley Preston.

The Pier, located at the south end of town, was a wonderful boardwalk filled with shops, eateries, a theater, and carney-style games. Fishing was a big draw as an activity in Crystal Cove, so there were boat rentals as well as sunset cruises available. The Theater on the Pier, which was located past Mum's the Word, one of my favorite diners, was set up like an old saloon with small wooden tables, footlights jutting up from the apron of the semicircular stage, and plush red brocade drapes framing the wings.

As we entered, we presented our tickets to a young woman, who handed us a crossword puzzle and pencils and ushered us to our table.

I spotted Noam Dixon seated at one of the front tables. He was tapping his pen as if primed to ask questions. I recognized a few other spectators because my aunt had shown me a playbill of the festival's participants. Eva Wainwright was sitting at the table to the right of Noam's. Sunny Shore, a woman in her forties who had helped Wesley research his puzzles, was alone at a table two back from Eva's. My aunt thought Sunny might be a shoo-in to win this week's tournament, saying she was very clever. Ulysses Huxley, a local who happened to be a renowned crossword puzzle solver, was at the table beyond Sunny's. Aunt Vera told me he'd won many time-sensitive competitions, and now he was purportedly trying his hand at designing puzzles.

Tito Martinez, Bailey's husband and a savvy reporter for the *Crystal Cove Courier*, was talking to Ulysses. The two were polar opposites. Tito was short, compact, and swarthy. Ulysses, who was tall and muscular with a strong jaw and prominent brow, could have been mistaken for an aging Norse adventurer. He swiped a meaty hand through his silver-blond locks as he answered Tito's relentlessly dogged questions.

Bailey waved to her husband, who acknowledged her with a brief nod, and continued on. A waitress brought us water and asked for our orders. Typically when Bailey and I attended an event at the theater, we drank wine, but for this one, we opted for sparkling water. We would need clear heads if we were to get through the rest of the day.

At the rear of the room, I noticed Flora sitting with her sister Faith. Both women were avid puzzlers. Faith, an amateur artist like her sister, was an artist's representative. Recently she'd sold all of the work of a talented young man who was murdered last year. As a result of that coup, five new artists had hired her to represent them. One was selling particularly well with watercolor seascapes of the coast of California. Though Flora and her sister were twins, the two sported completely different hairstyles. In addition, Faith preferred flashy, form-fitting clothing while Flora chose subtler, looser styles. A waitress brought them champagne in crystal flutes and returned to us with our beverages.

Bailey said, sotto voce, "I suppose for the Fairchild sisters, this is a cause for celebration. I've heard Faith has been swooning over meeting Wesley Preston, and he's not taken."

"He's not?"

"Nope. According to the articles I read, he is, indeed, single at the moment."

"You've been reading up on him?"

"Yep. I'm a fan, too." She sipped her sparkling water and set the glass down. "In fact, I did a deep dive. He married his childhood sweetheart—"

"But they divorced a year later," I said. "My aunt told me."

"Right. Then in graduate school, he fell for a woman named Yvette Simms, a photojournalist. They dated for nearly three years until it ended abruptly—no reason given—and he's been single ever since."

"Hmm." I wondered if that was the memory that had been nagging my aunt.

"One of the articles said since his failed marriage he has been intent on finding the love of his life and has been loath to settle for less."

"Sounds like he's hard to please."

"*Difficult* a few customers told me at the shop." Bailey snickered. "Others said picky, fickle, and fussy."

I laughed. "Leave it to crossword enthusiasts to come up with that string of adjectives."

"One woman joked that he has a Napoleon complex, you know, the small man syndrome, and tries to overcompensate with a domineering personality."

Over a loud speaker, a man said, "Good afternoon, everyone. Wesley Preston, here. You've each been given a puzzle. Try to finish it before we begin. Good luck."

Bailey and I hunkered down. I was stumped by a few clues, but I pressed ahead knowing I'd correctly answered the surrounding answers. The missing words would come to me. Hopefully.

Fifteen minutes later, the curtains opened to reveal a stage set with a pair of ruby red, brocade armchairs and a table positioned between them holding a pitcher of water and two crystal tumblers. My aunt emerged from the wings carrying a cordless microphone and a notepad. She checked the volume of her microphone with the audio technician. When she was cleared to begin, she sat in the leftmost brocade armchair and said, "Welcome, everyone. Seeing all of your eager faces, I'm pretty sure I don't need to introduce our guest. You all know who he is. Many of you revere him." That drew laughter. "For those who might not be up to date on his history, let me quickly state that Wesley Ewan Preston comes from humble means. He didn't go to Harvard or Yale. He grew up here in Crystal Cove, and ultimately attended University of the Pacific, as did I."

My aunt had raved about the liberal arts as well as business education she'd received.

"He graduated with honors and went on to become a crossword prodigy. He's been published in the *New York Times*, *Los Angeles Times*, *Washington Post*, and many more, including the *Onion*."

More laughter. The *Onion* wasn't considered a serious newspaper. It published satirical articles, parodying the tone of traditional news. I enjoyed reading pieces in it occasionally, especially the man-on-the-street interviews.

"But let's dig right in. Please welcome Wesley Ewan Preston." Aunt Vera rose to her feet, as did the audience, all of whom were applauding enthusiastically.

Wesley sauntered onto the stage, adjusting the knot of his tie, though it didn't need it. He waited through a solid minute of appreciative applause before taking his seat. Smoothly, he crossed his legs and regarded my aunt.

"Wesley," she began, "let's begin with your early years. When did you become—"

"Hold on, Vera. I'm sure our audience is eager to find out the answers to the puzzle they received upon entering, wouldn't you?" He surveyed the audience right to left. "For example, what in the heck is the six-letter answer for snacks? Snacks is a pretty generic clue, right?"

I bobbed my head, still mystified.

"*Eats* is too short," he went on. "So is *bites*. How about *morsels*? Nope, that's seven letters."

Some audience members grumbled, as mystified as I was.

Wesley chuckled. "Sometimes, when coming up with the answer to a clue, you have to look outside the norm. Perhaps using vernacular. Did anyone come up with the word *noshes*?"

Everyone groaned.

"I feel so stupid," I whispered to Bailey. "I had the *o* and the *s*."

Wesley sat back in his chair, smiling. "Now to your question, Vera. When I was five, the teacher handed out large pieces of paper. The girls would draw houses and unicorns and flowers. The boys drew weapons and dinosaurs. I, however, drew mazes."

"Mazes?"

"Yes. Really complex ones. I think those are what inspired me to make my first spiral crossword puzzle."

A spiral puzzle consisted of a long chain of letters that spelled out clued words when read in either direction. I'd never been able to complete one.

"What is it about crossword puzzles that draws you to them?" my aunt asked.

"I think it's the way the elements work in unison, like music."

"You're a musician, aren't you?"

"Yes. I play the piano and a couple of other instruments. I'm darned good on the kazoo."

That earned him more laughter.

My aunt referred to her notebook. "Tell us what it's like to attend the American Crossword Puzzle Tournament."

The tournament was held annually in the early spring. Founded by Will Shortz, it was the oldest and largest tournament in the United States. A couple of years ago, the event set an attendance record with over seven hundred competitors and two hundred rookies.

"Are you recognized?" my aunt asked. "Are you a superstar there, like you are here?"

Wesley nudged his glasses higher on the bridge of his nose and offered a toothy grin. "If I'm honest, I'm sort of like Han Solo at a *Star Wars* convention."

My aunt tittered. "You mean, you're swarmed by fans?"

"Something like that."

The questions continued. At one point, my aunt asked Wesley his favorite *crosswordese*, meaning words frequently found in puzzles but rarely used in everyday conversation.

"Sere, meaning dry," he replied. "Olio, meaning a miscellaneous collection of things. *Omoo*, a narrative of adventures in the South Seas."

"Written by Melville," my aunt said.

"Correct. The list continues. Etui, anoa, erne, nene." He adjusted the lapels of his jacket.

"Could you give us an example of a spanner, you know, the words that cruciverbalists rely on to get them out of a consonant-jammed corner?"

"Jai alai with Yoko Ono or Brian Eno, anyone?" Wesley joked.

The attendees roared with enthusiasm.

"We are all appreciative of your expertise," my aunt said. "Let's allow a few in the audience to ask a question or two."

"Fire away." Wesley turned in his chair to fully face the crowd.

Hands flew up. Wesley picked Sunny Shore, who stood, tucking her shaggy hair behind her ears before smoothing the seams of her olive green sweater dress. She was willowy, about my height, with an impish, sassy face. "Hi, I'm Sunny—"

"Hold on!" Ulysses Huxley shouted, and bounded to his feet. "Me, first."

The onlookers gasped. Wesley's gaze smoldered with malice.

21

Chapter 4

Antagonism: hatred, bitterness, antipathy

"Sit down!" Wesley barked. "We'll get to you."

"No, you won't," Ulysses said. "You'll skip over me like you always do."

I saw Flora murmuring to Faith. My aunt started rubbing the phoenix amulet she wore around her neck, a habit she resorted to whenever she was flustered or concerned.

"Sit!" Wesley commanded. His neck had reddened. The flush was creeping into his cheeks. Evidently, he was not a fan of Ulysses Huxley. "Sit, or you can bet I will ignore you."

Ulysses glowered, held his ground for a long moment, his antagonism palpable, but finally sank into his chair and began drumming the table with his fingertips.

"Now, Sunny" — Wesley offered a tight smile — "your turn."

Sunny cleared her throat. "I'm Sunny Shore."

"Yes, yes." Wesley rotated a hand. "I know who you are."

"Well, you know who I am, but they don't." She gestured to the audience. "I'm a crossword puzzle researcher."

"And an amazing violinist, mathematician, and amateur inventor," Wesley said. "Sunny has been working on coming up with edible popcorn bags."

That received a host of hoots and whistles.

"I believe she's also concocting an edible power bar wrapper."

"Same thing as the other," Sunny said. "What I wanted to ask — "

"Researchers can be extremely creative," Wesley added.

"And underfunded," Sunny said. "My question — "

My aunt said into her microphone, "For clarification, a crossword puzzle researcher will often create a list of words specific to a theme and share those lists with cruciverbalists. Miss Shore is brilliant at this."

Sunny muttered her thanks and continued. "Mr. Preston, who are some of your heroes?"

"Other than Arthur Wynne?"

"Wynne published the first crossword puzzle," my aunt interjected. "In the *New York World* on December 21, 1913. He'd dubbed it a word-cross."

"Other than him." Sunny tucked her hair behind her right ear again, even though it didn't need tucking. Bailey did the same thing when she was nervous.

"Let see, there's Patrick Berry," Wesley said. "His masterpieces are published on Fridays and Saturdays. Also Michael Shenk, the editor of the *Wall Street Journal*."

"Don't you admire any women like, you know, Elizabeth Gorski?" Sunny asked. "She's well known for her crafty grids."

Wesley cleared his throat. "Yes, of course. Miss Gorski," he said tightly, as if it pained him to do so.

"And your editor, Eva Wainwright?" Sunny acknowledged her.

Eva swiveled in her chair, waving to the onlookers like a princess on a float.

"Naturally," Wesley said. "Eva, rise, my dear."

She did.

"Eva is my editor, everyone. A marvelous woman who is fierce with a red pencil."

The audience applauded.

"Sit, Eva."

She obeyed.

"And me?" Sunny raised a hand. "Do you hold me in high regard?"

"Well, you, yes, of course."

"In that case, how come you haven't paid me recently?"

The audience gawked at her. So did Eva. My aunt blinked. Wesley slid a finger between the knot of his tie and shirt and gave a small tug.

"Why no response?" Sunny taunted. "Are you out of excuses? Pretexts? Defenses?"

"We'll discuss this later," Wesley said curtly.

"No, sir, now."

"It's not the time or place, Miss Shore. We'll discuss our business matter at the inn. As planned. Next question," Wesley said, cutting her off. "You. Noam."

Sunny huffed, kicked back her chair, yanked her oversized khaki-colored tote onto her shoulder, and stomped out of the building. At the same time, Noam Dixon rose to his feet. His shirt was still rumpled. His hair looked windblown. He had his ballpoint pen out, but unlike Tito, he wasn't prepared to write an article about today's chat. I wondered if his pen served as a device to help him stay calm, like a fidget spinner.

"Everyone," Wesley went on, undaunted, "meet Noam Dixon, one of my oldest friends."

"And mine," my aunt chimed in.

"Noam is an English professor at UC Berkeley," Wesley said. "Don't ask him about Geoffrey Chaucer and *The Canterbury Tales*, or he'll start talking and bore you to tears for hours."

"He will not bore you," my aunt said, coming to Noam's defense. "He'll charm you. He knows Chaucer like the back of his hand. For those who aren't familiar, *The Canterbury Tales* are about a storytelling contest where a traveling group of pilgrims head off to visit the shrine of Saint Thomas Becket. Do I have that right?"

Noam nodded. "Chaucer was seminal in the popularization of the English vernacular."

"Okay, okay," Wesley said. "I'm here to educate these folks, not you. What do you want to ask me, Noam?"

"How do you feel about Will Shortz?"

Wesley beamed as if he'd expected his friend to tee up the question. "I'll always be grateful that he created the World Puzzle Federation. Brilliant man."

"Do you—"

"My turn, Dixon." Ulysses bounded to his feet again. "Mr. Preston, what one or two words do you find hard to clue? I mean, we all like to see new clues, not the old tried and true."

Wesley pursed his lips. He lasered a scathing look at Ulysses.

Ulysses coughed out a smug laugh and shoved his hands into his pockets. Waiting.

"To be honest, I can't find a new clue for ale," Wesley said. "Suds, grog, malt, lager, porter, on tap." He ticked them off on his fingertips. "Yes, the list is endless, but they've all been used, ad nauseum. Please sit down."

"How about the clue *rhymes with nail?*"

"Too nonspecific," Wesley chided. "You'll only solve that once you've filled the squares around it."

"Unless I guess."

"And if you guess wrong, you have an erasure. This week's daily puzzles require there be no erasures." Wesley formed a zero with his fingers.

"I never have erasures," Ulysses said.

Really? I had never solved a puzzle without at least one. I tried not to mess up, but there was often one clue that tripped me up. A textbook example, in this morning's *Courier* puzzle, the clue was *check out quickly*. It started with *pe*. Six letters. I was certain it was *peruse* and jotted it in. But I was wrong. It turned out to be *peek at*. And I had to erase it. Dang.

Wesley said, "Guessing is unscientific, Mr. Huxley. You must always *know* before you put anything in a crossword puzzle box."

"For those who aren't familiar with me" — Ulysses turned to the audience in the same way Sunny had — "I'm a puzzle solver for a lot of cruciverbalists. In fact, I'm Wesley Preston's guinea pig for each new puzzle he creates."

"Guinea pig is a bit strong," Wesley countered.

Ulysses made a snorting sound.

"Okay, that's enough, Ulysses. Cut it out with the antics. This is my interview. My time to shine. Sit." Wesley motioned.

"Or else?"

"'The graveyards are full of indispensable men,'" Wesley intoned.

"Oho. A quote attributed to Charles de Gaulle," Ulysses said. "Good one."

"Sit." Wesley glowered at him.

Ulysses pulled his hands from his pockets. "Why are you cutting me off so soon, Mr. Preston? Are you feeling vulnerable?" He puffed up his chest, almost daring Wesley to lash out again.

"Actually, I'm feeling rather . . . *witty*." He stressed the word and narrowed his gaze. "Can't say the same for you."

Ulysses flinched, as if Wesley had struck him. He plopped into his chair with a huff.

"Noam, it's your turn," Wesley said, dismissing Ulysses. "Did you have something more to ask?"

Off to my right, Faith was talking to her sister under her breath. Flora seemed concerned by Faith's words. Faith flicked her sister on the arm.

"Noam, did you hear me?" Wesley asked.

Noam had resumed his seat and was clicking his ballpoint pen. Was the man always in motion?

My aunt said, "Noam, ask away."

Noam shrugged docilely in response. "That's okay. I'm good."

Ulysses waved a hand like a kid who knew the right answer.

But Wesley didn't acknowledge him. Instead, he chose a young woman with blue ombre hair. "You, miss."

"Which three games, other than crosswords, do you suggest to sharpen your mind?" She held up three fingers.

"Scattergories, Scrabble, and word searches." Wesley pointed to a man in a flashy Hawaiian shirt. "You, sir."

"Which three attributes make a good crossword puzzler?" The man folded his arms as if he'd provided a poser.

"A complete knowledge of language, spelling, and trivia." Wesley scanned the theater.

No one else's hand shot into the air.

Given the lull, Ulysses Huxley took to the floor again. "Mr. Preston, on a personal note, I hear you're a devoted nocturnal birdwatcher. Care to tell us about that predilection?"

Wesley scowled. "I don't consider it a predilection."

"A penchant or a fondness, then," Ulysses said, his lips curling into a sneer, like he was determined to goad our guest. "An affection. A proclivity. Do you look for owls?"

"Yes."

"Nighthawks? Nightjars?"

"Yes and yes."

"Isn't it true that you think nighttime birds are like vampires without the bloodsucking? Is that the allure for you, to see the bird conquer its prey? To watch it rip its quarry to shreds with its talons? To wait until it dominates its target, leaving the poor sap with no more fight left in it?"

Wesley shifted uncomfortably in his seat.

"Do you identify with this kind of bird?" Ulysses asked.

Wesley exchanged an anxious look with my aunt. Had Ulysses Huxley pressed some kind of emotional button, or was Wesley simply getting tired?

My aunt rose to her feet. "I think we've grilled Mr. Preston enough, everyone," she said. "How about a big round of applause?"

Looking relieved to elude any further taunts from Ulysses, Wesley rose to his feet and, when the ovation died down, reminded everyone that no cheating would be allowed on the daily puzzles. If caught, the entrant's puzzle would be automatically disqualified, adding that he would know. He had spies everywhere.

"Wait!" Faith leaped to her feet as Wesley headed in the direction of the wings.

Flora swatted her and said, "Don't."

But Faith wouldn't be dissuaded. "One last question."

Wesley signaled for her to continue. "Yes, beautiful lady in the burgundy halter jumpsuit."

Faith, who usually preened after a compliment, tinged the color of her outfit. Without a doubt, she was smitten with Wesley. "I hear you and Vera Hart had a set-to this morning."

My aunt sat taller in her chair.

"She accused you of stealing the first puzzle she ever created," Faith said. "Is that true? Do you poach puzzles?"

Chapter 5

Foodie: a person with an interest in food, a gourmet

The Pelican Brief, a delicious seafood restaurant on Buena Vista Boulevard, was bustling when my party of six entered. Nearly every one of the rustic tables was filled. As the hostess guided us to our large booth, she said it was a good thing we'd made a reservation; they intended to have a second seating.

After we ordered beverages, I recapped the day's events involving Wesley Preston. Out of the corner of my eye, I noticed many customers were poring over a crossword puzzle—tomorrow's, I presumed. A few appeared to be kibitzing for answers, but their counterparts seemed to be heeding Wesley's warning about being caught cheating and were keeping mute.

Rhett, my husband, was seated to my right, and my father and my aunt to my left. Her husband, Deputy Appleby, couldn't join us. Duty called. Seated across from us were our illustrious mayor, Z.Z. "Zoey" Zeller, and her husband, Jake Chapman. Lola, my father's wife and the owner of the Pelican Brief, was greeting customers but hoped to join us soon.

"Tell us more, Jenna," Z.Z. said. An energetic dynamo with the most direct gaze of anyone I knew, she not only kept our town hopping with interesting events, but she was also the top real estate agent for the past two years. "Then what happened? Sunny Shore really stormed out?"

Jake said, "She sounds like a diva."

"Oh, no, darling." Z.Z. patted her husband's arm. "I met her yesterday. She's charming. Not the storming out type. Wesley Preston must have really pushed her buttons."

"If you say so. I trust your assessment," Jake said.

"You do?"

"Indubitably." Jake was twenty years older than Z.Z., but you'd never know it. He was as spry and lively as my father.

"Then why do you question me all the time?" Z.Z. teased.

"Do not."

"Do."

Jake winked. With his weathered skin and keen eyes, he had the charisma of so many of the actors who'd starred in old-style cowboy movies. "Go on, Jenna."

"Wesley Preston was back on his heels." I started to explain further but paused when our waitress appeared with our drinks. After she left, I continued. "The audience sure got to see a different side of him. Flustered, red-faced, and seething under the collar."

Rhett slung an arm around me and gently caressed my shoulder with his fingertips. "I wonder how Tito will present the story in tomorrow's paper."

"Hard to say. When Faith asked the question about Wesley poaching puzzles, whewie!"

Rhett arched an eyebrow. "Poaching, as in stealing them?"

"In particular, mine," my aunt inserted.

"When they were kids," I added.

"The notion was taken out of context," my aunt said. "Wesley and I were at the Cookbook Nook, sparring like we used to. Trying to one-up each other. Flora heard us and, well, she certainly stirred the pot at the theater."

"It was Faith who asked the question," I said. "Flora tried to stop her."

"Flora and Faith." Z.Z. *tsk*ed. "What a pair."

"Wesley and I didn't get a chance to clear the air afterward." My aunt sighed.

"Why not?" Z.Z. asked.

"Because fans swarmed him."

"Wesley was livid," I said, continuing my story. "He bolted to his feet and denied any such behavior, and he defied anyone to prove otherwise. 'I'm honorable,' he shouted. 'Trustworthy. Principled.'" I spanked one hand against the other, mimicking Wesley. "People leaped to their feet and surged to the stage."

"Jenna, dear"—Aunt Vera fussed with the tie of her cream silk blouse—"you're blowing things out of proportion. His reaction wasn't that bad."

"My daughter . . . blow things out of proportion?" my father joked. "Get real. She's the epitome of a level head. She takes after me."

I glared at him. "As if."

Until a few years ago, my father had worked for the FBI. He'd claimed he was an analyst, but my siblings and I'd suspected he'd been an interrogator. The way he could grill us and always uncover the truth was astounding. And irritating. None of us could resist his tactics.

"Now, Daughter." He grinned his inimitable grin, the one that made him look like Cary Grant in his sixties. Over the years, he'd been teased for having the same first name as the iconic actor, as if my grandparents had foreseen there would be a resemblance.

"Now, Father," I replied. "How's the hardware business?" He'd purchased Nuts and Bolts so that, during retirement, he wouldn't go stir crazy. He was keen on keeping busy.

"Good enough, but don't deflect. Wesley Preston sounds as full of bravado as he always was. Is he, Vera?" My father had trailed my aunt by two years in school.

"I suppose."

Z.Z. said, "I hear his followers adore him."

Followers? That made him sound like the leader of a cult. "They do," I said. "But there were definitely a few non-fans in attendance." Ulysses Huxley and Sunny Shore came to mind.

"Hungry?" Lola approached the table with a platter filled with a variety of appetizers. Like her daughter, Bailey, she had short-cropped hair and a colorful sense of style. She held out the platter for all to see and set it in the middle of the table. "Mini fish tacos à la the Pelican Brief. They're inspired, if I do say so myself."

My father rose to give her a peck on her cheek. Though they'd been married for a while, they acted like newlyweds.

I took a taco and bit into it. "Oh, yum, Lola. Incredible." The tacos were made by forming fried wontons into little cups. Each was filled with a mixture of spicy cod and red cabbage slaw. "Am I tasting ancho chili powder?"

Lola said, "You've got such good taste buds, Jenna. You are a true foodie."

During my advertising stint, I'd gone out to dinner almost every night. I'd made it a point to appreciate fine food.

Rhett put a mini taco whole into his mouth and hummed his approval. "Delicious."

"The presentation is superb," Z.Z. said, selecting one for herself. "I love the dollops of guacamole, sour cream, and salsa."

"What's that one?" My aunt pointed to another appetizer, a firm white fish topped with elegant mango salsa and pierced with a toothpick.

"Poached halibut bites," Lola said.

The word *poached* made me think of Wesley and the puzzle he'd stolen from my aunt. I also flashed on a cookbook that we carried at the shop, *Oh! Top 50 Poaching Recipes Volume 4: Not Just a Poaching Cookbook!* It featured recipes for eggs Benedict as well as poached oranges, poached peaches, and poached chicken. I'd never poached anything. The thought petrified me.

"It's a new appetizer we're trying out. The chef came up with it after the lunch rush." Lola ambled to Rhett. "Don't you love when your staff concocts novel menu items?"

"It's a restaurant owner's dream," he said.

Before Rhett and I met, he'd been the executive chef at the Grotto, a popular fish-themed restaurant that burned down from a deliberately set fire. After that, he gave up owning a restaurant and bought Bait and Switch Sports Store, located on the Pier. Recently, though, the partners in his parents' restaurant in Napa lured him back to the restaurant business—to Intime—and I was thrilled they had. He was once again in his element and as content as I'd ever seen him.

"Look. There's Wesley Preston," Z.Z. said.

Wesley was entering the restaurant looking dapper in a pinstripe suit, white shirt, and multicolored bow tie.

I signaled my aunt. "*Psst.* Check who's with him."

On his arm was Faith Fairchild. She looked stunning in a chic but revealing fuchsia cocktail dress, spiky high heels, and chunky silver jewelry. A hostess led them in our direction. Flora and her fiancé lagged behind. Comparatively, they had dressed sedately, Flora in a beaded blue sheath and her beau in a navy sweater over slacks.

Upon seeing us, Flora whispered something to her fiancé, pecked his cheek, and made a beeline for my aunt. "Vera, I'm so sorry about what happened earlier," she said.

"It was nothing." My aunt shrugged.

"Faith shouldn't have done that. I'd spoken to her in confidence, but you know my sister. She likes to make a spectacle."

"I see she won the heart of Wesley in the process," my aunt said. "How did that come about?"

"She pursued him after the event to apologize, and he forgave her instantly. How could he resist? She's wily."

Vera chuckled.

Flora regarded her sister. "I'm worried that he's a womanizer. Is he, Vera?"

"Not exactly," my aunt confided, "but he has broken a heart or two."

"Um . . ." Flora shifted feet. "Are you and Wesley feuding?"

"Of course not. What you heard at the Cookbook Nook was stuff and nonsense. He and I have always been cheerful rivals. Back in the day, we competed all the time, giving each other a reason to strive for more at crossword puzzle tournaments, chess club, and debate matches."

"I'm so glad to hear that." Flora brushed my aunt's arm with her fingertips. "I thought you might have been putting on a stiff-upper-lip act. I hate to see anyone insult my friends."

"Forget it," my aunt reassured her.

• • •

Later, when Rhett and I returned home, Tigger and Rook, our adorable Labrador, greeted us at the door, eager for attention. Rhett and I kicked off our shoes, then he hooked a leash on Rook, and I tucked Tigger into his carry pack, and the four of us went for a walk on the beach. Rook adored walks. Given the opportunity, he'd romp morning, noon, and night.

I gazed at my husband and smiled. He'd thrown a Pendleton on over his button-down shirt. Moonlight graced his rugged features, and I thought how lucky I was.

"Listen and inhale," Rhett said.

I did. The salty aroma of the ocean was heady, the sound of the water lapping the shore soothing. I appreciated living close to the water. At first, when I'd moved to Crystal Cove, I'd stayed in the cottage next to my aunt's beach house, but it would've been too small for me and Rhett to reside in, and his cabin was too remote. We were shocked when my aunt bought the house across the street from hers and gave it to us as an early wedding gift. We didn't have a direct view of the ocean, but we were less than a hop, skip, and jump away from the beach, and we were enjoying the extra space. The pets were, too.

"How were sales at the shop today?" Rhett asked as we made our way along the sand.

We hadn't been able to catch up at the restaurant.

"Good enough. Lots of customers came in to gossip about the Q&A at the theater."

"Gossip?"

"Tongues were wagging."

He snickered. "As the saying goes, 'Strong minds discuss ideas, average minds discuss events, weak minds discuss people.'"

"True, but dishing dirt is what gets people to convene, and when they meet in my shop, sales go up. I won't tell them to stop." I swept an arm across my torso and bent at the waist. "I bow to the mighty dollar."

Tigger grumbled his disapproval at being jostled.

Rhett laughed. "Your aunt seemed okay about what went down between her and Wesley Preston."

"I think she hides her hurt well. Honestly, he was tart to her. She's got a strong spirit, but . . ."

"But what?"

"Something is bothering her. She won't say what."

"Could it be that she's jealous of his career?"

I thought of how he'd insulted her success as a businesswoman. "I doubt it. I think she's harboring an old wound."

Rhett steered Rook closer to the water's edge.

I followed and kicked up the surf with my heel. "Bailey and I endured a similar tug-of-war during our childhood years."

"One upmanship is natural. Tell me more about the people who were in attendance."

"Sunny Shore" — I described her — "in addition to being a crossword researcher, is a violinist, a mathematician, and inventor." I told him what invention she was working on.

He raised his eyebrows. "Very accomplished. Has she sold it yet?"

"I don't think so."

"Can she make money as a researcher?"

"If she gets paid."

"She claimed Wesley stiffed her?"

"Yep, and he didn't deny it."

"I'd imagine she'd make better money by doing any of the other three things she's competent at."

"She might. She left so suddenly I didn't get to hear her whole story. Maybe researching Wesley's puzzles is all she can do right now. Perhaps she needs to work from home. Or it's possible she's holding down other jobs that Wesley didn't enumerate."

"And the guy named Ulysses? What's his story?"

"He was big and blond and pugnacious."

"Fifty-cent word," Rhett teased.

"He had a beef with Wesley, too." I summarized their exchange. "I'm not sure he feels respected or appreciated."

"He's a master puzzle solver?"

"Yes, and my aunt thinks he's trying his hand at creating puzzles, too."

"Are we the only two in town who don't? We're slackers." Rhett elbowed me in jest. "Who else was at the theater?"

"An old friend of my aunt and Wesley's, Noam Dixon. Also, Wesley's editor, Eva Wainwright."

"Did they face off with him, too?"

I shook my head. "No, if anything, he slighted both of them with what he'd presumed were clever quips, dissing Noam for his extensive education and Eva for her heavy hand with a red pencil. When he told her to sit, she obeyed like a trained puppy."

"*Oof.*" Rhett let out a puff of air. "Is that Wesley's typical MO? To demean his supporters and friends?"

"Good question."

"Was he kind to your aunt, at least?"

"At the Q&A, yes."

Again, I wondered what was causing my aunt dismay. *A memory best forgotten . . .*

Chapter 6

Dredge: scour, comb, rummage; (food term) to lightly coat a food in a dry ingredient, like flour

The next morning, I parked my VW Beetle in the Fisherman's Village parking lot and climbed out with Tigger in my arms. The sun was radiant. A soft breeze caressed my face. I headed to the shop and spotted Wesley sitting on one of the benches outside the café. Katie had suggested we put the benches there for diners who were waiting for reservations. They had turned out to be a big hit.

Ulysses Huxley was sitting beside Wesley. Both men were dressed more casually than they had been yesterday; Wesley in white shirt, chinos, and loafers; Ulysses in jeans, plaid shirt, and hiking boots. Wesley was using a red pocketknife to clean beneath his nails. Ulysses was wielding a penknife, which was longer in design than Wesley's, to pare the wood around the tip of a pencil. *Paring*, I'd learned from a crossword puzzle clue, was a way to sharpen pencils before pencil sharpeners were designed. Shavings lay at his feet beside a leather satchel I presumed was his. To-go cups rested on the bench on either side of the men. The two weren't chatting but gave the impression that they were much less hostile toward one another. I was surprised not to see crossword fans hovering about. I supposed most were at the Center collecting their credentials for the tournament.

Wesley saw me, pocketed his knife, and grabbed his to-go cup. "Jenna." He caught up to me as I opened the shop.

"Good morning, Mr. Preston. What a nice surprise."

"Wesley, please. We're almost family. Your aunt is like a sister to me."

A sister he hadn't spoken to in years, I noted. Not as close-knit as they should have been.

"*Ahh.*" He stepped in after me and stretched both arms, as if he'd been sitting for a while on the bench. "What a fine morning."

"Indeed."

"You look lovely," he said. "That orange suits you."

"Thanks." I'd thrown on a rust-colored sweater over a denim skirt and brown sandals. "What brings you in?" I set Tigger on the floor, and he scampered to his kitty condo and bounded to the top of it. Then I crossed to the light switches and flipped them all on. The overhead lighting illuminated the room. Spotlights highlighted the display window. Even the lamp by the Queen Anne chair in the far corner flicked on.

"Will your aunt be coming in this morning?" Wesley asked.

"She will." I moved behind the register, stored my purse, and lifted a stack of books I needed to replace on shelves.

"Great. I want to apologize to her."

"Apologize to me for what?" My aunt swept into the shop, the folds of her copper caftan wafting as she moved. The fact that she was wearing a matching turban meant she had a client coming in for a tarot reading. She let the door swing shut behind her.

"For making you the target of jeers and suspicion, Vera." Wesley splayed his hands. "You didn't deserve that. If we spar, we need to make it clear to everyone that it's in jest, don't you agree?"

"Tosh," she said. "What's past is past. You know I adore you."

"I hoped you'd say that."

He drew her into a hug, which made her turban topple. She snapped it up and planted it on her head, smoothing the short strands of her hair that peeked from beneath.

"Sit with me, Wesley." She gestured to the vintage table. "I need to prepare for a client."

I moved to the endcap of a bookshelf near the table. "New deck?" I gestured to the cards she pulled from the pocket of her caftan.

"Yes. It's gentler in tone than my regulars, but I like the vibes."

"All tarot cards work the same, don't they?" Wesley asked.

"Not necessarily," Aunt Vera said. "It depends on the energy you convey."

Wesley took a seat. "I can't believe you continue to tell fortunes. You started doing so in eighth grade, if I'm not mistaken."

"It's all in fun. I don't do it for money."

"Tell me mine."

She viewed her watch. "All right. I have time for a single-card draw." My aunt had the uncanny ability to turn any card into something positive for a client. She handed the deck to Wesley. "Cut the cards and put the bottom half on top, then hand it back."

He did as told.

She turned over the top card. *"Ahh. The Three of Swords."*

I drew near to take a peek. I didn't believe in tarot like my aunt, but I understood the cards. The Three of Swords, or in this case the III of Swords, showed a heart pierced by three swords.

My aunt's gaze narrowed. She studied Wesley's face so intently that he recoiled.

"Wh-what does it mean?" His voice quavered.

"Wesley, dear Wesley," my aunt said in the serious way she addressed all her clients—it was an act. "You're feeling deeply hurt and disappointed."

"No, I'm not."

"Your heart has been pierced by the sharp blades of others' hurtful words or actions, hasn't it?"

"No."

"They have inflicted this pain to cause you grief and heart-break."

"Vera, this is hogwash."

"No bad reviews? No one dredging up the past? No one hurling cutting remarks at you like the ones you received yesterday?"

"They weren't cutting," Wesley sniped. "Sunny lashed out with reason—I do owe her money—and Ulysses is always good for a taunt or two. He considers himself a wit, but he's a clown."

"Hmm." My aunt lifted the card and held it in front of Wesley. "Be prepared, my friend, to suffer the slings and arrows of your enemies. Hurtful words may come out of the blue. I would urge you to pause, take personal account if you've wronged anyone, and make amends."

"I haven't wronged anyone," Wesley said.

"Oh, no?" She skewered him with a steely gaze. Was she trying to make him admit something he'd done, relating to the memory that she was doing her best to tamp down? "Look within," she intoned.

"Look within." Wesley scoffed. "As if I'd ever waste time doing that."

"You must take this seriously." My aunt set the card faceup on the table and swiveled in her chair. She clasped Wesley's hands. "You have focused so much on your career to the detriment of your heart."

"Honestly, Vera—"

"Wesley, I know you have a keen desire to be the most recognized cruciverbalist in the world. You're willing to go to great lengths to make that happen. Has what you've lost been worth it? Can your heart survive?"

Wesley stood up abruptly. "Vera, this is poppycock. Cut it out. You're nuts."

My aunt bridled and pushed to her feet. "How rude. I would never say such a thing to you."

"You, my dear, would have no cause to do so because I am perfect."

"Oh, are you?" Her mouth twitched with tension. "Have you found the love of your life?"

He winced.

"Do you rue letting Elyse go? You married her, only to dump her, like that." My aunt snapped her fingers.

"Stop, Vera."

"It was cruel, Wesley, and you know it. She's never been the same. And what about Yvette Simms?"

Wesley raised his chin imperiously. "She was never worthy of me."

"Worthy? Ha!" My aunt barked out a critical laugh. "You pompous fool. She was sensational. A treasure. Your equal. But she refused to give up her career to make you the center of her universe, so you ended it." My aunt brushed her hands together. "You shooed her away without a backward glance."

Wesley grumbled, "Give me a break."

My aunt persisted. "If I don't speak truth to you, who will?"

"You're one of these swords, aren't you?" He stabbed the tarot card with a fingertip. "It's your hurtful words I have to watch out for. Well, I want nothing more of it. Leave me be." He stomped out of the shop.

My aunt sagged, and I hurried to her and threw my arms around her. She shuddered, and I realized she was sobbing. "I shouldn't have done that, but the cards . . . the warning . . ."

She rarely took on a client so forcefully. What had driven her to do so? Her history with Wesley? Something else?

"Don't worry," I cooed. "Give him time. He'll cool down."

"I hope so."

"Is Yvette the memory you're holding on to? Did you know her? Was she a friend? Did he break her heart?"

"Yes, she is the memory. She was a precious friend. A budding photojournalist, musician, and amateur puzzler. She and Noam Dixon were dating in college, but when she met Wesley, he . . . he rocked her world. She gave up everything she would've had with Noam—a home, a family, the freedom to pursue her career—to be with Wesley."

I shook my head, not understanding.

"She adored him with all her heart, and he loved her, too, but in the end, what he really wanted was a wife who would cook and clean for him and look good on his arm. He asked her to give up everything. He didn't understand balance. He didn't appreciate the natural give and take of a relationship."

Like the kind she had with Appleby and I had with Rhett.

"He didn't realize that asking her to give up her dream would crush her. When Yvette grasped the depravity of his egoism," my aunt continued, "she said goodbye and fled the country."

"She didn't go back to Noam?"

"No. They . . . they couldn't repair what they'd lost."

Poor Noam. And poor Yvette.

"Where's Yvette now?" I asked.

"The last I heard, she was working for *National Geographic* documenting African villages."

"Have you harbored these bitter feelings about Wesley all these years?"

"Yes." She sighed. "I was worried I couldn't curb my tongue if I reached out to him . . . so I didn't."

What a memory to bury for such a long time. One friend ruining another friend's life. I petted my aunt's shoulder as I peeked at the tarot card. "At least it wasn't the *Ten* of Swords," I said to lighten the mood, half joking. That was a card that always shook me to my core. It featured a man lying facedown with ten swords in his back and signified the recipient of the reading was in for a big surprise.

"Yes, I suppose you're right." My aunt slid the card back into the pack, pocketed the deck, and sauntered to the sales counter. She shifted the freebie bookmarks to the left and the flyers for the tournament to the right.

I joined her. "Are you puttering to clear your head?"

"How well you know me." She spun to face me. "Are we ready to open?"

"I have to check the register, but sure. Why not prop the door ajar and let in some fresh air?"

She set the iron-cast stack-of-books doorstop in place. "Are Gracie and Bailey coming in today?"

"Yep. Oh, did I tell you Bailey found a nanny for Brianna?"

"That's great news."

Bailey's daughter was mobile now and a handful. Having her hang out in the bookstore during the morning had become too difficult to manage. Bailey had been more interested in keeping the child from pulling cookie jars onto her head than selling cookbooks to customers.

"Here comes Bailey," I said. She was running from her car in the direction of the shop. "She looks excited."

"What's she waving?" my aunt asked.

Bailey rushed in and skidded to a stop. She inhaled sharply, to refill her lungs, and blurted, "My very first crossword puzzle ever without erasures! *Huzzah!*"

Chapter 7

Connoisseur: authority, expert, enthusiast

"That's great," I said. "I completed mine, too." I pulled the puzzle from the cross-body purse I'd stowed by the register. "When we take a break, let's celebrate. I heard Latte Luck is giving free coffee crunch cookies to puzzlers who finish without erasures."

"Sounds good." Bailey disappeared into the stockroom and reemerged, finger-combing her short hair and fluffing the puffy sleeves of her lace top. "What's on the agenda today, boss?"

"How about you unpack the box of books that came in late yesterday? I think *Posh Kebabs: Over 70 Recipes for Sensational Skewers and Chic Shawarmas* is in the mix."

"What's its allure?"

"Tell customers it's the equivalent of taking a global foodie tour, including recipes like Moroccan lamb, South African sosatie, and Portuguese Beef espetada." I licked my lips, remembering my first *espetada*, a Portuguese way of cooking food on skewers—in my case, squid.

She returned to the stockroom and came out carrying a stack of cookbooks. "Love the bright pink covers and the picture of the satay on the cover. So fun! Hey, you and Katie and I should cook a feast soon. We could use this as our guide."

"We will, but before we do, Katie has promised to teach me how to make more hors d'oeuvres. I'm deficient in that regard. Want to join in when we get the evening scheduled?"

"Sure do."

I treasured our girls' nights out. They involved good conversation, delectable wine, and lots of giggles.

Through the shop window, I saw Eva Wainwright crossing the parking lot toward the Nook Café, her long, quick strides straining the seams of her pencil skirt, as if she was late for a date. With Wesley? If so, she might be disappointed. After his outburst, he'd sped away in his rental car. As Eva neared the café's entrance, she smiled, and Ulysses Huxley bounded to his feet. Quickly, he pocketed his penknife and pencil and extended a hand. Eva shook it, and he beamed. *Oho.* Was he the one she'd come to meet? Did

Ulysses hope to entice her to take a peek at whatever crossword puzzle he might have designed? I couldn't fault him for wanting his own success. Did Wesley know? Could he throw a wrench into the works?

"What are you staring at?" Bailey scrunched up her nose, looking in the direction I was. "Lovebirds?"

I regarded Ulysses and Eva again. He'd offered her his arm and was escorting her into the café. Was Bailey right? Was there something going on between the two of them? "Not my business," I murmured.

"But you're curious."

I grinned. "How well you know me. Okay"—I clapped my hands together—"give me a couple of those books. Let's set one or two on the main display table and put the others on the shelves."

At eleven, after a flurry of customers purchased nearly two-thirds of the crossword puzzle books and half of the themed paraphernalia, I approached Bailey and said, "I'm starved. Let's pick up our prize at Latte Luck, and then we'll come back and put in reorders." Gran had arrived and was helping my aunt at the register. They could easily manage the store by themselves.

Latte Luck Café was bustling as we entered. All of the wooden tables were filled. The brown leather booths were occupied, too.

"Yum. I adore the aroma of sugar and butter," Bailey crooned.

"What's not to love?"

A handful of customers were working on crossword puzzles. Many were sitting, as I might, with their tongues wedged between their teeth in concentration. A woman with a ginger-orange scarf tied dramatically around her hair was guarding her puzzle with arms and hands outstretched, like a student protecting the answers on a final test.

Her booth mate, an older woman with curly hair, snarled at her. "C'mon. One peek. Be a pal."

"Uh-uh. You heard what Wesley said," the woman in the scarf said. "No cheating. He has spies everywhere."

Did he? Had he hired tournament attendees to be on the alert? Was the man in the blue sweater one of his posse? He was definitely people watching and not filling in a puzzle.

"I'll be right back." Bailey excused herself to go to the restroom.

I joined the line, my eyes fixed on the teenaged clerk at the counter. As thin as she was, clad in her pink-striped apron and pink-striped cap, she resembled a peppermint stick. "What's she putting into that bag?" I said to the woman in front of me.

She turned slightly, and I recognized her instantly. Sunny Shore, the woman from the Q&A who'd clashed with Wesley. Her outfit was olive green again, but a dressed-down version—camo pants with a V-neck, long-sleeved tee. The oversized tote hanging from her shoulder was bulging, which made me wonder what she had stored in it. Rocks? A defensive weapon like a cudgel? A series of hard drives containing information about her inventions?

"Pumpkin caramel muffins," Sunny said in answer to my question.

"Ooh, I adore anything with caramel."

"What connoisseur of sweets doesn't?"

Bailey, I thought. She was a chocoholic through and through.

"I hope there're some when we get to the front of the line," Sunny added. "Everyone has been ordering them."

"I hope so, too." Suddenly, a coffee crunch cookie, free or not, didn't sound like nearly enough to satisfy my sweet tooth. "That's a hefty bag you're toting around."

She patted it. "I'm a mom. Always prepared. Wipes. Tissues. Hand sanitizer. And if a job interview comes my way, a change of clothes." Her gaze sharpened. "Hey, I know you. You were at the theater yesterday."

"I was. I'm Jenna Hart. Vera Hart is my aunt. I'm sorry Mr. Preston was sort of, um, curt to you."

"Wesley." She sniffed. "Do you—does anyone—honestly think he could've come up with foodie-themed puzzles on his own? *Not.* He doesn't have enough zest in his brain to add zing. Enough flavor to add pizzazz. He wouldn't know the difference between yellow pudding and lemon mousse. I've helped him research every puzzle for the last three years. *Me.* I—" She stopped; her cheeks tinged pink with embarrassment. "That was horrible of me. I shouldn't have said that about the pudding. It was mean."

"It'll be our secret." I raised a finger to my lips. "Did you and he have your meeting last night?"

"Meeting?" She blinked as if not understanding my question.

"At the theater, he mentioned that you and he had a meeting scheduled at the inn. Were you able to iron things out?"

"Oh, the meeting isn't until tonight. After the soiree."

"Well, you might be happy to hear that he visited the Cookbook Nook today. That's the culinary bookshop in Fisherman's Village that I own with my aunt." I motioned in the general direction of the shop. "And he said you'd lashed out at him with good reason. He agreed he *did* owe you money."

"Well, how about that? The man speaks out of both sides of his mouth. Big surprise. Between you and me, if he doesn't come through, my kids won't get new shoes."

Sensing she was kidding, I said, "How many children do you have?"

"Two."

"Boys? Girls?"

"Girls. Skylar and Sloane. Fourteen and eleven. They're my sweet angels. They're . . ." Her eyes grew misty. "They're with their father right now."

"Where do you live?"

"Santa Barbara."

"Do you love it there?"

"It's beautiful."

Santa Barbara was on Rhett's and my bucket list of day trips starting next year. We weren't taking any long vacations until Intime was firmly back on its feet; the restaurant had just completed renovations last week.

"My aunt says the symphony in Santa Barbara is very good," I said. Aunt Vera and Appleby had visited the town to go wine tasting and had taken in a performance.

"It is."

"If I heard correctly at the Q&A, you're a violinist. Do you play professionally?"

She shook her head. "It's a hobby. Do you play?"

I snorted. "I can barely carry a tune, let alone play an instrument. Mr. Preston also said you were a mathematician."

"I am, but I'm not doing anything with it right now. I worked for a small computer company at one time, designing computational techniques and algorithms, but the job was eliminated. I'm looking for another job now. Hence, the interview apparel." She tapped her tote.

"And you're an inventor?" I asked. Okay, I knew I was prying, but Rhett's questions yesterday had made me curious about everyone who was in town for the tournament. "Exactly what is an edible popcorn bag?"

"Exactly what it sounds like. Once you're done with the popcorn, you down the bag. No fuss, no muss. No trash to dispose of." She brushed her hands together.

It sounded disgusting, but I smiled.

"I've patented it, but"—she brushed a stray hair off her cheek—"I have yet to find a buyer. It's a competitive market."

"I'm sure it is."

The line inched ahead.

"In addition to researching crossword puzzles, I design them, too," Sunny said.

"You do? How do you go about selling them?"

"It's complicated. I haven't had any success in that regard, either, but I will. Wesley was supposed to . . ." Her voice drifted off.

"Give you a leg up?"

"Something like that. He hasn't, to date."

I couldn't imagine how she was scraping by. Researching puzzles couldn't produce a substantial amount of income. Perhaps her husband earned enough to support the entire family. "I hope your luck will change this year, and you win the event." I crossed my fingers for her.

"We'll see. Twenty thousand could help a lot."

"It might even cover the cost of shoes," I joked.

She chuckled. It became her turn to order, and as expected, she requested a pumpkin caramel muffin.

"Last one," the clerk said.

"Oh, then let her have it," Sunny said, indicating me.

"No, thanks, that's nice of you, but it's all right." I held up my completed puzzle sheet. "I'll take the free coffee crunch cookie instead."

"You'll get a recipe card with that, too, Jenna," the clerk said.

"Win-win," I said and smiled.

As Sunny was paying for her purchase, Bailey rejoined me. "Just in time," she said, pulling her puzzle from her purse. "Did I miss any gossip?"

"Nothing to write home about." To Sunny I said, "Will I see you at the cocktail reception tonight?"

"I'll be there, but if Wesley Preston has anything to say about it, I'll be persona non grata."

Chapter 8

Wit: wag, comic, joker, clown, satirist

When I entered Intime Wednesday night at half past six, the excitement from the group of conference participants was palpable, the timbre of chatter and laughter at a fevered pitch. Gone were the array of bistro tables, which created an open space. The light emanating from the candelabra-style chandeliers seemed brighter, as if matching everyone's mood. Guests stood in clusters, serving themselves from a buffet teeming with raw shrimp as well as a wealth of cheeses, patés, chilled items, and fruit. The staff was moving through the throng with serving trays filled with hot appetizers. I caught the delectable scent of onion tarts, one of my favorite hors d'oeuvres, and nabbed one as a waiter passed by. I bit into it and hummed my appreciation. Then I scanned the restaurant for Rhett and caught sight of him standing in the archway leading to the kitchen, giving orders.

Deciding not to disturb him, I searched the sea of humanity for my aunt as I polished off the tart. It was hard to find her in the blur of black cocktail dresses and black suits. Wesley had requested the party attire be black-and-white, in keeping with crossword puzzle colors. Nobody had bucked the suggestion. I was wearing my slinky sheath with cap sleeves and a draped back. I'd clipped on a spangly bracelet and matching earrings to add a bit of bling.

As I neared the buffet, I noted Wesley Preston was engaged in a heated argument with a florid-faced man and a beady-eyed woman. She was aiming a finger at him. The man was spanking the back of his hand against his palm, as if to drive home a point. They were probably taking Wesley to task over the difficulty of one of his puzzles. He threw up his hands and marched away from them.

Ulysses Huxley bumped into him. On purpose?

Wesley drew up short. Shock registered on his face. "What now?" he carped.

"It's the last time," Ulysses mumbled. "Do you hear me?"

"I heard you the first time," Wesley said, and moved on.

The two men parted ways, and I weaved through the multitude to join Aunt Vera, who was standing with Deputy Marlon Appleby, a moose-jawed, big-boned man, who came across as tough as a bouncer at a bar but was a pussycat at heart. In his black suit, he looked debonaire. His warm brown eyes were drinking in my aunt's face. Both of them were holding flutes of champagne. They clinked glasses and sipped.

"Cheers, Jenna, darling," my aunt said when she caught sight of me.

I pecked her on the cheek and said hello to Appleby. "Are Dad and Lola here?"

"Haven't seen them." My aunt jutted her chin in Rhett's direction. "Your sweetheart is earning raves for the food."

"He always does."

Appleby stopped a waitress who was carrying gougères and mini spinach quiches and nabbed two of each. He offered them to my aunt and me.

"No, thanks," I said. "I'll indulge soon." I adored gougères, a cheese-stuffed pastry, and wished I could make them at home. Rhett assured me the recipe wasn't hard, but French delicacies were not my forté. However, recently, I'd decided to tackle pie crusts and wasn't half bad at making them, so I put the quiches on my to-try list.

I spied Sunny Shore standing near Noam Dixon. He was saying something, but she didn't appear to be listening. Was he relaying the misadventures of being an English professor and tales of the odd students he'd taught over the years? Sunny, in a mid-calf-length black sheath fitted with a crossword puzzle brooch, was staring off in the distance. Discouraged by her lack of interest, Noam moved on.

Ulysses, on the other hand, had joined Eva Wainwright near the buffet and was charming the socks off of her. He said something, and she laughed, making it impossible for her to polish off the slice of cheese she was holding or take a sip of her champagne. I imagined Ulysses reciting kooky crossword clues to her. What's an eight-letter word for anteater? Aardvark. What's a five-letter word for supercilious? Aloof, surly, bored. At one point, Eva shook her head in awe, clearly blown away by his wit, and again I wondered if their meeting at the café earlier had been a date or a business meeting.

My father and Lola pressed through the crowd to join us. He toasted my aunt. "It's a success, Vera."

"It certainly is," Appleby said.

"Do you know everyone here, Vera?" Lola asked.

"Not all, but many," my aunt replied. "Wesley, of course. And Noam Dixon."

"Back in grade school, Noam was an egghead," my father said. "If I recall correctly, he was valedictorian in eighth grade as well as twelfth grade, right?"

My aunt nodded.

Lola said, "Cary told me that you, Noam, and Wesley went on to college together."

"Also correct." Aunt Vera nodded. "I got a degree in economics, Noam in English, and Wesley, to prove he was better than us, earned degrees in five different fields."

"Five." Lola whistled softly.

"Noam had planned to write a novel or two," Dad said. "Did he do that?"

"No," my aunt replied. "He settled for being a professor."

"Settled?" Lola echoed. "Being a professor is a worthy career."

"Not for someone who had huge dreams. Noam . . ." My aunt sighed. "After the love of his life left him, his dreams waned and his creativity dwindled."

"You're talking about Yvette Simms," I said. "She's the woman who went to Africa after Wesley dumped her."

My aunt hummed, *"Mm-hm."*

"Wesley sure has caused a lot of hurt," I said.

"I'm afraid Noam brought some of it on himself," she said. "He lacked confidence."

"But he was so smart," I countered.

"Smart people can be filled with self-doubt," my father said.

"Shh," my aunt cautioned. "Wesley's coming this way."

"Vera." He sauntered to us, looking dapper and pumped up on adulation. He raised his flute of champagne. "Thank you for all you've done. What a delightful evening."

I raised an imaginary glass. I was waiting for one of the waitstaff to pass me with a tray of beverages. I could have gone to the open bar across the room, of course, but I'd chosen to stay with my family.

"However, I must say"—Wesley lowered his voice—"that the language skills of this year's field seem to be lacking."

My aunt's mouth dropped open. "Wesley, what a horrible thing to say." With Z.Z.'s help, my aunt had cherry-picked all of the participants. According to her, they were the cream of the crop.

He sniffed. "I've spoken to a few who don't know the difference between zinc and synch, and heaven forbid they know how to spell perambulate or preternatural."

Aunt Vera gasped. "Did you quiz them? Here? Wesley, that's obnoxious."

He knuckled my aunt's arm. "C'mon, Vera, you know how I am. I like to be provocative."

"You mean confrontational. Incendiary. Insulting."

"Aggressive."

"Vexing."

"Annoying."

My aunt sputtered and placed a hand on her chest.

"What's wrong, my old friend?" Wesley smiled wickedly. "Have you run out of synonyms?"

Aunt Vera glowered at him. The hand on her chest balled into a fist, and for a long moment, I worried she might slug him, but then she burst out laughing. "Oh, you! I do miss our rousing exchanges."

He laughed, too, and looped a hand around my aunt's elbow. "Come. Let me introduce you to everyone." He steered her to a group of puzzlers.

"Well, that was fun," I gibed.

"Fun," my father echoed.

Lola, who stood frozen in place like a woman in a tableau, wheezed with relief. "Was it fun? You could've fooled me."

"Is this how it's always been between them, Cary?" Appleby asked, shrugging the tension from his shoulders.

"I don't recall."

"Jenna?" Appleby eyed me.

"She hasn't said much about him other than he's an excellent cruciverbalist with a bit of an ego. Hasn't she told you anything about him?"

"She hasn't said squat." Appleby gazed after them.

So did I. Seeing Wesley and my aunt talking animatedly, I drew in a deep breath, deciding they'd simply staged another of their legendary sparring sessions for our amusement. Not far from them, I noticed Noam Dixon staring at them. Was he wishing they'd beckon him to join in their frivolity? Was he feeling dejected because they hadn't included him?

Rhett appeared on my right and kissed me gently on the cheek. "Hey, darling, is everything okay?"

I swiveled to face him. "Fine. My aunt and Wesley put on another show."

"Is that what you call it? A show?" Appleby screwed up his mouth. "I'm not a fan of their banter."

My father tilted his head. "For heaven's sakes, Marlon, it was all in jest."

"Don't get me wrong. Your sister likes to kid around, I get that, but what went down between them . . ." Appleby's nostrils flared. "I've been on the receiving end of that look. I could tell it took all of her reserve not to clock him."

"Wesley Preston is brash," my father said. "He always has been."

"That's the problem," Appleby said. "He's brash and arrogant, like he thinks he's smarter than everyone else."

Lola leaned in. "Between you and me, I'm not sure he's an iota smarter than anyone else in this room, but he does have an assured air about him. When I was practicing law, I was often cautioned to keep my defenses up whenever I ran into a handful of killer attorneys."

"Like who?" Dad asked.

"No one you know, but I was forever on the alert." Lola had given up law to run the Pelican Brief and had no regrets.

Someone tapped a microphone. I recognized the mayor's voice as she said, "Ladies and gentlemen."

The crowd parted, and I glimpsed Z.Z. standing on a raised platform.

Rhett bussed my cheek. "I've got to check on the kitchen staff. I'll be back soon."

"Welcome to the Crystal Cove Crossword Puzzle Tournament cocktail soirée," Z.Z. said. "We're so glad you could join in the festivities. I'd like to thank our host, Intime, for putting on this delicious shindig. Rhett Jackson, bravo."

51

"Hear, hear," a cluster of guests chanted.

Rhett paused to wave and then disappeared into the kitchen.

"There is plenty of food, folks," Z.Z. went on, "so don't go back to your hotels, inns, or homes hungry. But do go back as sober as you can because tomorrow you will need to do everything you can to boost your mental acuity for this weekend's events. Practice puzzles. Bone up on your vocabulary. Take a nice relaxing walk on the beach. Clear your heads. And then on Friday" — she raised a glass of champagne in a toast — "may the cleverest among you — "

Bang! Crash! Clatter!

Chapter 9

Knife: (noun) dagger, stiletto, penknife, scalpel; (verb) to spear, stick, wound

My insides jolted at the sound of glass shattering. I swung around to scan the restaurant. Where was Rhett? Was he all right? Instinctively, I visualized the night when a bomb went off in Intime and almost killed him, hence the reason for the renovations.

"Rhett!" I cried, unable to fight the dread searing my esophagus. "Rhett!"

Everyone was bleating with panic. Many were demanding to know what had happened. I didn't see smoke or fire. I didn't smell the stench of gunpowder, either.

"Do you see Rhett?" I asked.

"Jenna, breathe." Lola rested a hand on my arm. "Everything is fine. A tray of glasses bit the dust." Being a restaurateur, she would know the sound. "Look. Rhett is right there. See him waving to you? Wave back."

Relief swept over me. I gave him a thumbs-up and said to my father, "Where's Aunt Vera?"

"By the hostess's stand. With Deputy Appleby."

Noam Dixon was near them, peering past, trying to peek inside the kitchen. I didn't see Wesley Preston in the vicinity, but that didn't mean a thing. I didn't see Sunny Shore, either. The disturbance had probably given both of them the opportunity to bow out early.

• • •

The party ended at a little past eight. When I arrived home, I was still shaking from the stupid tray of glasses fiasco. Despite my distress, I crawled into bed without doing my ablutions, and I slept without dreaming.

At dawn, Rhett roused me. "Time to get up, sleepy head."

"It's dark out," I muttered.

"Yes, but we made a promise to Rook to take him for a walk."

Even though Rhett worked nights, we'd made it our Thursday

morning ritual to take a hike with our lab, opting for midweek when tourists wouldn't be flooding the trails. Rhett's cabin, where he liked to go to decompress and fish, was located at the top of the mountain near a small lake and a perfect halfway point on our treks. The place was fully paid for, so keeping it wasn't a financial burden on us. We only had utilities and taxes to consider.

"How much sleep did you get?" I asked.

"Enough."

I'd felt him slip into bed around two a.m.

He kissed my neck and said, "I've made coffee."

"You're a saint." I scrambled to the bathroom, washed up, and threw on leggings, T-shirt, hoodie, and sneakers. I roused Tigger with a kiss on the nose, but he promptly went back to sleep in his cozy spot on the comforter. Then I fixed two cups of to-go coffee with cream and sugar, stowed treats for Rook and power bars and bottled water for us in a backpack, and met Rhett by the front door. I handed him his coffee.

"Record time," he said, jokingly regarding his watch.

I jutted a hip. "It took me fifteen minutes tops."

"Sixteen."

"But who's counting?" I took a sip of coffee. "Let's go."

Rhett drove south to the trailhead parking lot across the road from the Pier. There were four vehicles in the lot. Rhett pulled in between a Ford Explorer and Chevy Tahoe and set the brake.

Two trails, unimaginatively named North and South, led up and down the mountain. We chose North to go up and would take South on our return. Rook was a good walker. He followed Rhett's lead and only tugged when he needed to relieve himself.

Early-bird hikers were already on the trail. Some were using trekking poles for balance. Most were wearing broad-brimmed hats and sporting backpacks or fanny packs. Like us, none were using flashlights. There was enough emerging sunlight to be sure-footed.

"It's beautiful this morning," I said, "though a bit breezy." Loose dirt and leaves were kicking up around our feet. Luckily, my sunhat had a drawstring to hold it in place. "The scent of the pines is heady, isn't it?"

"*Mm-hm,*" Rhett murmured. "Did you know there are eight conifers native to the Santa Cruz Mountains?"

"I did not." Gardening was not my specialty. With the help of a landscaper, I'd planted year-round color in our backyard, and I knew the names of a few flowers, vegetables, and bushes that grew on the Central Coast, but that was the extent of my knowledge.

"Yep. The variety is driven by our unique climate, topography, and geology. The upwelling of subsurface cold water off the coast produces our fog."

"Now *that* I knew." I had taken a meteorology class in college to fulfill one of my science requirements.

"The coast redwood is the best known of the conifers. It's part of the cypress family."

I glanced sideways at him. "Well, aren't you a bundle of trivial information this morning? You should take up doing crossword puzzles." As it was, I was the only one of us who was fond of doing them.

"Not a chance."

"C'mon, you're smart."

"But I can't spell." Rhett let loose with a laugh. He did struggle with knowing the difference between *they're*, *their*, and *there*. Homonyms, he joked, should be drawn and quartered.

We veered off the North Trail in the direction of the cabin. Rook strained at his leash as we neared it. Rhett released him. The dog scampered away, and we made our way to the backyard to enjoy our snack. Rhett's vegetable garden was thriving. The spinach was green and healthy, as was the kale. He grew the vegetables for us as well as for Intime. We didn't talk. We decided to eat our snacks while quietly enjoying the view of the ocean. The sun was creeping over the mountain behind us and casting a golden glow on the water below.

A minute later, Rook bounded around the corner of the house and skidded to a stop beside Rhett. He bark and whimpered.

"What's up, boy?" Rhett scratched the dog's ears.

Rook yowled.

"Did you bag a squirrel?"

Rook butted his head against Rhett's leg and nabbed his leash between his teeth.

"You're ready to leave?" Rhett gave me a curious look. "This is unlike him."

I'd known the dog long enough to know that was an understatement. A breeze kicked up, sending my power bar wrapper flying. I snatched it before it hit the ground. "Maybe he wants to show you something. Like Lassie. Follow him."

Rhett chuckled. "Okay, let's get going." He hopped to his feet, shoved our trash into the backpack, and slung the pack over one shoulder. "Here, boy," he said, but before he could clip the leash onto Rook's collar, the dog tore off.

We raced after him and saw him head down the South Trail. At the first bend, Rook halted and bayed. It was a haunting sound that sent a shiver down my back.

"What the heck?" Rhett ran faster.

I followed.

When we caught up to the dog, he was as immobile as a statue, staring off the trail into a cluster of trees and a stand of evergreen bushes. Though the wind was flapping his ears, he remained stock-still. An English pointer couldn't have been more explicit about pinning down a location.

Rhett pushed through the bushes, and I followed. He stopped, and I bumped into him.

"Oh, crap," he muttered.

"What's wrong?"

"Look."

Wesley Preston was on the ground, lying stomach-down, his head turned to the left, his face pasty gray. His arms were bent at the elbows, his hands by his neck. He was wearing a collarless camouflage shirt, cargo pants, and hiking boots.

Rhett started to crouch. "Wesley, buddy, are you—"

"Wait." I shot out my hand. "Is that blood?"

Something dark and viscous had formed beneath Wesley's shoulders, neck, and head.

"Is he . . ." The word *dead* caught in my throat.

Gingerly, Rhett bent down and checked Wesley's wrist for a pulse. He nodded to me.

"Oh, no!" I cried.

"I'd guess he's been dead for a few hours. His skin is cold."

"Did he hit his head on something?"

"Hard to tell. His hands are bloody."

I pulled my cell phone from my jeans pocket, swiped the screen, tapped the flashlight icon, and aimed the beam of light at Wesley.

Rhett said, "I think the blood's coming from his neck, but I can't be sure without moving him."

"Don't," I cautioned, knowing the police would frown on us tampering with the scene, even though we were smack-dab in the middle of it.

"No, I won't, but we need to call—"

"Nine-one-one. On it." My insides roiled as I pulled up the phone app and stabbed in the numbers. A dispatcher answered. I explained the situation to her. After asking for my location, she told me the police were on their way and to stay put.

Neither Rhett nor I moved. Dutifully, Rook sat on his haunches beside Rhett, his tongue lolling from his mouth.

Rhett's gaze remained riveted on Wesley. "Why would he have been out here?"

"To bird watch."

"Huh?"

"During the interview at the theater, he was asked about his predilection for studying nocturnal birds. I bet he went back to the inn after the party, changed clothes, and came here straightaway. The wildlife along this trail is pretty spectacular."

"Would he come alone?"

"Well, he wasn't alone if he was . . ." I couldn't say *murdered*. "Unless . . ."

"Unless what?"

"Could a bird have killed him? With its beak?"

Rhett crouched again to inspect what he could see of the wound, bending so low his head nearly touched the ground. "No, I think his throat has been slit."

I flashed on the tarot card Wesley had drawn from my aunt, showing a heart pierced by swords. Had the reading forewarned of his death? Had my aunt sensed it? Was that why she'd been rattled?

A siren disturbed the silence. The paved road to the top of the mountain lay to the right of us. Two vehicles screeched to a halt. Doors slammed.

"Over here!" Rhett hollered. "Off the South Trail."

Chief Cinnamon Pritchett pushed through the bushes from the

direction we'd come and drew to a halt. Appleby followed her. He towered over her, but Cinnamon was no slouch. Some might think she was an amiable camp counselor with her sweet face, short hair, and athletic build, but she was far from it. Once a rebellious teen, after guidance from my father, she became a fierce defender of justice.

Neither Cinnamon nor Appleby was wearing a uniform. Like me, Cinnamon had donned jeans, hoodie, and a pair of sneakers. Appleby had on workout clothes and high-end running shoes. Our emergency call must have roused them before they'd dressed for work.

Cinnamon stepped to the body, crouched as Rhett had, and felt Wesley's wrist. From that position, she eyed me. "Again?"

"Hey, the dog found him, not me, okay?" I sounded defensive, but, yes, I had come across more victims than a person ought to in one's young—youngish—lifetime. "It's Wesley Preston, the cruciverb—"

"I know who he is," she said with a bite as she donned latex gloves. "His face has been on the front of the *Courier* every day for the past week."

"How did he die?" I asked. "Rhett thinks his throat has been slit. Could a bird do something like—"

"No!" Cinnamon lifted Wesley's head an inch and peeked beneath. "He's been murdered. His carotid artery has been severed." She said to Appleby, "The wound is narrow, about four inches wide."

"Check," he replied.

I gagged, my hand flying to my own neck. "Mr. Preston has a few enemies."

"And you know this how?" She rose to her feet.

"I was at the theater when he was interviewed. There were some caustic exchanges. And then at the soirée last night, a couple of people argued with him, most likely questioning the answers in some of his puzzles, but I won't speculate," I added hastily, knowing how much Cinnamon hated for me to do so. Sure, I'd been helpful in solving a few murders in town, but she was always quick to remind me that it wasn't my job and to butt out.

"Good," she said flatly. "Don't speculate."

"However, if he—"

"Don't, Jenna."

I pressed my lips together.

Appleby was taking photographs of the crime scene with his cell phone. I peered in the direction he was aiming the lens, beyond the body, and wondered if the area had been swept clean of footprints. The wind could have done so, I supposed. I didn't see loose leaves or branches anywhere.

"Our dog found him," Rhett said.

"Your dog." Cinnamon regarded Rook, who hadn't moved from Rhett's side.

"I let him off leash," Rhett said. "He sprinted away and returned in minutes to alert us."

"Have you seen other hikers?"

"A half dozen. Some were ahead of us, others behind us." Rhett caressed the lab's head. Rook took in his master with fond affection. "Yes, you're a good boy," Rhett cooed, and returned his gaze to Cinnamon. "We set out before sunrise up the North Trail."

"To have breakfast at the cabin," I said.

Cinnamon knew where Rhett's cabin was. They'd dated briefly years ago. Now she was married to a deliciously charming fireman. They had a handful of cats and were trying to decide whether they wanted to try to get pregnant again. They had once, but she'd lost the baby early on.

"Actually, it was a snack," I revised. "Not breakfast. A power bar."

"I don't care what you ate," Cinnamon snapped.

I shifted feet. She and I were friends. We'd gone out for wine as recently as last week. But at the moment, she was treating me like a hostile witness. I scowled at her. She stared daggers at me.

The phrase *stared daggers* caught me up. "What kind of knife do you think the killer used?" I blurted.

Cinnamon gawked at me.

"They come in all shapes and sizes," I went on. "I doubt it was as large as a hunting knife, if the wound is narrow like you said. Could a Swiss Army knife have been the weapon?"

"Why a Swiss Army knife?"

"Mr. Preston owns . . ." I hesitated. "He *owned* one. A red one. I saw him using the nail file tool to clean his fingernails yesterday."

Cinnamon mumbled under her breath.

"Lots of other people own them, I'm sure," I continued. "I do. Rhett does. I saw one of Mr. Preston's colleagues using a penknife yesterday, too," I added.

Cinnamon met my gaze. "What's a penknife?"

"It's like a pocketknife but longer and originally designed to sharpen or thin quills."

She frowned.

"It's a crossword clue." I exchanged a look with Rhett.

"Don't expect me to corroborate that," he said. "Puzzles are not my thing."

"Mr. Huxley, the colleague, was using it to tweak his pencil," I said.

"Mr. Huxley?" She arched an eyebrow.

"Ulysses Huxley is a renowned crossword puzzle solver. He was Mr. Preston's guinea pig." I halted. "That didn't come out right. He worked with Mr. Preston to help him hone his puzzles. I suppose he refined the clues. For example, did you know there are fifty-nine seven-letter answers for the clue *tightens*? Shrinks, relaces, adjusts —"

"Stop." She held up a hand.

"Right. Sorry. By the way, Mr. Preston was a nocturnal bird-watcher," I went on. "That could explain why he was out here."

As if on cue, a bird hooted. Not an owl. It sounded more like a mourning dove. Rook startled and yipped. Rhett hushed him. When the bird repeated its call, "Coo-ah, coo-coo-coo," I was certain it was a dove. On previous walks, Rhett had tutored me in birdcalls.

"The other day, a lot of people at the Q&A Mr. Preston held at the Theater on the Pier learned about this affinity," I said. "Mr. Huxley made mention of it. Anyone who attended might have known he'd come here."

"Oh," Cinnamon murmured, not looking at me, too captivated by her visual search of the surrounding area.

"I think someone sneaked up on him, don't you?" I went on.

Cinnamon grunted. "That would be my guess."

"Do you think the killer used a branch to mess up his tracks? Or did the wind wipe them out? It looks, you know, cleaned up."

"Hard to say." Her eyes narrowed as she continued to study the surroundings.

"The killer could have done so to obscure hiking boot prints," I said. "But then everyone wears hiking boots up here, so finding one set of prints wouldn't help you much, unless the treads were distinctive."

"You don't," Cinnamon noted.

"Don't what?" I inclined my head.

"Wear hiking boots." She motioned to my shoes.

"True. I don't own a pair."

"I wear them," Rhett said, indicating his Timberlands.

"Mr. Huxley is a large man," I offered. "Taller and bigger than Deputy Appleby. His shoe size must be at least twelve to fourteen. Those would be distinctive."

"I've taken pictures, Chief." Appleby held up his phone and swiped through a few photos to show her.

"What else did you notice, Deputy?" Cinnamon asked.

"There are a few broken branches in the wax myrtle. Low down." He hooked a thumb at the evergreen bushes. "I'm guessing the killer arrived first and crouched, lying in wait."

Cinnamon bobbed her head. "Meaning the killer knew Mr. Preston would be at this exact location."

"Possibly. He might have mentioned the route he planned to take to someone," Appleby said. "Lab techs should be here in a few. Coroner, too."

"I don't see a flashlight," Rhett said, scanning the area.

"Do you think Mr. Preston went walking without one?" I asked Cinnamon.

"You did," she said.

"Rhett and I started at sunrise. There was plenty of light," I said. "But Mr. Preston might not have. Rhett said his body is cold. He's conceivably been dead a few hours. He'd have needed to use a flashlight. Does he have a phone on him? I don't see a backpack anywhere."

Cinnamon squatted again and patted Wesley's pants pockets. She rotated her head to take in Appleby. "Empty."

"No room key or car key?" I asked.

"I can't tell. I'll leave a thorough search to the techs." She pursed her lips and rose to her feet. Turning in a circle, one hand shielding the sun from her eyes, she said, "Okay, Deputy, let's set a perimeter.

Jenna and Rhett, if you'd both go back the way you came, in case there are incriminating footprints coming up the South Trail. Be available if we need to ask you more questions."

I felt like saluting but tamped down the urge.

She sighed. "With all the people who've come to town for this tournament, this is going to be one heck of a long day of interviews."

Chapter 10

Enigmatology: the study of all puzzles

Rhett, Rook, and I hurried home. My aunt's Mustang wasn't in her driveway, meaning she'd already left for the shop. Not knowing if Appleby had informed her about Wesley's death, I decided to wait to tell her the news until I saw her in person. A phone call wouldn't cut it. I texted that I was running behind schedule, threw on my denim skirt, an *I love books!* T-shirt, and cropped cardigan sweater with oversized buttons, slipped into a pair of leather sandals, and raced out the door with Tigger in tow. Rhett would see to Rook.

When I entered the Cookbook Nook, the place was empty. The shop wasn't open yet, but the lights were on. I heard my aunt humming in the storage room, so I set Tigger on his kitty condo and pressed through the drapes.

Aunt Vera was unpacking a box of books and placing them on the metal shelving. "Morning," she trilled.

"Morning." I wasn't sure how to begin. "Um, did you get the text that I was running late? You didn't respond."

"Yes. Is everything okay? Car trouble?" She stopped what she was doing and brushed her hands on her ocean blue caftan. When she took in my gaze, her face fell. "What's wrong?"

"I'm so sorry to have to tell you this, but—" I swallowed hard. "Wesley Preston . . . is dead."

She staggered backward, bumping into the shelves. I rescued her, guided her to the chair by the desk, and made her sit.

She stared up at me. "Are you sure?"

I nodded.

She fluttered a hand. "Oh, oh, oh. What happened? How? When?"

I told her about Rhett and me finding him. Well, actually Rook finding him and then guiding Rhett and me to the location. "He was lying on the ground. His throat . . ." I reached for mine and balked. "His throat was slit."

Aunt Vera gasped.

"I think the killer used a knife." Cinnamon hadn't corroborated that. "I'm not sure when he died, but his body was cold. So, last night sometime."

Tears leaked down my aunt's cheeks. She swiped them away with her fingertips. "I can't believe it. He was so . . . so . . . vital. Who would want to harm him?"

"I don't know. Cinnamon and Marlon are on the case. They'll find out who did this." I fetched her a glass of water from the cooler and forced it into her hands. "Drink."

"Wesley had rivals, of course," she murmured. "And he'd certainly ruffled a few feathers. I can think of many who were disgruntled with him." She sipped the water. "He could be prickly and a braggart and self-righteous, but that's no reason to be killed. If it were, fifty percent of the world would be dead."

A quiet moment passed between us. Tigger sauntered into the storage room and flicked my aunt with his tail, as if knowing she needed him. She set the glass aside, picked him up, placed him on her lap, and stroked him steadily.

I said, "Wesley broke a few hearts in the past, I gather."

"Yes."

"Anybody other than Elyse and Yvette? Is it possible one of them might have come to town to exact retribution?"

"Now? Years later? *Pfft.* No, I can't see a former lover as the killer. They were upset and baffled by his rejection, but to a person, they still loved him." Aunt Vera heaved a sigh and scrubbed Tigger under the chin. "Poor Wesley. He was such a clever cruciverbalist. So devoted to enigmatology."

I hadn't heard the word before but pieced it together by its roots, *enigma*, meaning puzzle, and *otology*, the study of. Back when I was preparing to take the SATs for college, I'd delved into words and their roots, knowing it would aid me on the English portion of the exam. To my surprise, that review had helped me throughout my career in advertising as well as when solving crossword puzzles.

"He was always in search of perfection and not willing to settle for less."

What a sad pursuit. Nobody was perfect.

She set the empty glass on the desk. "How will we go on with the event? He was the glue that held these kinds of things together. And he was supposed to be the primary judge. And his fans . . ." She placed a hand on her chest. "Oh, my. They will be distraught."

"Turn the event into a tribute."

"While a murder investigation is underway?" She squinched up her nose. "How tacky. How gauche. No, no, no."

"It's not tasteless," I said. "I'm sure everyone who's here for the event will want to grieve for him."

"Not everyone," my aunt said snidely.

She was right. One person was happy he was gone.

I said, "You could have a memorial at the end of Sunday's session and toast him."

She mulled that over.

I added, "I'll bet the police will demand everyone stay in town until they're done with their investigation. There are a lot of participants. It'll take days."

My aunt said, "I'll touch base with Z.Z. She'll know what to do." She reached for the telephone on the desk but didn't lift the receiver. A broken sob escaped her lips. She clapped an arm across her chest as if to hold herself in check. "I loved him, Jenna. Yes, we could go at it like enemies, but we weren't. Ever. We were like siblings. We enjoyed the banter. The challenge."

"I know."

"He was family."

"He said the same to me about you." I gave her shoulder a squeeze. "Why don't you take some time for yourself? Go home. Lie down. I'll open up the shop. Bailey will be here soon."

"Oh, no. Never. Work is a salve for me. I'll be fine."

As I pressed through the drapes I heard her murmur, "Dead. Who would want to kill him?"

I returned to the sales counter and prepared to open as I normally would. I checked the till. I reviewed yesterday's receipts. And then I roamed the store, dusting shelves and arranging books.

When I opened the front door at nine, a line of customers streamed into the shop. No one was gossiping about the murder, so I figured the police hadn't released the news.

Around noon, a police cruiser pulled into the parking lot. Cinnamon, riding solo, climbed out and strode to Beaders of Paradise, the shop that was cattycorner from ours. The proprietor, her mother, Pepper Pritchett, popped outside, the work apron she had on over her beaded sweater and trousers billowing up. She clutched Cinnamon by both elbows, and the two exchanged a few words. With her short silver hair and harsh features, Pepper looked nothing like her daughter. In some regard, life hadn't treated her well. Years ago, she'd been in love with my father, but she'd lost out to my mother. When she did find love, she married, but soon after Cinnamon's birth, the man walked out, leaving her to raise her daughter by herself. Pepper's crafting shop and the classes she taught had become the mainstay of her existence.

Pepper turned her head and yelled something in the direction of her shop. Seconds later, Flora Fairchild came into view. Like Pepper, she was wearing an apron over her clothes. Apparently, the two of them had been immersed in a project. I wondered whether Flora had finally convinced Pepper to make items to sell at Home Sweet Home. She'd been nagging her to do so for months.

Flora's mouth moved, and she jutted her hand in the direction of the Cookbook Nook. Pepper bobbed her head profusely. When Cinnamon cut a look in our direction, something inside me twinged with unease. I told Bailey I needed to see what was up and sprinted out the front door.

Cinnamon saw me. "What do you want?"

"What do you mean *what do I want*?" I gestured to Flora. "Obviously she's talking about something or someone at the Cookbook Nook, and your mother is agreeing with her. I'd like to know the substance of the conversation." I realized my voice was rising in pitch and took a deep breath. "Please loop me in."

"Miss Fairchild was telling my mother—"

"Call me Flora, Cinnamon. For heaven's sake," Flora muttered. "I babysat you."

Cinnamon started again. "Flora was telling my mother about a set-to your aunt had with Wesley Preston, and my mother, in turn, told her about the murder."

"How did she learn of it?"

"It so happens that my mother"—Cinnamon scowled at Pepper, who was studying her fingernails—"has invested in a police scanner and heard about the murder when we requested backup."

"And you think my aunt had something to do with it? Ridiculous." I faced Flora. "My aunt told you the *set-to*"—I made air quotes—"between her and Wesley was nothing. They laughed about it, don't you remember? She didn't . . . She wouldn't . . ." I squinted, trying to ease the tension that was taking hold of my forehead but couldn't. I addressed Cinnamon. "Aunt Vera doesn't go out at night. Not on her own."

"So?"

"Mr. Preston died at night. Not this morning."

Cinnamon shifted feet.

"She doesn't own a pair of hiking boots, eith—" I drew up short. Yes, she did. Appleby had coaxed her into taking hikes a few months ago.

"We didn't find boot prints," Cinnamon said, "so that's neither here nor there."

"Look, there's no way she could have killed Wesley Preston." I stuck out a hand. "Ask Deputy Appleby. He was with her last night at the reception. He'll vouch for her whereabouts."

"I've already asked him." Cinnamon held up her cell phone, displaying a text message from Appleby. "After dropping her at home, he left for his weekly poker game."

I groaned. *No-o-o-o.* "With whom?"

"That doesn't matter. He was out until two a.m."

"And you think Mr. Preston died before that?"

"The coroner guesses the murder occurred sometime between ten and midnight." Cinnamon narrowed her gaze. "Miss Fairchild tells me—"

Flora cleared her throat to remind Cinnamon not to be formal.

"Flora," Cinnamon revised, "tells me your aunt owns quite a selection of specialty cheese knives."

I sputtered out a laugh. "No way a cheese knife was used to kill Wesley Preston."

"A skeleton knife, to be specific," Cinnamon said.

Oh, heck. She was right. A skeleton knife was small and sharp. It was designed with three large holes on the blade to reduce the surface area of the blade so sticky foods wouldn't cling to it. "I have two in my kitchen drawer," I said defiantly. "Does that make me the murderer?"

"Don't get huffy," Flora said.

"Right," Pepper chimed in. "Don't get huffy."

I glared at the two of them. Flora withered. Pepper folded her arms across her chest.

"I'd like to see her knives," Cinnamon said.

"Chief," I said, "how could you possibly think my aunt had anything to do with this?"

Flora said, "If she's innocent—"

"The police will figure it out," Pepper finished.

I whirled on them, not knowing which of the two disgusted me more. Both were friends of my aunt's. What had possessed them to throw her under the bus? The idiotic sparring between Wesley and Aunt Vera? Get real.

My aunt passed through the shop's doorway. "Jenna, customers need—" She paused and frowned. "What's going on? Why are all of you huddling out here?"

Cinnamon strode toward her. Flora, Pepper, and I followed.

Bailey stepped outside while shrugging a light cardigan over her turquoise top. She joined me. The weather had turned crisper, the wind stiffer, as if in honor of the tragedy that had occurred. "What's going on?" she whispered.

"The chief wants to see my aunt's knives."

Cinnamon said, "Vera Hart?"

"Yes, young lady, you know who I am." My aunt squared her shoulders. She was taller and bigger-boned than Cinnamon, and the slight adjustment of her spine made her seem fearsome.

"Aunt Vera, she thinks you killed Wesley!" I cried.

"What?" She flapped the air with a hand. "Nonsense."

"Flora said you have a knife, a knife that—"

"I have lots of knives, Jenna. For all occasions. So do each of you." My aunt leveled her gaze on her accusers. "You can't be a good chef without the proper knives." My aunt loved to cook. She made a mean spaghetti and her Beef Wellington was incredible. "Knives are the backbone of any decent kitchen."

"Aunt Vera"—I rounded the chief, scuttled to my aunt, and gripped her elbow—"stop talking." Did she need an attorney? I was afraid to ask Cinnamon, fearful she'd say yes.

Bailey rushed to my aunt's other side and also clasped an elbow. I imagined we resembled a poor imitation of the three musketeers.

"Where were you last night between the hours of ten p.m. and midnight, Miss Hart?" Cinnamon asked.

"It's Mrs. Appleby, now," my aunt said staunchly, "but you should call me Vera."

"Vera," Cinnamon acquiesced. "Ten to midnight?"

"I was at home. Why?"

"Was anyone with you?"

"My husband, your deputy, dropped me off after the soirée and left to attend a poker game." She raised her chin ever so slightly, refusing to be cowed. "He came home at two."

"What did you do during that time?"

"For the first hour, I worked on tomorrow's specialty crossword puzzle, like everyone else in town, I imagine. I wanted to win the free appetizers at Brick's Barbecue. I was stumped, however, by a handful of clues. Wesley outdid himself . . ." Her voice snagged. She began again. "He outdid himself on this one. It was rather challenging." Her shoulders started to vibrate. Her lips quivered. "For the next hour, I puttered. I was wound up after the cocktail party. It was such a success. Everyone had a—" She choked back the rest. "I didn't kill him, Cinnamon. I adored him like a brother."

"Flora said he threatened you during your set-to," Cinnamon stated. "He said something to the effect of, 'Over my dead body.'"

"It was in jest," my aunt said. "All in fun. One of our favorite games to play as kids was Clue."

Cinnamon gawked. "That game had been invented by then?"

"It was created in 1947," my aunt stated, "but because of war shortages, it wasn't released until 1949."

"Trivia for one hundred!" Pepper exclaimed.

Cinnamon threw her a dirty look. "Mother, please."

"I happen to like *Jeopardy!*" Pepper said. "I'm good at it."

"I know you are, but now is not the time. Vera," Cinnamon said to my aunt, "I'd like to visit your house right now if you don't mind. I want to see your collection of knives."

To my relief, Cinnamon didn't handcuff my aunt or stuff her into the backseat of her vehicle. Instead, she fetched her a few tissues from the cruiser and then allowed me to chauffeur my aunt home. Perhaps Cinnamon was going easy on my aunt because she was the wife of a deputy. Maybe it was because she had great respect for Aunt Vera and didn't believe she was guilty. Even so, in my heart of hearts, I hoped this step in the investigation was giving her indigestion.

My aunt's beach house faced the ocean and was about the same size as Rhett's and my home. The living room led to the lanai. The dining room abutted the living room. She'd recently redecorated in shades of blue and green.

"As you can see," Aunt Vera said to Cinnamon as she led her into the kitchen, "the knife block is complete."

The kitchen was streamlined but comfortable with white granite counters, white subway tile backsplash, and white cabinets, with accents of turquoise and emerald. The knife block in question stood to the left of the stove. Every knife was, indeed, in its slot.

"I'll give you a tour if I may," my aunt said.

"You may," Cinnamon said.

Aunt Vera opened a drawer below the knife block. "Here are more of my knives."

I peeked in. She had inserted a sixteen-slot organizer. Every slot held a knife, blade down.

"There are steak knives as well as carving knives, each in its place. And here" — my aunt moved to her right and slid open another drawer, "you'll find my cheese knives." There were five lying in separate sections of a bamboo tray, blades turned to the left. "The first is a *Laguiole en Aubrac* handmade cheese knife," Aunt Vera said. "For Francophiles, there is no knife more iconic than this. Named after the city in southern France, these knives are synonymous with quality."

Cinnamon kept quiet.

"Now, please note they are not a brand, but they represent a craftsmanship beyond compare. See the gorgeous curved wood handle?" Pointing to the next knife, she said, "This is a Boska soft cheese knife. Boska is a Dutch company that has been around for over a century. With its slim blade, the Boska knife is designed to slice your favorite soft cheeses. Next is a Boska cheese slicer. It's not exactly a knife, but it can cut."

She was referring to the utensil with a triangular head and a carving space perpendicular to the handle. In my opinion, it was the best for cutting a brick of cheese, the resulting slices perfect for grilled cheese sandwiches.

"The one beyond that is a stainless steel knife with holes, skeleton-style I believe you called it," she said, an edge to her voice. "It's inexpensive but practical."

I breathed easier. It didn't look like it had been used to kill a man. Of course, she could have washed it and replaced it in the drawer, but wouldn't the killer have discarded the murder weapon? Had Cinnamon's crew scoured the crime scene for a knife? Had they dug through the garbage bins positioned along the trail and in the trailhead parking lot?

"Last but not least, the Casaware five-inch Santoku knife," my aunt said. "It's a thin knife and features a sheepsfoot blade—that's the corrugation. It is an extremely well-balanced knife, but lacking a tip, it would be worthless as a murder weapon."

"How did you learn so much about knives?" Cinnamon seemed impressed by my aunt's knowledge, or she was astounded, as I was, by how well my aunt was holding herself together.

"I've been cooking all my life. I even went to culinary school in France for a year."

I gawked. I'd had no idea, but there was a lot of my aunt's history I didn't know. She shared it with me one revelation at a time.

"And the cheese knives?" Cinnamon asked.

"I frequent Say Cheese Shoppe," Aunt Vera said. The gourmet shop wasn't far from my father's hardware store. "Charlene loves to offer advice. If given the chance, she'll wax rhapsodic about cheese all day long."

Cinnamon knew that was true. Over the past few months, her husband had become a cheese connoisseur and frequently picked Charlene's brain for new cheeses to try. The last time he and Cinnamon had joined Rhett and me for a barbecue, he'd brought his new favorite cheese, a *tomme du Savoie*, as an appetizer.

Cinnamon studied the knives and said, "Do you mind if I take the skeleton knife?"

My aunt stiffened but kept her composure. "Feel free. I have nothing to hide."

Cinnamon produced a paper bag from her pocket as well as a pair of latex gloves. She donned the gloves, lifted the knife from its slot, and inserted it into the paper bag. I remembered my father telling me once that wet evidence went into paper, dry into plastic. The knife didn't look wet, but if there was a trace of blood on it . . .

I bit back the bile rising in my throat. No. I couldn't think that. Cinnamon's action was procedure. My aunt was not guilty!

Chapter 11

Tête-à-tête: (noun) a private conversation; an S-shaped sofa on which two people can sit face-to-face; (adverb) between two people in private

By the time my aunt and I returned to the shop, a horde of customers were mingling inside. Many had solved today's specialty puzzle and were carrying disposable boxes from Brick's Barbecue. The savory boneless baby back ribs smelled divine. I adored the restaurant's selections of mild, moderate, and spicy sauces. None of the customers seemed to know that Wesley Preston was dead. Yet.

Now that Pepper and Flora were spouting off and my aunt had been questioned by the police, it was purely a matter of time.

Gran was at the sales counter ringing up purchases. She gave me a worried look. Bailey, who was helping a couple of customers on the floor, did the same. I threw them both a thumbs-up sign and forced a smile. Aunt Vera was fine. *Fine*.

Pepper and Flora must have been waiting in the breezeway for our return because they bustled through the archway the moment we entered and shadowed my aunt to the sales counter.

"Vera, I'm so sorry," Flora said. "It's not my fault. Pepper and I were chatting about your tête-à-tête with Wesley, and then she heard—"

"I didn't *hear* anything," Pepper cut in. "I got an alert on this." She held up her cell phone. "I've got an app."

Everybody had an app for something nowadays. If only there was an app for solving a murder. As if sensing my musings, Tigger brushed against my ankles, eager to be picked up. I obliged him, holding him close to drink in his good vibes.

"I heard about the"—Pepper lowered her voice to utter the word *murder*—"and knowing you were intimately involved with Wesley, I informed my daughter about the altercation between you two."

"We weren't intimately involved," my aunt said. "Intimately implies a love relationship. We were friends. That was all. Good friends. And it wasn't an altercation."

"Flare-up, then," Pepper said. "A squabble."

Flora huffed. "I distinctly told Pepper it was a tête-à-tête."

"I don't care what either of you called it or what you did afterward," my aunt said. "What's done is done. I'm innocent."

"Did Cinnamon find the murder weapon at your house?" Pepper asked.

"No!"

"You have so many cheese knives."

My aunt leveled a glare at her. "Pepper, listen and listen good. I'm not guilty. End of story. All I want is for the police to find my friend's murderer."

My aunt hadn't used her indoor voice. This time the word *murderer* swept through the crowd. Instantly, questions circulated. *Was there a murder? Who was killed? Where did it happen?* Gran answered a cluster of customers eager for the news. Bailey handled another set of inquiries. I tuned them out and remained focused on Flora, Pepper, and my aunt.

"Please don't hate me, Vera," Flora said.

"I don't hate you." My aunt put a reassuring hand on Flora's arm. "How could I? You don't have a vicious bone in your body."

Flora nearly wept with relief.

"You are a gossip, though. I wish you weren't, and you would do yourself a favor if you'd try not to be, going forward. I'm sure your fiancé would appreciate that. As for you . . ." My aunt turned her gaze on Pepper, her lips thin with exasperation. "You can be . . ." She bit back whatever she was going to say.

Pepper gulped. "Vera, let me explain."

"No need." My aunt held up a hand to stop her. "I understand. You're the mother of a policeman. That can't be easy. You feel it's your duty to report whatever you hear."

"Precisely." Pepper swung around as if to convince onlookers that she was guiltless on all charges.

"Which is what Jenna does, at times. She wants justice. She wants answers." My aunt slung an arm around me and gave a squeeze. "Why, Pepper, you and Jenna even teamed up once, didn't you?"

Pepper sputtered. "We did."

My aunt was referring to the time Pepper actually came to my rescue when I was facing off with a killer. After that, Pepper had warmed to me and I to her. She wasn't a mean-spirited woman, just single-minded at times.

"That must've irked the heck out of your daughter," Aunt Vera said.

Pepper laughed. "That's an understatement."

"All right, everyone." My aunt clapped her hands and addressed the crowd. "You've now learned that dear Wesley Preston has been killed. The police are doing everything they can to find the culprit. I know some of you will want to join in a memorial for Wesley. I will be speaking to our mayor to set that up. In the meantime, if you know something, speak up. If you see anything suspicious, contact the police. If—" She wheezed as if all the reserve energy she could muster had drained from her body. "Good day." She proceeded into the storage room. Alone.

"That's all, folks," I said. "Show's over. Those who are ready to finalize purchases, please form a line at the counter." I set Tigger on his kitty condo so he wouldn't get trampled. "And any of you who are hungry, feel free to take one of the mini cupcakes Chef Katie put in the breezeway." Daily, Katie came up with a treat that might entice customers to visit the café. Today's goodies were an array of chocolate and vanilla cupcakes, and a pink one that I presumed was peppermint. Katie fancied experimenting with minty flavors.

A few of the customers tried to get more details from Gran, Bailey, and me about the murder, but we didn't take the bait. My aunt was innocent. Why muck up the water with suppositions?

When the line of customers dwindled, Bailey moseyed to me. While smoothing the sleeves of her top—she'd removed the cardigan sweater she'd thrown on earlier—she said, "Are you okay?"

"Don't worry about me." I told her about Cinnamon confiscating a skeleton knife at my aunt's house. "It's not the murder weapon. It can't be."

"Of course it's not."

"But the sheer act of her taking it really unnerved my aunt."

"And you."

"If I'm truthful, yes."

When Cinnamon and I first met, she suspected me of killing a friend I'd met in college. Living under the weight of her mistrust had been unbearable. Having the police comb through all the reasons I might have wanted my friend dead was unsettling. "Aunt Vera is acting like it was no big deal, but she's good at hiding her emotions."

On cue, my aunt emerged from the storage room. "Jenna."

I told Bailey I'd be back and darted to her. "Yes? Do you want to go home? Do you need to rest?"

"No, dear," she said, sotto voce. "I need you to find whoever killed Wesley."

"Aunt Vera, you know the police and Marlon—"

"The police will do their best, of course, but that might not be enough." She pressed a hand to her chest. "And Marlon is a very effective deputy. He's stalwart and true and the love of my life, but he can be narrowly focused."

Only once in the years that I'd known Marlon Appleby had he willingly asked me to discuss a case with him and that was solely because Cinnamon had been in the hospital and was feeling stymied by an investigation.

"But Cinnamon is in charge," I said. "You know she's determined and smart."

"Yes, she is excellent at what she does, but she, too, can be . . ." My aunt pursed her lips. "I can't think of the word. It'll come to me. But, let's face it, she'll never be welcomed by the puzzlers who are in town for the event. She isn't a crossword enthusiast."

"How do you know that?"

"Can you imagine her taking private time to solve one? Not on a bet. To let off tension, she roller skates." Cinnamon was an excellent skater. "She's athletic," my aunt went on. "She won't sit idle for a second. On the other hand, you, when you worked at the advertising agency, were praised for your ability to think outside the box. You delve. You ruminate. You lose yourself in a novel. You get immersed in an art project."

Occasionally, I painted. I'd never be a professional, but I enjoyed the peace that filled me when doing so. My mother had been the real artist in the family.

"Also, you are a people person."

"So is Cinnamon."

My aunt chortled. "You know how to get people to confide in you. Given your strengths, you are the one who will be in tune with all the tournament participants. You talk their language. Therefore, I'm expecting you to befriend them and slyly question them."

Slyly. Yeah, right. I was not very sly.

"You, my dear girl, look at clues and attribute multiple meanings to them. That's what this case might need." She seized my arm. "Please promise me you'll do everything in your power to bring the killer to justice."

I threw my arms around her and cooed, "I promise."

"Jenna," a woman called.

Eva Wainwright was weaving through the customers who had remained to finalize purchases. Her black leggings, seamless black top, and running shoes accentuated her slimness. Her hair was slick with perspiration. Her skin was flushed—from exercise, I presumed. She hadn't put on a stitch of makeup, not that she needed to. She had exquisite bone structure.

"I heard you have crossword puzzle cookie jars, and I simply must have one," Eva said breathlessly, removing a credit card from a zippered pocket. "Please tell me you have some in stock. I want to give one to Wesley as a thank-you present for deigning to take part in this week's events. Yes, yes, he can be a snob, refusing to appear unless he is the star, but he came, and for that he deserves a pat on the back."

Oh, my. She hadn't heard. I glanced helplessly over my shoulder at my aunt, who quickly joined the two of us.

"Eva"—Aunt Vera clasped the woman's elbow—"come with me."

"What's going on?" Eva asked.

"I have some bad news." My aunt guided Eva to the vintage table and settled her into a chair. I followed. "Wesley—"

"He'd better not have left town." Eva's gaze hardened. "He threatened to do so at the soirée last night after all those fans kept riling him, but I made him promise—"

"Wesley is dead," Aunt Vera said.

"What?" Eva turned pale. "No. That's not possible. Last night, he was the epitome of health. He's dead?"

My aunt nodded glumly.

"What happened?" Moisture flooded Eva's eyes. "Did he have a heart attack? He did, didn't he? Ooh, I've been telling him to slow down. Telling him he didn't need to turn out so many puzzles or put in so many hours. He was a workhorse, you know. Each puzzle was part of his legacy." She paused. *"Was.* What a horrid three-letter word." She clapped a hand over her mouth and spoke between spread fingers. "Dead." She gulped in air as tears leaked down her cheeks. "Tell me what happened."

I fetched some tissues from a container on the sales counter and hustled back. I passed them to Eva. She dabbed her eyes and crumpled the tissues into a wad.

"He went hiking last night," my aunt began.

"To see nocturnal birds we think," I inserted.

"He was fascinated by them," Eva said. "Birding after dark, he told me, was the best way to experience the incredible creatures. He couldn't view as many, but he could listen." Her eyelids fluttered. She slurped back more tears. "Did you know he created the most marvelous puzzle about owls a year ago? He was so proud of it, using words like *snowy* and *hootercells* and *screecher* and *tuwhittuwhoo*." She spelled the word. "That's the sound an owl makes. He—" She covered her mouth with the tissues. "Did he have a heart attack, Vera? You didn't say."

"No, dear. Someone, um, met him on the trail."

"Met him? I'm not following."

"Someone slit his throat. With a knife."

"No!" Eva swung her gaze between me and my aunt.

"Jenna and her husband found him," Aunt Vera added. "This morning. On their hike."

Rhett had been texting me frequently since I'd dropped him and Rook off at the house, asking me how I was faring. *As well as can be expected, Fine*, and *Okay* had been my go-to responses. His, too.

"No, it's not possible," Eva drawled, her accent thicker from the shock. "Someone killed him? No!" She must have realized she was shouting because she covered her mouth again. "Why would anyone do that? He was the most marvelous man."

The way she was gushing over him made me wonder if she'd been in love with him. Had she flirted last night with Ulysses Huxley to make Wesley jealous? When he didn't rise to the bait, did she take that as a rejection and kill him?

Jenna, stop, I chided. *Do not jump to conclusions.* If I intended to help my aunt solve this mystery, I needed to be deliberate and thoughtful and consider every clue. Besides, a woman as remarkable as Eva wouldn't fly into a rage over being rejected. I'd bet she had plenty of suitors. On the other hand, she had been Wesley Preston's editor. Who knew what kind of contentious business relationship they might have had?

"I . . . I . . ." Eva stammered. She bounded to a standing position. The chair's feet scraped the floor. The sound sent a chill down my spine. "I need to go back to the inn. I need to lie down. I need to—"

"You shouldn't drive," my aunt said.

"I won't. I mean I can't," Eva said. "I'm on foot. I left my T-Bird at the inn. I was on my daily run when I decided to drop in here."

"You're not walking back, either." Aunt Vera put a hand on Eva's shoulder. "Jenna will drive you. Jenna, dear, please make sure Eva gets settled in. Order her some soothing tea." To Eva she said, "Do you have any family or friends in town?"

"My brother lives in San Francisco."

"Would you like us to call him?"

"No." She said it so abruptly I got the feeling that she and he didn't have a warm relationship. "I'll be okay," she whispered as if to convince herself. "Once I get over . . . over the shock."

"I would imagine the police will be reaching out to you soon," my aunt added.

Eva's red-rimmed eyes widened. "Why would they need to speak with me?"

"You were Wesley's editor. You've known him a long time. Talking to you will help their investigation."

"I'm not a suspect, am I?"

"Doubtful," my aunt said. "I'd guess you were asleep by ten last night, what with all the activities and excitement." My aunt rarely made such pointed remarks. Was she fishing for answers? Was she wondering, as I was, whether Eva killed him?

Eva blinked. "Yes, I was," she murmured, but it sounded like a lie. Had she been out and about? Could a witness place her somewhere other than in her hotel room? Was she, at this very minute, trying to fashion a credible alibi? "I was in my room. Not asleep. Reading. My e-reader. A historical novel." Fresh tears bloomed. She mashed the wad of tissues against her eyes and held it there for a good thirty seconds. When she lowered the tissues, she was composed. "I can't believe it. Murdered."

A series of synonyms coursed through my mind. *Slain. Snuffed.*

Done in. Then a list of alternative words for motive followed. *Aim. Intention. Purpose.*

Other than rejection, did Eva have another reason to want Wesley dead?

Chapter 12

Editor: responsible for selecting and editing crossword puzzles, and moderating the clues to match the desired degree of difficulty

"It's so kind of you to give me a lift, Jenna," Eva said, sitting in the passenger seat of my car.

"I'm glad to be of help, and I could use a bit of fresh air myself."

We were driving up Seaview Road in the direction of Crystal Cove Inn, which was located near the top of the mountain. Most of the tournament attendees were staying at the place. Z.Z. had reserved a block of rooms. She hadn't planned to hold any events on-site, but she'd wanted there to be a central location so participants and fans could hang out.

"I can't believe you and your husband found Wesley," Eva said. "How did you —"

"Our dog discovered him and alerted us."

"Did he, you know" — Eva swallowed hard — "suffer?"

"He died quickly," I said, knowing it wasn't a sufficient answer. However, with all I'd absorbed about crime scenes over the years, from my own experience as well as watching popular TV shows, I was certain a slice to the carotid artery would cause death instantly. "How long have you known him?"

"Years. Thirty-eight, to be exact. He was the first cruciverbalist I brought to the *Gazette*. There were many constructors providing puzzles by then, but he was . . ." She turned to peer out the side window. Not for a view, unless she was fascinated by businesses like Chill Zone, Enchanted Garden, or the Cultural Center. I figured she didn't want me to see her cry again. "He was a standout and my discovery," she finished.

Her tone was wistful and again I wondered if their relationship had been more intimate than it had appeared on the surface.

"Thirty-eight years," I said. "Gee. I thought he was producing puzzles for other papers by that time."

"He was, but not on the West Coast. I was twenty-four and eager to make my mark."

"Isn't that young to become an editor?"

"Oh, I wasn't a full-fledged editor at the time. I was an assistant copy editor. I was artless but dogged." She sighed. "When I reached out to Wesley, I convinced him to send the *Gazette* a few of his best puzzles. His work impressed the editor in chief so much, he fired the entertainment editor and gave me the position as long as I got Wesley on board." She drummed her fingertips on the passenger door. "I owe . . . *owed* Wesley everything."

Falling silent, she turned her face toward the window again.

"There are tissues in the glove compartment," I said gently.

"Thank you." She took one and dabbed her eyes with it.

Minutes later, I pulled into the upper parking lot at the inn and found a spot. Like most buildings in town, the inn was painted white with a red tile roof. Calling it an inn didn't do it justice, though. It was expansive with two wings of rooms as well as a dozen private cabanas. With its coveted views of the ocean and Crystal Cove below, the place was consistently full. The exquisite grounds of azaleas and crape myrtles called to mind gardens in a Jane Austen novel. In addition to the breakfast room, there were two notable restaurants.

Eva hurriedly exited the car.

I got out, too.

"You don't need to come in," she said.

"My aunt will be upset with me if I don't see you to your room and order that tea."

Eva made a face. "I hate hot tea."

"How about sweet iced tea?"

She scrunched up her nose. "Heaven forbid."

"Coffee?"

"Okay," she said, resigned, realizing she wasn't going to get rid of me until I'd followed through on my promise. She led the way through the lobby.

A number of guests were enjoying the fire in the big stone fireplace. Some were sitting in the wing-backed chairs filling out crossword puzzles. Others were perched on the hearth, warming their backs. Many were holding copper cups, which I presumed were filled with hot cocoa, the inn's specialty.

The concierge, a perky woman named Ginny, greeted us from her desk as we passed. I responded half-heartedly and followed Eva.

We walked along the colonnade in silence. As we made the turn toward the cabanas, Eva halted and gasped. "What're they doing here?"

Cinnamon Pritchett and Marlon Appleby were standing outside a cabana, its door ajar. I was surprised to see them, as well. I hadn't spotted any squad cars in the upper parking lot. They must have found ample space in the lower. The manager of the inn was standing nearby speaking with a blunt-haired housekeeper. Cinnamon gave a command to Officer Foster, a female cop my age who I'd mistakenly believed was in her twenties when we'd first met, due to her sprightly nature and pert features. She saluted Cinnamon and returned inside the room. Cinnamon and Appleby, consumed with the work at hand, didn't look in our direction.

Eva's cabana was two shy of Wesley's. She opened the door with a magnetic key and entered. I followed her inside. The room, like all the cabanas, was well-appointed with an adjoining kitchen area to the left and a bedroom to the right. A brocade sofa and a pair of comfortable-looking chairs faced the gas fireplace.

"Didn't you say Wesley died on the hiking trail?" Eva asked, removing her jacket and tossing it on the sofa.

"Yes."

"Then why —"

"Often the police will sift through items in the deceased's room to get a feel for the individual." *Listen to you, Jenna, sounding like a seasoned pro.* "They'll look through his computer. They'll scour his cell phone for messages and texts."

"His cell phone?"

"He didn't have one on him."

"How do you . . . Oh, right. You and your husband found him. You must've searched him."

"No, we didn't. We wouldn't tamper with a crime scene. But we were there when Chief Pritchett checked."

"Oh." She dragged her teeth over her lower lip.

"The police will also look for clues to see if anyone visited him before he went out on his hike," I went on. "Perhaps a fellow birder."

"Why, oh, why did he have to go birding?" She spanked the side of her leg. "Here of all places?"

"We aren't sure he did." But it sounded reasonable. "Lastly, the police will look for evidence that they can connect to the crime scene, like a weapon."

"How would it have ended up in his room if he was killed on the trail?"

"The murderer might have come back, broken into his room, and left it."

"That makes no sense."

She was right. It didn't. Why would whoever had done this risk entering Wesley's room after the fact? Unless there was something of value that the killer wanted to find. Did Wesley travel with a lot of cash? Did he carry works in progress with him? Had a budding cruciverbalist eliminated him in hopes of stealing his trove of puzzles so they could submit them as their own?

"Coffee," I said, and strode to the room's landline phone on the kitchen counter. I dialed room service and ordered Eva a pot of black coffee.

"With cream and sugar," Eva said, moving into the bedroom.

I peeked around the corner, hand over the phone's mouthpiece. "Do you want anything to eat?"

"I don't think I'll ever be able to eat again," she said dramatically.

"The scones here are excellent."

"Fine. A scone." She slumped onto the edge of her queen-sized bed, shoved the black canvas bag that rested on it to one side, and finally the dam burst. Her body heaved. Her sobs tore at my heartstrings.

I completed the order, ended the call, and joined her on the edge of her bed. She hoisted the canvas bag and threw it on the floor. It landed with a metallic thud. What the heck did she have in there? Jumper cables? An anvil? I put a hand on her back to console her. She sobbed until someone knocked on the door.

"Room service," a man said.

Eva mopped her face with her palms, rose to her feet, and allowed the waiter to bring in the tray. She directed him to set it on the dining table. "You don't have to stay, Jenna," she said after he left. "I'll be all right on my own."

"If you need anything . . ." I pulled a business card from my purse and handed it to her.

She thanked me and saw me to the door.

When I returned outside, I caught sight of Deputy Appleby standing by himself close to the foyer, a cell phone pressed to one ear. He ended the call and beckoned me. "How is your aunt doing?"

"She's holding up under the pressure. Are Officer Foster and Cinnamon inside Mr. Preston's room?"

"The chief left. Foster is in there with Ford."

I knew Ford. He was a freckle-faced rookie with an easy grin.

"I'm sure Cinnamon doesn't believe your aunt killed Wesley," Appleby said without much conviction.

"And you know she didn't," I said forcefully.

He remained neutral. "The cheese knife is at the lab."

"If . . ." I paused and stressed, "*if* a cheese knife was the weapon, has anyone thought to visit Say Cheese Shoppe and ask Charlene about the knives she sells?"

Appleby scratched the back of his neck. "Not to my knowledge, but it's a good suggestion."

"The only reason Cinnamon suspects my aunt is guilty is because of what Flora and Pepper said."

"And the fact that she argued publicly with Wesley Preston."

"You know they had a friendly rivalry. They sparred. It's their . . ." I paused. "It *was* their thing. One-upmanship, as it were. She had no reason to want him dead." I opened my hands. "And do you honestly believe she went hiking near midnight on an unlit trail? That's inconceivable."

"It is."

"Then go to bat for her."

"I can't. Not this time. I have to let the investigation lead wherever it will."

I glowered at him. "Will you have to recuse yourself? I mean, talk about conflict of interest. You're married to her."

"For now, I'm allowed to observe but not investigate."

"Does she need an attorney?"

"Not yet."

A cool breeze kicked up. I folded my arms to warm myself. "Did your team find Mr. Preston's Swiss Army knife in his room?"

He shook his head.

"And it wasn't on his person or nearby?" I asked.

"Nope."

"So, it could very well be the murder weapon," I reasoned, "and the killer could have tossed it anywhere along the hiking trail."

"We've got officers searching the area."

"The garbage bins, too?"

"Yes." He peered soulfully into my eyes. "Don't worry. I won't let anything happen to your aunt."

From your lips to God's ears, I prayed.

I headed into the lobby wondering who had motive to want Wesley Preston dead. He'd stiffed Sunny Shore, and he'd undervalued Ulysses Huxley. Noam Dixon certainly had an axe to grind with him; he'd lost the love of his life because of Wesley. And what about Eva? I wanted to rule her out. She had seemed genuinely shocked and upset that he was dead.

I crossed the peg-and-groove floor to the concierge desk. "Hey, Ginny." I took a seat and leaned forward on both elbows.

Her back was to me. She swung around with a paper she'd collected from a printer and smiled at me. "Hi, Jenna."

"Got a moment? Am I interrupting something important?"

"Nope." She set the paper down and smoothed the lapels of her green uniform. "I was finalizing a guest's itinerary. How may I help you?"

"I suppose you heard about Wesley Preston . . ."

"I did." She leaned forward, lowering her voice. "What is Crystal Cove coming to? Another murder. Should we be scared?"

"No. I think this was a personal, one-time attack. There are a lot of people in town for the crossword event, and Mr. Preston ruffled a few feathers, to put it mildly."

"He was nice to me."

"What can you tell me about guests staying here?"

"They're awfully clever. Always asking each other questions, like 'What's a four-letter word for this or a six-letter word for that?' Me? I can't do a crossword puzzle to save my life. My mind doesn't think that way. Give me a knitting pattern, no problem. I don't think in black and white."

I smiled. "Do you know Sunny Shore?"

"Sure do. Cute face. Devil-may-care eyes."

That pegged her. "She was supposed to have a meeting with Mr.

Preston last night. After the soirée at Intime. Do you know if they met?"

"Yep. Right over there. By the fireplace. Around a quarter past eight."

Not long after the glass-shattering incident had given Wesley and others an out to leave.

"How was their encounter? Friendly?" I asked.

"At first. Both of them were sitting down. She was drinking white wine. He had champagne. They were smiling and chatting." Ginny peeped left and right to make sure the area was clear before continuing. "But then things turned sour."

"Sour," I echoed.

"Yep. He said something, I don't know what, and all of a sudden, she threw the wine in his face."

"Oh, my." That seemed like an overreaction just because he'd refused to pay her what she was owed. "What did Mr. Preston do?"

"He howled like he thought that was the most hysterical thing in the world, then he said, 'I didn't know you had it in you, girl.'"

"Girl?" I gawped. "He called her girl?"

"Yep," Ginny said. "Needless to say, that ticked Miss Shore off. She jumped to her feet and stomped the floor, which startled a number of guests."

"Throwing the wine didn't?"

"I'm not sure anyone noticed. I was, um, observing, you know? We were having a slow night. With most everyone attending the gig at the restaurant, I didn't have very many reservations to make and no wine tours to set up." Ginny repeated her left-right glancing maneuver to ensure she could continue confiding in me without others hearing her. "Next, Miss Shore said—and I caught this as clear as day—'You'd better hope the Boogie Man doesn't get you for all the bad juju you're putting out in the world.'"

"The Boogie Man? Bad juju?"

"Uh-huh. She was really angry. She said, 'You're done screwing me over. I'll sue you.' Then Mr. Preston's face got really dark, and he lowered his voice, and I couldn't hear what he said next, but it sounded like, 'You don't have the guts to follow through.' Miss Shore said, 'Watch me!' and stormed out of the place. I rushed after her, afraid she was going to climb into her car and tear off. I hate to see anyone drive angry because . . ." She sighed. "Because that's how my father died. He and my mother had a fierce fight. My mother has never forgiven herself."

"I'm so sorry."

"It was twenty years ago. I only know because my mom told me the story." She rapped her knuckles on the desk. "Suffice it to say, I felt obliged to run after Miss Shore to see if I could soothe her, but I couldn't catch up to her. She peeled out of the lot in her Acura. The stench of burning rubber was awful. I was relieved when I saw her return about an hour later all cool, calm, and collected. She greeted me, and I greeted her, and it was like nothing had happened."

"Jekyll and Hyde-ish?"

"No. More like she'd taken a valium and a long walk along the beach. That's what I do when I'm wound up. Not the valium. I don't do drugs. But the long walk and the sound of the surf soothes me." Ginny peered at the archway leading to the room. "Huh. Come to think of it, I haven't seen her today. She probably got up early for her morning stroll. She told me listening to birds relaxes her. She must have stayed out longer to sightsee. She was asking about the lighthouse yesterday."

Interesting. Was Sunny a nocturnal bird watcher like Wesley? When she returned from her drive, had she gone to his room to have it out with him one more time? Did she see him leaving and follow him to the trail? Being a birder, would she have been able to make her way in the dark without a flashlight, and therefore, go undetected?

Chapter 13

Grid: a pattern of straight lines that cross over each other, forming squares or rectangles

I climbed out of my car in the Fisherman's Village lot and drew in a deep breath. The sun was sinking over the ocean. Wisps of tangerine and yellow clouds painted the sky. I closed the driver's door and auto-locked the car with a *beep*. At the same time, I spotted Ulysses Huxley once again whittling outside the Nook Café, his leather satchel beside him on the bench. He saluted me with the edge of his penknife. I shivered. The gesture seemed cavalier on the heels of Wesley's demise. Maybe he hadn't heard.

"Waiting for someone?" I approached cautiously.

"Eva Wainwright," he said. "We have business to discuss."

"Eva, of course. Um" — I hooked my thumb over my shoulder — "I dropped her off at her hotel. She wasn't feeling well. She . . ." I perched on the bench alongside him and studied his outfit — plaid shirt, jeans, and hiking boots. *Dusty hiking boots,* I noted. Rather than launch into Eva's state of mind, I pointed to his creation. "That's nice."

"Thanks. I made it."

"Wow." It wasn't a pencil, as I'd seen him paring before. It was a ten-inch-long tapered stick. On one end, he'd tied a string of decorative beads and crystals. Along the length of the stick, he'd glued sparkly stones. "What is it?"

"A spirit wand. Whoever owns it will be able to tap into the energy of the universe."

I'd heard about spirit wands. They could be made out of a variety of materials, but they should include wood, crystals, or stones.

"There are some that have been crafted of gold and silver, but that's too rich for my blood. This one" — Ulysses held it up for me to inspect — "will tap into the owner's individual frequency, allowing her to resonate with the energy of the universe."

"Her?"

His cheeks flamed red. "Eva."

"Ah. You like her."

"No. I mean, yes, but purely as a friend. I've got my sights set on someone else. I made this because Eva told me she's been suffering from doubt about her career and her future. She's trying to decide if she should retire."

"And this will help her resolve the issue?"

"If not, it should bring her peace, and, hey, it might make her amenable to considering my puzzles for the *Gazette*."

"Why did you carve such a pointy end?"

He chuckled softly. "It will be a good metaphor for what she does. She edits. She makes drastic cuts. It's lethal-looking, don't you think?"

I shuddered, thinking of the way Wesley died—a *drastic cut* to his neck.

"Did Eva get the flu or something?" he asked. "Should I take her chicken soup?"

"No, she's not sick. She's distraught because she heard that Wesley Preston died, and she—"

"What? He died?"

I was shocked he hadn't heard by now.

"How?" Ulysses's face was riddled with concern. "He seemed in good health. Okay, sure, he drank too much, but, hey, everyone does. You're allowed to when you cross the sixty threshold, aren't you? Was it his liver? Come to think of it, he was looking pale last night."

"He didn't die of natural causes. He was killed."

Ulysses's jaw dropped open. "Murdered?"

Butchered, slain, slaughtered.

I nodded, not offering more.

He transferred the wand to his other hand. "I guess, like all of us, he had enemies."

I'd like to think I didn't, but maybe I did. "Do you?" I asked.

"Of course." He settled back against the bench. "Truth be told, I'm astonished I haven't been done in by now. Puzzle constructors are an interesting lot. They can be conceited, so they don't like being made to look foolish. They want to believe that their puzzles are the hardest ever."

"And you've made some look foolish?"

"A few times."

"Did you make Wesley feel that way?"

"Sure did. He was not happy with me. He always thinks his puzzles are unsolvable." He whistled softly. "I mean *thought*. He always *thought* his puzzles were unsolvable. Are the police looking into it?"

"Yes." I studied his dusty boots. "Did you go on a hike today?"

"Sure did. Big guy like me has to exercise. 'You don't use it, you lose it,' my father said." He started carving the wand again. "I try to hike a different trail every day."

"Which one did you take?" There were dozens in and around Crystal Cove.

"The Seaview Trail. I picked it up north of the fire station and headed into the hills."

"Wesley was killed on a trail."

He stopped whittling. "No kidding. Which one?"

"South."

"By the Pier?"

"Yes." I motioned to his penknife. "That's sure unique. Where'd you get it?"

"Sunny Shore made it for me."

"She crafted that?"

"Yep. Polished rosewood handle. Damascus steel." He held it up so the sun would glint off the blade. "If you didn't know, Damascus steel was the forged steel for knives smithed in the Near East. They're reputed to be tough and resistant to shattering. They . . . Sorry." He stopped and tapped his head with the side of the knife. "I know too much for my own good and sometimes go on and on. You'd think the brain would get cluttered with all this info, but so far, so good. I can spit out data like a computer."

"I didn't realize you and Sunny knew each other."

"We met a few years ago at another of these events. This group is a close-knit family, come to think of it. We've all crossed paths. Sunny and I have been corresponding ever since then. She gave this to me as payback for helping her with one of her own puzzles."

"She mentioned that she was trying her hand at creating some."

"She's good at it. She's made dozens. I proof them for her and tell her if a clue is too darned easy. She hasn't sold any, but she will."

"She's amazing, isn't she? Violinist, mathematician, inventor."

"She's talented."

"Is she the one you've got your eye on?"

"Sunny? Nah. She's married."

"Then who . . ."

He locked his lips, refusing to reveal the woman's identity, and folded and pocketed his knife. "Hey, it dawned on me that the police might want to question Noam Dixon. I heard him and Wesley arguing last night."

Okay, that felt like a sudden left turn. To end my inquiries into Sunny or into himself? Had he held a grudge against Wesley for making him feel like a guinea pig? Was that a big enough motive to kill someone?

"Where did they quarrel?" I asked.

"At the inn. They were in Wesley's cabana. I'd gone there to apologize for pressing him so hard at the Q&A in front of all those people, all his fans. I was out of line. I was about to knock when I heard voices. The door was ajar. Noam sounded upset. Wesley was calling him names. Noam told him to stop."

"What kind of names?"

"Loser. User."

Those sounded like high school taunts, but Wesley hadn't been above hurling those at my aunt.

"I didn't stick around and went back to my house. I figured I could chat with Wesley today, thinking apologies don't have a time limit. Except . . ." He paused; his jaw started to tick. "Except maybe they did this time." He rose to his feet and hoisted his satchel. "I sure hope the police catch whoever did it."

"They will."

A minute later, I entered the Cookbook Nook and stowed my purse by the register. Half a dozen women were browsing the aisles. A man was flipping through one of the crossword puzzle books. Gran was chatting with an elderly woman in the cake cookbook section. I recognized the book she was holding up, *All About Cake* by the fabulous Christina Tosi. The book featured everything from microwaved coffee mug cakes to buttery Bundt cakes to her signature naked layer cakes. I owned the book and had tried my hand at making cake truffles. I'd failed but intended to try again. And again. I'd bet with Rhett or Katie's deft guidance I could master them.

I moseyed to the children's corner, where Bailey was guiding a handful of kids in the art of shortbread cookie decorating. Katie had made a slew of square-shaped cookies and had decorated each with a blank crossword puzzle grid. With a fine-tipped icing pen, Bailey was showing the children how to write letters in the squares. She advised them there were no wrong answers for any of the puzzles. They were to be personal. One little girl had nabbed an icing pen and had written *Happy*. A boy had written *I love cookies*.

"Meow!" Tigger greeted me plaintively.

I bent to scratch his neck. "What's wrong, fella? Aren't the children paying you enough attention?" I pushed his rump. "Mingle with their ankles. They'll warm up to you when they're done concentrating."

My aunt pressed through the drapes from the storage room, her face pinched with fatigue. She was shuffling a deck of tarot cards. "Hello, dear. How did it go with Eva?"

"She's forlorn, of course."

"Poor thing." She fanned the cards and held them out to me. "Draw one."

"I don't need my fortune told."

"For Eva."

"You know that won't mean anything. It'll be random."

"Humor me."

I obeyed and gasped when I viewed the card. The Three of Swords again. My aunt swooned. I braced her and guided her to the vintage table. I made her sit in a chair. "You're going home," I said. "Doctor Jenna's orders."

She threw me an exasperated look.

I dashed to Bailey and told her my plan. "I'll be back shortly."

After driving my aunt home and settling her in the living room with a hot cup of tea, I phoned Appleby. I couldn't reach him, so I left a message. When I returned to the shop, Cinnamon was there toying with the jigsaw puzzle on the vintage table.

"Need me?" I asked.

"No. I'd hoped to talk to your aunt again, but I hear she's left for the day."

"She's under the weather. Can it wait until tomorrow?"

"I want to ask her about her alibi again."

I glared at her. "She told you she was home."

"She did," Cinnamon said. "But that was a lie."

Chapter 14

Alibi: excuse, defense, reason, account

"She was seen at Crystal Cove Inn by one of the housekeepers," Cinnamon went on.

"No way."

"Way."

I wondered if the witness was the blunt-haired housekeeper that I'd seen standing outside Wesley Preston's room with the inn's manager.

Cinnamon exited the shop. Hurriedly, I informed Bailey and Gran that I was leaving for the day, fetched Tigger, and chased after Cinnamon, but she was already veering the cruiser out of the lot.

She was a fast driver. I had a hard time keeping up. But I did and pulled into my aunt's driveway right behind her. She climbed out of her car and shot me a critical look.

"I have a right to be here." I jostled out of my car with Tigger in my arms. "And I have something to tell you about Sunny Shore, a researcher who helped Wesley Preston develop his puzzles."

"Hold that thought."

"Aunt Vera is expecting you," I added. I'd dialed my aunt from the car to prepare her for the visit. "Will Deputy Appleby be joining us?"

"No. He's investigating a home robbery. Someone broke into a safe and stole a slug of bank notes."

Evidently, after the police had finished sifting through Wesley's cabana at the inn, Cinnamon had reassigned Appleby to a mundane case to keep him at arms' distance from this one. Rats. I'd hoped to be able to pry information from him, given his relationship with my aunt.

I jogged up the stairs to the porch and rapped on my aunt's door. Then I opened it and poked my head in. "Aunt Vera?"

"In here, dear." She was sitting in the living room where I'd left her, but she'd changed clothes. Her capris and blousy T-shirt nearly matched the sofa she was sitting on. A pitcher filled with ice water rested on a tray on the coffee table. "Cinnamon, lovely to see you," she said. I detected fear in her eyes, but far be it from me to betray her feelings.

I perched on the sofa beside her. Tigger squirmed in my arms. I placed him in my aunt's lap for moral support. She petted him and cooed to him.

Cinnamon sat in one of the armchairs. "Vera," she began. At least she hadn't called her Miss Hart or Mrs. Appleby this time. "It has come to my attention that you went out last night. You were seen at Crystal Cove Inn. Why did you lie — "

"I didn't lie," my aunt interrupted. "At least I didn't mean to. I was so keyed up by the successful night that I wanted to celebrate. I hoped to surprise Wesley and buy him an after-dinner drink. The bar at the inn with a view of the town below is so lovely. But when I pulled into the parking lot, I reconsidered the idea. With Marlon being out at his poker game, I realized it might be unseemly for me to be seen with Wesley alone. I didn't want to promote gossip. Therefore, I made a U-turn and drove home. I didn't go into the hotel. When you asked if I went out, I didn't think about it. A ten-minute drive didn't seem to warrant mentioning."

Cinnamon propped her elbows on the arms of the chair and pressed her fingertips together. "A housekeeper saw you, Vera."

"If she did, she saw me in my car. I never got out. I didn't even open the car door."

Cinnamon mulled that over.

"It sounds reasonable," I said. "Did the housekeeper give you — "

Someone knocked on the front door. It opened before I could answer, and Rhett poked his head inside. "Is everything okay? I saw the cruiser." He stepped in, leaving the door ajar, and hooked his thumb over his shoulder.

"Yes. Cinnamon wanted to speak with my aunt," I said. "What're you doing home so early?"

"I took the night off." He kissed my cheek and glanced at Cinnamon. "What's up? Why're you here?"

I said on her behalf, "She was just leaving."

"Wait! Don't go!" Faith Fairchild flew into the house and skidded to a stop on the area rug. In dark green leggings, chartreuse tank top, fanny pack, and multicolored sneakers, she was a sight to behold. Her skin was glistening with perspiration, her short hair damp from exertion. "I'm so glad I caught you all. Chief Pritchett, I was planning to go to the precinct, but since you're here, I've got to tell you what I saw last night." Faith eyeballed my aunt. "Flora phoned me, Vera. She told me what went down with Pepper. She's mortified."

My aunt harrumphed.

"She adores you, Vera. You know that. She couldn't help what Pepper did." Faith addressed Cinnamon. "Face it, your mother can put her nose in where it doesn't belong."

Cinnamon threw me a dirty look. "So can Jenna."

"We all do it," Faith said. "It's human nature. We want to right the wrongs of the world, and that's precisely why I've barged in. I saw Vera last night. Here at the house."

Cinnamon shrugged. "So?"

"I'm her alibi. See, I was running on the beach, back and forth from the Pier, and I saw Vera's lights go on and off numerous times between ten and twelve. That's the time of death, isn't it? Ten to twelve? Flora got that from your mother."

"You were running alone?" Cinnamon raised a skeptical eyebrow. "That's not safe."

"I wasn't alone. My friend and I are getting ready for a marathon. We have to put in the hours. I was running this evening, too. Solo. But it's safe at dusk. That's why I saw your cruiser pull up." She ran her fingers through her hair to comb it. "Like I said, I was planning to come see you after I showered, but there's no time like the present, right?"

Cinnamon mulled over what Faith had seen before addressing my aunt. "Are any of your lights on timers?"

"No. Marlon suggested we get some, but we haven't gotten around to it."

"You see?" Faith jutted a hand in the direction of my aunt. "She's innocent. She did not kill Wesley Preston."

"Faith," I said, "you had dinner with Wesley Tuesday night."

"So?" She straightened her back. "You can't think I had anything to do with his death."

"No, no," I assured her. "I was wondering —"

"I'll ask the questions, Jenna," Cinnamon said curtly. "Miss Fairchild —"

"Call me Faith, young lady," Faith cut in. "I babysat you, for heaven's sake."

I smiled. She and her sister must have shared sitting gigs.

"Faith," Cinnamon revised, "did Mr. Preston mention any squabbles?"

"Squabbles," my aunt said, and tittered. "A squabbler did not murder him. Someone who despised him did. Faith, did he mention whether anyone threatened his life?"

"Of course not," she replied. "It was our first date."

A last date, as well, I reflected.

"We talked about art and puzzles and opera. He adored opera. He suggested we take in a performance of *Così Fan Tutte* the next time he traveled to California. We'd go to San Francisco and make a night of it. Not a *night* night," she stammered. "We wouldn't spend the night together. He . . . I . . . We weren't . . ." Her voice drifted off.

"He didn't mention anyone with whom he had an issue?" Cinnamon asked.

"I questioned him about the few who'd pressed him at the theater Q&A, but he wouldn't talk out of turn."

That had to have frustrated Faith. Like her sister, she relished chin-wagging.

Cinnamon said, "Faith, who was running with you last night?"

Faith wriggled with displeasure. "Are you doubting the validity of my statement?"

"Not at all. The more witnesses we find to corroborate what you saw regarding the lights going on in this house, the better for Vera."

"Charlene Grater," Faith said.

I gaped at her. "Really? She plans to run a marathon?" I wouldn't have guessed Charlene would attempt a slow jog, let alone a long-distance run.

"She's adamant about doing so because her sister bet her a year ago that she couldn't complete it. You'd never know it, but Charlene is extremely competitive. Back in February, she begged me to be her running buddy because I was so disciplined." Faith chuckled. "How could I say no after that kind of compliment?"

Cinnamon told my aunt that if the Crystal Cove Inn housekeeper confirmed my aunt's story and Charlene substantiated Faith's, she was in the clear. The fact that our staunch chief of police was willing to be openminded made me breathe easier.

After she and Faith left, I told my aunt that Rhett and I would get some takeout for dinner and be back in a while. She said she wasn't hungry, but I didn't care. She would have us for company whether she liked it or not.

Rhett and I went home to drop off Tigger. Rook was dumbfounded to see us earlier than usual and showered me with kisses. Then Rhett did. I melted into his arms, trying to shed the weight of all that had happened. Finding a dead man. Hearing my aunt suspected of murder.

"What do you want to bring in for dinner?" He stroked my hair with one palm.

"We could swing by the Pelican Brief and pick up bento boxes with Cajun fish and some of those spicy tacos."

A bento box was the Japanese form of a single-portion take-out meal.

"Sounds good. Why don't we also get a cheese platter, in case peppery food doesn't appeal to your aunt tonight?"

"Great idea."

We went to Say Cheese Shoppe first. It was a darling place situated not far from the Pelican Brief. To drive home the name of the shop, Charlene had plastered the walls with cartoon-style smiles and cameras. She'd even hung mirrors so customers could test out their grins.

As we were entering, Charlene was chatting with Posey, the owner of Crystal Cove Flowers, the florist who did the arrangements for our wedding. She was a cheery woman with rosy cheeks and a penchant for wearing floral dresses. Her husband, the pastor of the church Flora went to, was a sweet man, as well. He didn't like that Posey worked, but she wouldn't have it any other way. The business had been in her family for generations.

Charlene and Posey were talking low, as if sharing a secret. When Charlene spotted us, she jerked backward. Posey let out a nervous giggle.

"We didn't mean to frighten you," I said.

"Hi, Jenna and Rhett," Charlene said.

Posey echoed her and hurried out of the shop without making a purchase.

Odd, I thought, but put it out of my mind as I sidled past a display table set with a ring of homemade jam jars. In the center of the circle, Charlene had staged a wide selection of gourmet items. I chose some fig jam and a box of buttery crackers, and then made a beeline for the cheese case.

Charlene beamed at me. "Jenna and Rhett, the happy couple. What brings you in?" She untied and retied the string of her Say Cheese apron. Mother of a college-aged daughter and teenaged son, she was a warm and caring woman who valued her customers. I couldn't remember her ever saying hello without a smile on her face.

"We're making a cheese platter for three or four people." I wasn't sure if Deputy Appleby would be home when we returned.

Rhett removed a wedge of prepackaged smoked gouda from a side refrigerator and showed it to me. "Your aunt's favorite."

"Excellent," I said, amused. Of course, he would remember a detail like that. As a former chef, he paid attention to what his customers enjoyed.

"Why don't you choose the other cheeses?" I said to Charlene.

"Well, I happen to know Vera loves manchego as well as a sharp cheddar. My personal favorite is this Beecher's Flagship." Charlene held up a wedge enclosed in the Beecher company's wrapping.

"Super. You're looking fit, by the way," I said. "I hear you're getting ready to run a marathon."

"Who told you that?"

"Faith Fairchild. Isn't it true?" I held my breath. If Faith had lied . . .

"Oh, it's true, but I wouldn't use the word *run*," Charlene said. "It's more of a trot or a hop-skip. I'm not sure I'll finish the whole thing, but I intend to try, even if it takes me nine hours to complete." She chuckled. "That's approximately how long it takes to walk if you never break into a run. I'm certain I can do that. Heck, I've chaperoned my nieces around every theme park in California, and those places are huge. I'm certain I've clocked twenty-six-point-two miles in less than nine hours. But, yes, I intend to try to run it."

"Faith said you were with her last night. You were doing sprints up and down the beach."

"We did. Back and forth, back and forth." Charlene let out a *whew*. "She is a taskmaster. I think we did six or seven miles."

"Faith said she saw lights going on and off in my aunt's house at that time."

"That's correct. We giggled at how attentive your aunt was to her electrical usage. Me? I leave lights on all over the house." She tilted her head. "Why do you ask?"

"You're my aunt's alibi."

"For . . ." Her eyes widened. "Oh, no. The murder. I heard. Wesley Preston was killed, and your aunt and he argued the other day."

"They didn't argue," I protested.

"Had a set-to, then."

"It wasn't . . ." I stopped and released an exasperated breath.

Charlene shook her head. "The police couldn't possibly believe Vera had anything to do with it. She's the kindest woman in the world."

"They're looking into all possibilities."

"That's good. Keep an open mind." Charlene pulled a wheel of manchego from her cheese case and cut a wedge. She weighed it and wrapped it in white butcher paper and affixed a label to it. Next, she opened a white carry bag with twine handles and inserted the cheeses. She reached out to accept the items Rhett and I were holding.

"Have the police spoken with you?" I asked.

Rhett smiled. "Sweetheart, Chief Pritchett only heard about Charlene's running habits a short while ago."

I explained how I'd suggested to Appleby that the police talk knives with Charlene.

She gasped. "The murder weapon was a knife?"

"Seems so." I pointed to a set of cheese knives encased in a wooden box on an easel-style stand to the right of the register. "What a lovely array." Each had a polished burlwood handle. "Have you sold a lot of these sets?"

"Three this week. The foodie puzzle themes have brought a lot of buyers my way. The puzzle Mr. Preston created for tomorrow"— she halted as if a moment of silence would honor his passing—"is entirely about cheese."

I knew it was. I'd almost finished it, though I was stumped on a nine-letter word for lover of cheese, plus a few of the words that crossed it.

"One of my customers, a woman who came in yesterday, was a

true turophile," Charlene said as she finalized the sale. "She couldn't stop talking about cheese."

Turophile. That's the word! Had Charlene read my mind? Would her help disqualify my puzzle? Who would care at this juncture? Not Wesley. He was dead. *Bad, Jenna,* I chided, instantly wanting to pinch myself for having such a heartless thought.

"Thirty-four dollars and eighty cents," Charlene went on. "Cash or credit?"

"Credit," Rhett said.

"Anyway, the woman and I must have chatted for an hour yesterday," Charlene said, continuing her story as Rhett swiped his card in the payment terminal. "She's not from around here. She's a puzzle editor."

"Eva Wainwright?" I mimed wisps of hair on my cheeks. "Athletic woman with a stylish cut?"

"That's the one. She waxed rhapsodic about a truffle cheese she had in France and went on and on about how the rules for making cheese in Europe are much different from the rules for making cheese in the U.S."

"Eva bought one of these sets?" I motioned to them.

"*Mm-hm.* She said she has loads of knives at home, but she wanted to have a cheese platter last night before the event at Intime. She was *starving.*" Charlene stressed the word.

"Did the set she bought have a skeleton cheese knife like this one?" I indicated the knife with holes in the blade.

"Skeleton?" Charlene puffed out a laugh. "I don't refer to those as skeleton knives. That puts customers off. I refer to them as hole-y knives. Get it, as in holy? To be revered?" She tittered. "But yes, her set had the same four knives you see there. One for soft cheeses, one for smooth, one for semi-hard like Parmesan, and the cleaver for hard cheeses." She handed the bag with our items to Rhett.

He said to me, "Why does it matter if Eva bought a set?"

"Because Cinnamon went to my aunt's house to have a look at her cheese knives. She confiscated the skeleton — the *smooth* — knife from a set like this."

He raised an eyebrow. "She thinks a household knife was used in the murder?"

I nodded.

"A fine-tipped one would create a similar incision," Charlene said.

"Fine-tipped?" I asked.

"Notice the pointy end of that knife." She wiggled a finger. "That's super sharp. There are lots of knives that could make a similar incision. A vegetable knife. A paring knife. A deejo knife."

I tilted my head. "A what?"

"I'm sorry. I sound much more knowledgeable than I am. Oh, the travails of being a *CSI* buff. A deejo knife is one of the most striking knives in the world. They're all handcrafted. I gave my brother a set with coralwood handles for Christmas. As for Eva and the knives" — she batted the air — "what do I know? Don't listen to me."

But I had, and if Eva had purchased a set of knives then Cinnamon should know about it.

Chapter 15

Cryptic: having a meaning that is mysterious or obscure, puzzling

"Your father is here," my aunt said as Rhett and I returned to her house with our purchases.

"Why?" I handed her the takeout from the Pelican Brief and headed into the kitchen.

"He'd heard Cinnamon came to see me and was concerned. I asked him to stay. He's on the lanai having iced tea. Would you like something to drink?"

I raised the chardonnay we'd bought. "I'll take a glass of this."

"Let me handle that." Rhett took the bottle and rounded the kitchen island to the drawer that held the wine opener.

"Charlene says hello, by the way," I said.

"That's nice." Aunt Vera started unpacking the food. Bento boxes from the Pelican Brief to the left, cheese, jam, and crackers to the right.

"She'll be contacting you for another tarot reading," I added. "She wants to see what the future holds for her daughter."

"She knows where to find me." Aunt Vera removed a bamboo cheeseboard from the stack of platters she housed in a lower cupboard and passed it to me. "I'll let you plate the cheese."

"You won't believe what we learned from Charlene." I unwrapped the manchego as I told her about the revelation that Eva Wainwright had purchased a set of cheese knives yesterday. Then I glanced at my cell phone. I'd texted Cinnamon and left a voicemail message on the way back to my aunt's house, but she had yet to respond.

"Eva didn't kill Wesley," my aunt said. "You heard her. She was in her room last night."

My father moseyed into the kitchen and saw Rhett pouring wine. "I'll take a glass of that. I'm ice tea'd out."

"You've got it, Cary," Rhett said.

Dad set his tumbler in the sink and sneaked a cracker from the cheeseboard I was preparing. "Who was in her room, Vera?"

"Eva Wainwright."

"The puzzle editor?"

"Yes."

I said, "Eva told us she was reading last night, giving her an alibi for the time Wesley was murdered."

"A historical novel," my aunt added.

"But what if she wasn't?" I proposed. "She was staying at the same place as Wesley was. What if she followed him from the inn to the trail and slit his throat with her newly purchased cheese knife?"

"To follow him, she'd have needed to drive," my father said. "He would've seen her."

"Cars are on the road at night," I countered. "No big deal."

Rhett said, "True, but following the guy all the way up the trail to the spot where he was murdered and him not picking up on her doing so is highly unlikely. It was dark. She would've needed a flashlight."

"Unless he was using one, and she followed the beam from his," I said.

Rhett removed four Baccarat clear crystal wineglasses from a cupboard, poured wine into each, and gave one to my aunt and father and then to me.

"Or" —I took a sip of the wine—"what if she accompanied him?"

Rhett shook his head. "Remember what Deputy Appleby theorized? The killer might've crouched in the bushes, waiting, meaning the killer knew Wesley would walk that route."

"If only they'd found a footprint," I groused.

"What would Eva's motive be?" my aunt asked.

"They had a lover's spat," I said.

My aunt harrumphed. "They weren't in love."

"Or a contract issue. She was his employer."

"One of his employers," my aunt said. "He didn't need Eva. She needed him."

"What if he told her he was through with the *Gazette*? That could jeopardize her career." I gestured with my wineglass. "There could be a bunch of reasons."

"Could you be more cryptic?" My aunt frowned.

Rhett said, "No matter what, Vera, you're not guilty."

"Cinnamon hasn't confirmed that," she said.

"She will," I assured her.

"Let the police handle the investigation," Rhett said. "Cinnamon will find the culprit."

Aunt Vera sipped her wine and set the glass aside. "Will they? When?" The plaintive tone in her voice broke my heart.

"Aunt Vera, it's only been a few hours."

"But listen to us," she said. "We're trying to come up with answers. We can help the police solve this."

"No, *we* can't," my father said firmly. "In particular, you, Jenna."

"Hey, Dad, ease up." I raised both hands. "Can I help it if people talk to me?"

"Or you talk to them?" he chided.

"Look, if someone offers information, I will pass it along to the authorities."

"And not act on it."

"Dad, please." I picked up the cheeseboard and my wine and headed to the lanai. I set them on the rattan coffee table and turned to listen to the sound of the ocean lapping the sand.

"Tootsie Pop," my father said, following me.

I spun around. "No, Dad, don't baby me." During his stint at the FBI, he'd seen the seedier part of life, I imagined, but that didn't mean he had to protect me, not to mention I hated when he used the term of endearment he'd given me when I was three. "I won't interfere, but Aunt Vera's good friend is dead. Forgive me if I care."

He seemed stunned by my snarkiness and sat in one of the rattan chairs. The floral cushion wheezed beneath his weight.

My aunt perched on the front edge of the other chair.

Rhett moved to me, slung his arm around my back, and whispered in my ear, "Tread lightly, my darling firecracker. Your father means well."

I wriggled free and settled onto the rattan sofa. I spread a cracker with fig jam, topped it with a piece of the Beecher cheddar, and ate it whole. My stomach grumbled, and I wondered if hunger could explain why I was feeling so testy. My father hadn't deserved my sarcasm, but I ached for my aunt. She needed resolution. Not to mention, it was unsettling that there was another killer loose in Crystal Cove. We needed him or her apprehended so our town could heal.

"I'm worried about Marlon," my aunt said. "He called while you were out."

"To give you an update on his robbery investigation?" I asked.

"No. To tell me Cinnamon has directed him to steer clear of Wesley's investigation. No ifs, ands, or buts."

Meaning my aunt was not yet cleared of murder.

• • •

After we finished our meal and cleaned up the dishes, Rhett and I headed home. My father opted to stay with my aunt until Appleby returned.

Rook and Tigger were delighted to see us. I petted them both, let them out in the backyard for a quick romp, and then brushed my teeth, switched into a nightgown, and crawled into bed.

Rhett was already there reading text messages sent by his executive chef about the evening's business. He set his phone aside and extended his arm. I cozied into him.

"What're you thinking?" he asked.

"I'm wondering what other motives Eva Wainwright might have had to kill Wesley Preston."

"Jenna."

"Cut me a teensy bit of slack. I just—" I kissed his cheek. "I want answers. Eva was his staunch supporter. She adored his puzzles. At one point earlier today, when I drove her back to her hotel—"

"Hold on. You drove her back? When did you plan on telling me?"

"I forgot. Eva had been out for a run. She stopped into the shop to buy a gift for Wesley . . ." I shuddered. "Needless to say, she was rattled after hearing the news. My aunt instructed me to drive her to the inn." I turned on my side and propped myself up on one elbow. "We got to chatting, and from what she said, I began to wonder if she had been in love with him. My aunt might not believe it, but—"

"If she was, then she didn't kill him."

"Unless the love was one-sided, and he rejected her."

Rhett hummed. "Who else do you suspect?"

I told him about Sunny's encounter with Wesley at the inn following the event at Intime. As I did, I realized I hadn't informed Cinnamon about that. I'd meant to when she'd pursued my aunt, but she'd put me off. "And then there's Ulysses Huxley, the puzzle solver. He was quite contentious during the Q&A."

"I'm not sure contentious ranks as a motive for murder," Rhett teased.

"Why did he taunt Wesley?" I asked. "Did he see Wesley as competition in the crossword world? Did he believe he'd have a chance to shine with him dead? He's been trying to make headway with Eva Wainwright."

Rhett motioned for me to continue.

"When I ran into him in front of the café earlier and told him about the murder, he seemed shocked, but I got the feeling he was overacting. As an afterthought, or as a diversionary tactic to avoid answering my questions—I can't be sure—he told me about an argument he heard between Noam Dixon and Wesley. Noam is my aunt and Wesley's old friend."

"When did he hear this argument?"

"He'd gone to the inn to apologize to Wesley for mistreating him at the Q&A, but he stopped short when he heard Noam and Wesley going at it. Wesley called Noam a loser and a user. I suppose the *loser* slur was because Wesley robbed Noam of lifelong happiness when he won Yvette's heart."

"And *user*?"

"I'm not sure. Maybe Noam relied on Wesley for something, or perhaps he bragged to colleagues about his relationship to Wesley to boost his own standing." I flapped a hand. "Ulysses is a big guy. He could have easily overpowered Wesley. And he was wearing hiking boots when I saw him. Dusty hiking boots."

"Well, that seals it," Rhett said. "Dusty hiking boots. You've found your killer."

"Cut it out." I ran a finger along his jaw and jolted. "Hey, would the angle of the slit to Wesley's throat reveal how tall his attacker was?"

"I'd assume so, but that doesn't rule out many folks. Wesley wasn't a big man."

I thought of the woman at the shop who'd joked that he suffered from a Napoleon complex. "True, but he had a huge ego."

Rhett laughed heartily. "If having exaggerated self-esteem is cause for murder, there would be a lot more deaths in Crystal Cove, like . . ." He recited names of a few overly arrogant locals while counting off his fingertips.

I batted his hand down. He gripped both of my wrists in one hand and tickled me with the other. Laughter cascaded out of me.

Rook, wanting in on the action, bounded onto the bed. Tigger, who had nestled by my feet, was not pleased. He hissed. Rook barked merrily in the cat's face. Tigger leaped off the bed and settled onto Rook's pillow, grumbling at us, waiting for the fun to die down.

"Stop!" I begged.

Rhett didn't. He knew how ticklish I was. I squealed. Rook licked my face. When I really couldn't take any more, I cried, "Please. Really. Stop."

Rhett released me, gently shoved Rook off the bed, and then kissed my face. "No more thinking about murder," he said. "Cinnamon's got this."

"But what if she doesn't? She hasn't responded to my news about Eva's knife purchase—"

My cell phone buzzed on the side table. I rolled over to take a peek. "Speak of the devil," I muttered.

Cinnamon had texted, thanking me for my info. Nothing more. I considered telling her about Sunny's argument with Wesley as well as Ulysses overhearing Noam and Wesley going at it, but given her terse reply, I pushed the cell phone aside. Morning would come soon enough.

Chapter 16

Crosswordese: words frequently found in crossword puzzles but seldom found in everyday conversation

"I did it!" Bailey cried as she entered the shop Friday morning, her short-cropped hair windblown and going every which way. A cool breeze followed her in.

"Did what?" I was packing up a pair of ceramic crossword-themed salt and pepper shakers for a ponytailed customer.

"I finished today's puzzle," Bailey said as she stuffed her purse into one of the cubbies behind the sales counter. "The cheese-themed one. And now I can't wait to go to Mum's the Word for my appetizer. They're serving mini potpies." She pumped an arm. "Hurrah!"

"Hurrah!" I echoed as I finalized the sale and rounded the counter. The skirt of my burnt-orange, cap-sleeved dress fluted up around my thighs. I patted it down.

The shop was busy, in fact, so busy that I'd propped open the front door to let in fresh air. A mother was in the kids' corner helping her children choose a baking kit. My aunt was answering questions about *Martha Stewart's Appetizers: 200 Recipes for Dips, Spreads, Snacks, Small Plates, and Other Delicious Hors d'Oeuvres, Plus 30 Cocktails: A Cookbook*, which I often joked had one of the longest titles in the history of cookbooks. However, it was one of my favorite ones because the recipes were easy and the pictures amazing.

As I neared the display table, I saw Noam Dixon, who was unshaven and looking slightly rumpled in a blue plaid shirt, blue tie, blue blazer, jeans, and loafers. He was advising an elderly woman as to the best of the crossword solvers' dictionaries we'd stocked. I heard him say that knowing crosswordese was vital to one's strength as a puzzle solver. I guessed his untidy appearance could be the result of having heard the news about his friend and it had unsettled him, or because he was wrestling with the shame of having killed him and hadn't slept a wink. What motive would he have had? Revenge for stealing Yvette Simms so many years ago seemed likely. So did payback for Wesley's selfish actions having ruined Noam's future as a writer.

Stop, Jenna. Not everyone is guilty.

On the other hand, Ulysses claimed to have heard Noam arguing with Wesley the night he died. Was that the truth? Could Noam provide an alibi for later on?

"I almost didn't finish the puzzle," Bailey said, following me while brushing a piece of lint off her aqua skirt. "I was stuck on a nine-letter word for—"

"*Turophile.*"

"That's the one."

"Turophile," Noam Dixon said, holding up the book he'd been touting. "The irregular formation of the Greek word for cheese, *tyros*, and the word *phile* for lover. Turophile. First coined for cheese aficionados in 1938. However, it wasn't until the 1950s that the term really caught on."

"Why then?" Bailey asked.

"Because it wasn't until a popular writer and radio host used the word while musing about cheese, and then, bingo!" Noam snapped his fingers. "Others started using it."

The woman he'd been advising said, "Aren't you a font of information, young man."

Noam said, "I'm hardly young, ma'am."

"Younger than I," she teased in a flirtatious way. Chuckling, she headed in the direction of the exit without making a purchase.

Noam made a beeline for the sales counter, and I followed him.

"Yoo-hoo." A redheaded woman by the apron display waved a hand. "Can one of you help me?"

Bailey went to assist her.

Noam handed me the book he was holding. "I'd like this, and I'll take those three books with my name on it." He pointed to the pre-orders wrapped in twine and arranged on the shelf beyond the register. A Post-it note designating the purchaser was affixed to each group. "I wanted to buy them yesterday," he said, "but I left the hotel without my wallet."

"Absolutely, Mr. Dixon," I said.

"Noam, please."

"Noam."

Up close, his face was puffy and his eyes were bloodshot. His lower lip was chapped, as if he'd been chewing it nonstop.

I fetched the stack and removed the twine and sticky note. "Good choices," I said as I rang them up. None were cookbooks. Each was a fictional work. "I adored *Cooking for Picasso*." I'd read it last summer. It detailed a little-known interlude in the artist's life.

"I've heard good things about it."

"I saw you giving our customer advice. Want a job?"

"Got one. Thanks. And you'll notice I didn't make a sale."

"She probably forgot her wallet," I joked, and then sobered. "Hey, I'm sorry about what happened to your friend." I set his books into one of our gift bags. "You must be devastated."

Noam's gaze grew serious. "Wesley sure didn't deserve to die. Murdered. What is this world coming to?"

"Noam." My aunt made her way to him and gave him a hug. "How are you holding up?"

"The better question is how are you, Vera?"

"I'm managing."

"Someone said you're a suspect in Wesley's death." He peered into her eyes. "That can't be possible. You?"

"Yes."

"Unthinkable. Do you know what happened? All I've gleaned is that he was killed Wednesday night. The police are keeping a lid on details. Was he shot or something?"

"I'm not allowed to disclose anything," my aunt said. "On advice of counsel."

I gulped. She'd spoken to a lawyer? Hadn't Cinnamon received corroboration of her innocence from Charlene and the housekeeper at the inn by now?

"Vera, it's me you're talking to." Noam gripped her by the shoulders. "I know you didn't kill Wesley. You're the gentlest woman I've ever met next to . . ." He didn't fill in the blank.

"Yvette," my aunt murmured.

"Yes." His right cheek ticked below his eye. "Why do they suspect you? Did they find evidence of you being at the crime scene?"

She didn't answer.

"Where was he killed?" Noam asked.

"On a hiking trail not far from the Pier," Sunny Shore said, striding into the shop. Yet again, she was dressed in olive. Other than her cocktail dress, had she only brought one shade of clothing for the tournament? And if so, why that one? Someone ought to clue her in that her coloring would go better with jewel tones.

I said, "How do you know he died on a trail, Sunny?"

"I got the skinny from an officer who was searching Wesley's room at the inn." She hitched her tote higher on her shoulder. "It's horrible, isn't it? Just horrible."

Foster wouldn't have divulged anything to her. She was a by-the-book cop. Cinnamon or Appleby wouldn't have, either. The rookie, Ford, was a distinct possibility.

"When did he die?" Noam asked.

"Between ten and midnight," Sunny went on, looking green at the gills as she relayed the information. "In fact, Jenna was the one who found him yesterday morning. That must have been awful for you, seeing him with his throat slit."

"Ugh." Noam gagged. His hand reflexively went to his neck.

Boy, if Ford was the leak, he is certainly going to get an earful from Cinnamon after I clued her in.

"What was he doing on a trail at that time of night?" Noam asked.

Sunny said, "Nocturnal birding, I presume."

"He actually had the time to go birding?" Noam shook his head. "I've barely had time to prep for the tournament."

"Honestly, his work was done after the seminar, Q&A, and reception," Sunny said. "And he'd completed creating all the daily puzzles, so he only had to show up as a judge."

Noam's hand was trembling as he inserted his credit card into the payment terminal and pressed the buttons on the keypad to finalize the sale. I handed him his package, and he mustered a smile. For Sunny. "Will I see you at this afternoon's event?"

"Bet on it." She extended a hand.

Noam took hold. "Listen, I know Wesley was your employer, but he told me that you were close. If you ever want to talk . . ." His gaze was sad. Bereft, actually. Did I truly think he'd killed a lifelong friend?

"Thanks," Sunny murmured. "I appreciate that."

As Noam left the shop, I returned to the display table. It needed straightening.

Sunny trailed me, the color returning to her cheeks. "I'm here for the cooking demonstration."

"Great. We'll be setting up shortly."

Today was the day Katie would give her demonstration on how to make bread. Understanding proofing, she said, was key to the art.

"It won't start for a while," I said. "You have time to grab a coffee at the café next door."

"Good idea." She continued to follow me as I moved from the display table to the grouping of aprons. "I heard you were asking the concierge at the inn about me."

"No, I—"

"It's okay." She flicked one hand. "I don't mind. It was bound to come out that I threw a glass of wine at Wesley the night he died. It didn't mean anything. Like that quarrel your aunt had with him didn't mean anything."

"It wasn't . . . They didn't . . ."

"Don't worry. I think she's innocent."

I shook the tension from my shoulders and asked, "What did you argue about?" Ginny hadn't picked up the full gist.

"Wesley poached one of my puzzles," she said, a hint of venom in her tone.

"Poached it?"

"Stole it. Pilfered it. Nicked it, as they say in England. But I'm not the only one he scammed. He ripped off one of Ulysses's puzzles, too."

Was that why she'd warned Wesley about messing with bad juju?

"Ulysses didn't take it well. He's hoping to make his mark as a cruciverbalist. He'd like to be the premier one in the world."

I arched an eyebrow. "Big dreams for a man his age."

"Don't discriminate," she said. "There's no age limit for constructors."

"Noted," I said, feeling sufficiently chastised. "What puzzle did Wesley steal from you?"

"Last month, I showed him my inventor-themed one. I wanted his take on it. After all, he said he'd be my mentor. It was all about Alexander Graham Bell and Thomas Alva Edison and Samuel Finley Breese Morse. It's my best effort ever. Can you believe that Wesley had the gall to claim I'd filched it from him and demanded to know how I'd accessed his computer?" She chopped one hand against the other. "I didn't. I'm not a hack. But if the police find my work on his computer, it means he hired someone to break into mine."

Oh, man, the many reasons to want Wesley Preston dead were getting as complicated as a diagramless crossword. When I'd seen the police at the inn searching his room, I'd wondered if the killer might have sneaked in to swipe one of his puzzles. Should that theory be flipped on its head? Were police searching Wesley Preston's room looking for things he might have stolen?

"Have you told the police?" I asked.

"Better believe I will."

"Your puzzle sounds very clever."

"Darned straight. I even included a clue for one invention that each of them created. It's brilliant."

She certainly didn't lack for ego. I pulled an apron off a hook, smoothed it so the puzzle image would be more visible, and rehung it. "Can you earn a good living creating puzzles?"

"Depends. Lots of things determine price. Distribution and the size of your audience, plus whether the constructor is freelance or on staff. Wesley was pulling down well over seventy-five K a year."

I whistled.

"But he was a star. Me? I'll barely get a couple of hundred dollars for one of my puzzles." Sunny sounded deflated. So much for having an oversized ego. "I need to develop street cred first."

Killing someone for stealing a puzzle that was worth two hundred bucks didn't seem a likely prospect. On the other hand, one of the motives I'd attributed to Ulysses came to mind. With a star like Wesley out of the way, could the path for Sunny's future in the crossword world be smoother?

"Why would he need to steal from you or anyone?" I asked.

"Because he lost his mojo." She placed a hand on her chest. "His heart wasn't in it any longer. He felt he'd created all the puzzles he had in him." She peeked down the breezeway. Katie was setting a tiered plate of cookies on the table. "Ooh, treats. Are they—"

"Free. Yes. Help yourself."

"Don't mind if I do. Would you like a coffee? A latte? On me."

"No, but thanks."

I returned to the sales counter.

Bailey sidled over to me. "I couldn't help overhearing. She sure didn't have the best relationship with Wesley Preston. He poached one of her puzzles?"

"So she says."

Bailey raised an eyebrow. "Good motive for murder."

"However . . ." I revealed that Wesley had stiffed Sunny for the research she did for him. "Even though he told me and my aunt that he intended to pay up, now that he's dead, I imagine it will take a long time to work out any payments from his estate, which seems enough reason for her *not* to have killed him."

A handsome older woman with lustrous golden hair sauntered into the shop. Clad in chinos, ecru camp shirt, and sandals, she reminded me of a model, camera-ready for a Ralph Lauren shoot. When I'd worked the Lauren account at Taylor & Squibb, I'd held many casting calls searching to hire beauties like her.

"Help you?" I detected the scent of sandalwood with notes of orange and jasmine.

"Is Noam Dixon here?" she asked, her voice as sultry as her look.

"He left a bit ago."

"Oh." Her disappointment was palpable.

"He might have gone to the café for breakfast," I suggested, though I couldn't be sure. I hadn't seen which direction he'd turned after leaving the Cookbook Nook. "You can go through the breezeway to check."

"Thank you."

My aunt exited the storage room as the woman disappeared into the breezeway. "Who was that?"

"Not sure. Another puzzler, I imagine." I rounded the sales counter, prepared to call Cinnamon and fill her in on recent events, when she trooped into the shop.

With all the foot traffic, I was glad I'd propped the front door open. The notion of the door opening and closing that often in such a short time gave me a headache.

"Talk to me," Cinnamon said. Her uniform was crisply pressed, her minimal makeup fresh.

"Good morning to you, too," I teased. "Is my aunt cleared of the crime?"

"Yes. The housekeeper at the inn confirmed she did not see your aunt get out of the car."

"And have you spoken to Charlene Grater?" I asked.

"We'll get to her."

I breathed a huge sigh of relief and glanced at Aunt Vera. She'd heard and was visibly pleased, too.

"Yesterday, outside your aunt's house, you mentioned you had information about Sunny Shore," Cinnamon said. "I told you to hold that thought."

"Your ears must be burning. I was about to call you."

"Does it concern something other than her bankruptcy?"

"Bankruptcy?"

Cinnamon rotated a hand. "Never mind. Your turn."

Knowing she wouldn't reveal more, I recapped Sunny's argument with Wesley at Crystal Cove Inn, the wine she threw, the way she'd stormed off in her car but had come back composed. Then I told her about the information Sunny knew about the crime scene. "I'm not sure how she got it. I doubt Officer Foster would have spilled the beans. Maybe Ford did."

Cinnamon didn't comment. "What else?"

I filled her in about Sunny's claim that Wesley had not only stolen a puzzle she'd created but had also filched one that Ulysses Huxley had designed. "Toss in the puzzle he swiped from my aunt in grade school, and that makes him a serial puzzle thief. If he presented them as his own to any of his publishers, that's plagiarism."

"Is everybody in town a cruci—" She stopped short. "What's a puzzle constructor called?"

"Cruciverbalist. And, yes, I suppose many in town this week aspire to be one." I explained the minimal amount of money involved when it came to someone like Sunny, with no track record. "Not enough to warrant killing him for," I said. "But Mr. Preston did owe her for research she'd done. He told me and my aunt he planned to pay her . . ." I spread my arms. "She'll have to put in a claim, I suppose."

"That's how it works. Creditors reach out to the executor of the estate."

"Will the fact she filed for bankruptcy complicate that?" I

remembered her saying that if Wesley didn't pay her, her kids wouldn't get new shoes. At the time, I'd thought it was a joke, but maybe it wasn't.

"Anything else you'd like to share?" our intrepid police chief asked, dodging me again.

"Actually, yes. I was talking to Ulysses outside the café yesterday. He was whittling. And get this, he was using a knife Sunny made for him."

"She makes knives?"

"Not only is she a mathematician and violinist, but she's also an inventor."

Cinnamon's mouth formed an O. "She's a real overachiever."

"Like you."

"I don't have a clue how to play an instrument."

"But you can sing and roller skate." I grinned. "FYI, she isn't making a dime from her creations."

"Go on about Ulysses Huxley." She signaled for me to continue.

"Supposedly, he went to apologize for the way he'd treated Wesley at the Q&A, but he overheard Noam Dixon—he's one of Wesley's oldest friends; my aunt's friend, too—arguing with Wesley inside Wesley's room, so he decided to wait until the next day to make amends."

Cinnamon hummed.

"Ulysses wasn't sure what the dispute was about." I repeated the words he'd heard Wesley say. "Noam Dixon was in a bit ago. He acted saddened by the news of Wesley's death."

"Acted," she echoed.

"I wasn't sure whether or not he was sincere." Truth be told, I was questioning everyone's innocence at this point. "You got my text message about the set of knives Eva Wainwright purchased, right?"

Cinnamon clasped my elbow and guided me beyond the sales counter, stopping beside Tigger's kitty condo. He was lying languidly on it, one paw dangling over the side. She tapped it fondly. He purred with contentment, then withdrew his arm and tucked it under his torso.

Lowering her voice, she said to me, "Look, I don't know what it is about you that gets people to open up, and I'd like to warn you off discussing the case with anyone, but if they do talk to you, stay alert and keep me in the loop."

I saluted.

She swatted my fingers and left.

Chapter 17

Proof: (verb) establishing the truth; (noun) stages in the resolution of a math problem; (printing) trial impression of a page before corrections; (cooking) stage of fermentation

At nine fifteen, Bailey and I started rearranging the shop for Katie's demonstration by moving the portable bookshelves away from the center of the room and then setting up folding chairs we kept on hand in the storage area. Customers began to file in around nine thirty. Many made a beeline for the display table where I'd set out *Mastering Bread: The Art and Practice of Handmade Sourdough, Yeast Bread, and Pastry* as well as *The Bread Baker's Apprentice, 15th Anniversary Edition: Mastering the Art of Extraordinary Bread.* Reviewers of the first book were happy the author had explored different grains and approaches. Reviewers for the second said the cookbook was for the professional as well as the home cook, which would please many of our customers.

"Look who walked in," Bailey said as she unfolded the last chair.

"Who?" I wasn't sure if she was talking about Z.Z., whose face was as ashen as the suit she'd donned, or Flora, who was chatting with a passel of puzzlers carrying conference tote bags, or Ulysses and Sunny, who'd entered together.

"The puzzlers," Bailey said. "Did you think so many of them would be foodies?"

"Well, the theme for the competition is food, so it makes sense. You know, baking bread has become a big thing over the last few years."

Sunny and Ulysses stopped near the display table. While unfolding my last chair, I listened in on their conversation, curious about their relationship. I recalled him saying he wasn't interested in her because she was married, so what was their story? Each was drinking from a to-go cup. Perhaps they'd innocently met up at the café.

"I hear everyone's trying to master the art at home," Sunny said.

"Me included," Ulysses said. "I'm partial to sourdough."

"You bake?" she sounded incredulous.

"I find it relaxing."

"Let's grab two seats together before everyone else sits down," Sunny said.

"Good idea." He snagged a cookbook and took it with him.

"I'm here!" Katie pushed her mobile cooking cart through the archway. She centered the cart in front of the rows of chairs and locked the wheels in place. Then she smoothed her chef's coat and righted her toque. "Hello, everyone." She raised her voice above the chatter. "We'll start in five minutes. Find a seat. You'll have a good view from any of them."

Five minutes would give Bailey and me enough time to ring up customers who were ready to make their purchases.

As I handed the last customer a bag tied with raffia ribbon, I saw my aunt and Z.Z. leaving the shop. I was eager to know what they were discussing. Had they decided to have a memorial for Wesley yet? Or were they debating what might happen to Crystal Cove's reputation as one of the most charming places on earth now that another murder had occurred here?

After a brief opening with Katie introducing herself as well as the shop and café, she launched into her spiel. "We're making bread today. How many of you know what it means to proof something?"

A young woman's hand shot up. I recognized her. She worked with Tito at the *Courier*. "I have to proof copy at the newspaper."

"Good one. Who else?" Katie asked.

"I have to proofread my manuscripts before turning them in," an aspiring romance writer said. She visited the shop often to talk about her works in progress.

"I have to proof my canvas to make it waterproof," another woman said.

"It can also mean impervious, impenetrable, or resistant," a slender man chimed in, hand raised overhead.

"Excellent," Katie said. "You all must be whizzes at crossword puzzles."

That elicited laughter.

"I know one." Flora raised an arm, causing the sleeve of her pumpkin-colored blouse to slither down it. "The police have to find evidential proof to convict a killer."

Covertly, I eyed Sunny and Ulysses. Neither reacted to Flora's comment. Neither regarded the other, either. Did that mean they were innocent of Wesley's murder?

"Yes, indeed, they do," Katie said. "And our police force is very good at doing so." She smacked her hands together. "Moving on. How many of you know how to *proof* dough? That's the definition I was looking for. In baking, proofing refers to the final rise of the dough, which takes place after we've shaped the dough into a loaf."

One tentative woman said, "I try to proof my dough, but I stink at it."

That earned more laughter from the crowd.

"Well, let's teach you how to do it right," Katie said. "Proofing occurs before the bread is baked." She showed the group the floury contents in the bowl of her stand mixer. Then she held up a measuring cup; it contained something brownish and foamy. Via the cart's overhead mirror that was slanted toward the audience, the viewers could see whatever Katie was doing. "First, I'm proofing the yeast. That means I'm testing to make sure it's hardy enough to make my dough rise. If it is, I'll add it to my bread base and then knead." She winked. "This yeast is perfect, with exactly the right amount of foam. I started proofing it right before I entered the shop. Now, the only yeast you really need to proof is yeast you suspect of being old. To proof yeast, you dissolve it in warm water and sugar and wait until it's creamy-looking. Lots of tiny bubbles should form at the top." She whistled a tidbit of Don Ho's famous "Tiny Bubbles," which garnered her more chuckles as she added the mixture to the bowl, turned the mixer on, and let it beat on low.

"Dough should be a little sticky." She switched off the mixer and turned the soft dough out onto a floured cutting board. While kneading, she said, "There are lots of reasons we don't want to proof bread too fast. First and foremost, the fermentation that produces good flavor takes place after the yeast has exhausted its oxygen supply. If the bread rises too quickly, we'll get lots of CO_2 but less alcohol, meaning our bread won't taste as yummy. Also, gluten is less temperature-sensitive than yeast, meaning if we get our dough too warm, like putting it into a hot oven, the yeast will inflate rapidly, and the gluten structure will be diminished."

"That's what I did," the tentative woman who'd commented earlier said.

"Don't rush the bulk rise," Katie cautioned. "The proof is in the pudding."

"Except you're making hot cross buns," Flora countered.

The ad for today's demonstration was clear about Katie's plans.

"The pudding is a metaphor for the end result," Katie said. "Be patient with bread, and it won't disappoint you."

Sunny leaned into Ulysses and said something. He grinned.

Katie turned the kneaded dough into a greased bowl and covered it with a clean kitchen cloth, explaining each step. "Like a watched pot that won't boil, dough never rises if you stare at it. Do something else. Sing. Dance. Complete a crossword puzzle . . . or three or four. Distractions are your best friend. Two hours later, you should have something that looks like this." She displayed another bowl containing dough that had risen to the audience. She always came prepared with the next few steps completed in a recipe. Otherwise, her demonstrations could take six or more hours.

"Now, let's punch this little sucker into submission." She slid the dough onto her cutting board, dug her knuckles into it, and divided the dough into sixteen equal portions. "We'll let these rise for another hour."

The audience groaned.

"Like I said, baking is not for the impatient." She placed the buns in a greased nine-by-thirteen-inch pan and set the pan aside. "When the second rise is complete, the buns will look like this." She pulled a duplicate rectangular pan from the cabinet beneath the cart's counter. The buns had risen impeccably.

The collective group *ooh*ed.

For the next hour, she showed how to bake and ice the buns while regaling the audience with personal baking mishap stories. Over the last couple of years, she had sent me numerous links to humorous YouTube videos to make me feel better about my failed cooking adventures.

When the buns were complete, she cut them into fourths and said she would serve them in the breezeway. The audience cheered. I was eager to taste one, too.

"Pick up a free recipe card at the sales counter," Katie added, "and remember, I'll be offering a bread baking class once a month at the Nook Café starting next month. The first one will feature sourdough."

"Did you know about the classes?" Bailey asked me.

"Yes."

Ulysses said something to Sunny that made her roar. Had he told her a joke, or had he relayed a story about a kitchen disaster like Katie had?

"We should consider coming up with a TV show for her," Bailey went on. "That might attract new customers to the café."

"I think we're fine sales-wise," I said. "Besides, what would we do if she became a sensation? I can't afford to lose her. Reynaldo is good, but he's no Katie."

"True." Her stomach grumbled. "I need to go to Mum's right now."

"In a sec."

Katie met customers by the counter, shaking their hands, and calling each by his or her name.

Flora skirted the crowd. "Jenna. *Psst.*" She crooked a finger and moved to the children's corner.

I followed. "What's up?"

"I have some news," she confided.

"News?"

"*Mm-hm.*" She peered beyond me before returning her gaze to me. "I saw that puzzler at the bank yesterday."

"Which puzzler?"

"The one that wears that horrid green color."

She was referring to Sunny. I started to swivel to take Sunny in, but Flora blocked the move.

"Don't. She might glance this way. Honestly . . . ugh." She grunted. "Who wears that tone nowadays? It makes her skin look sallow. She should consider emerald green if she's determined to wear something in the green family. It's the trend color that debuted during Fashion Week."

I never paid attention to trends. "You should tell her," I teased.

"Me? Oh, no, I wouldn't even tell a friend that."

Um, yeah, you would, I thought snarkily. I'd heard Flora share her opinions with total strangers who ventured into Home Sweet Home, but that was beside the point.

"Anyway, to continue, she was meeting with that adorable loan officer," Flora said. "The young man with the golden hair."

I knew the one she meant. Bright eyes, winsome smile. He reminded me of my brother, albeit a little more buttoned down.

"He kept shaking his head as though he couldn't help her. Between you and me, she seemed suspicious." The word hissed out of Flora.

"Why?" I bit back a snort. "Did you think she was there to rob the place?"

"Not suspicious in that way. She . . ." Flora twirled a hand, unable to elaborate. "I think she wanted to secure a loan."

Surely, Sunny wasn't trying to deal with her bankruptcy situation while she was here. Her bank in Santa Barbara would be the better choice to help her out of a bind. To put an end to the gossip, I said, "Trying to borrow money doesn't make someone suspicious. Thanks for coming today."

Flora clasped my arm. "Hold on. What if she's broke? Don't you remember the other day when she said Wesley Preston had stiffed her on a payment? Being in debt might make someone desperate. What if she snapped, and—" Flora drew a finger across her throat.

I winced.

"And one more tidbit," Flora said. "I saw that skinny one with the spiky hair, the editor, outside Say Cheese Shoppe on the night of the murder. I was doing my constitutional. Three miles in forty-five minutes. So good for the heart. Anyway"—she flapped a hand—"the editor—"

"Eva Wainwright."

"That's the one. I heard she told your aunt she was in her room at the inn reading that night. Wrong." She made a buzzing sound. "She lied."

I couldn't believe how much Flora loved to dish the dirt.

"But that puzzler in green?" Flora peeked discreetly over her shoulder and back at me. "I think she's the one who killed Wesley Preston. She's got that look in her eye." She tapped the corner of her own eye and then, pleased with herself, bustled away.

I turned to look for Sunny and caught her staring at me.

She mouthed, *What?* and weaved through the throng to me, tossing her to-go cup in a trash can on the way. "You're gawking at me, Jenna," she said when she drew near.

"No." I felt my cheeks warm. "No, I wasn't. Not at you. I mean, I was, but it was because . . ." I scrambled for an answer. "Because I was startled to see Ulysses here. At the demonstration."

"Why? Because he's a man? There were others in the audience."

True. It was a lame response.

"And, if you didn't know," Sunny went on, "he's an amateur baker. A real bread aficionado. He loves to make sourdough."

"*Ooh*," I said, acting impressed. "He and Katie should exchange notes."

"They should, but back to you. Why were you staring at me?"

"I wasn't."

"Well, Flora Fairchild was." She aimed a finger at Flora's retreating figure. "Everyone in town says she's a rumormonger. What was she saying about me?"

I didn't realize so many knew about Flora's penchant for spreading hearsay. "Nothing," I said breezily. "She saw you at the bank yesterday. That's all."

"Oh."

"She said you were talking to a loan officer."

"Oh," she repeated.

"Like you needed a loan."

"I did. I do. Because"—Sunny clutched the strap of her khaki tote like a lifeline—"I was robbed the first day I got here."

"How horrible. Did you tell the police?"

"No, because whoever fleeced me didn't take everything. Only the largest bills out of my wallet and my ATM card."

"That's a big deal. Where did this happen? At the inn?"

"No, at the diner on the Pier."

"Mum's the Word."

"*Mm-hm.* My bag was on the stool beside me." She uttered an overly dramatic, "*Sheesh.* Was I stupid! I shouldn't have taken my eyes off of it. I know better. I've been mugged before."

"Did you tell the owner about the robbery?"

"I was too embarrassed."

That sounded sketchy, but I kept my opinion to myself. "They might have installed security cameras. You should go back and ask. There have been a few burglaries in Crystal Cove lately. Not a rash of them, but enough to make folks—businesses—take more precautions."

"That's a good idea. I will." She fidgeted with the fold-over top of her tote, flipping it one direction, and then back again. "Anyway, I only have one credit card, and it's maxed out with the fee for the inn, so I couldn't simply get more cash. I went to the loan officer to arrange for a short-term loan. To make it through this week."

"Your husband couldn't wire you some money?"

She shook her head. Something flickered in her eyes. Bitterness? Resignation? "By the way, Katie's demonstration was great. She's so bubbly and funny. I learned a lot."

That was an odd segue, but I rolled with it. "Do you bake?"

"No, but I love to make savory dishes."

"Do you cook with your daughters?"

"Every chance I get."

"What do your girls like to make with you?"

"Pasta loaded with everything. Peppers, mushrooms." Sunny viewed her watch. "I'd better get ready for this afternoon. Lots to do. See you."

I watched her hustle out of the shop and veer right, checking her cell phone as she went. Something about her hasty exit gave me pause. Had our conversation about the bank loan or her girls upset her?

Chapter 18

Deep dive: investigation, probe, search, trawl

"Mum's. Now." Bailey tapped my shoulder. "I've told your aunt where we're headed."

"But—"

"No buts. I'm starved, and you're driving. My car's in the shop for a tune-up."

My pal could be a force, so I didn't argue with her. I grabbed my completed puzzle and slung on my purse.

Minutes later, I parked in the Pier parking lot, and Bailey and I hightailed it to the diner, referred to by locals as either Mum's or The Word—rarely the whole name, Mum's the Word. We weren't the only crossword solvers eager to receive our free potpie. At least thirty customers holding puzzles were waiting in a line outside, including Ulysses and Eva, who continued to wear black. The dress she had on was the kind you could wad into a ball, shove it into a suitcase, and it would still hang out wrinkle-free. They were standing together, chatting. Though he was brawny and she so slim, they made a handsome couple. She said something that earned her a one-armed hug from him. I imagined they were talking about Wesley.

When Bailey and I made it inside, I drew in a deep breath. The aroma of garlic and thyme was incredible. I'd eaten Mum's regular pot pies. If their appetizers were one-tenth as good as the main dish, we were going to be happy campers. I scanned the cheery restaurant with its turquoise checkered tablecloths and yellow window treatments. Lunch customers filled each of the tables. No one seemed disappointed with their meals.

We proceeded toward the sales register.

"Hey, Jenna. Hey, Bailey," a woman said from behind us.

I turned and saw Cinnamon. She was holding her cell phone in one hand and a puzzle in the other.

"Well, hi there," I said. "You do crossword puzzles?"

She pocketed the phone. "Not all cops are dumb."

"I didn't say . . . I didn't mean . . ." Playfully, I mock-glowered at her. "I simply meant you'd be too busy to take the time, and when and if you do take a break, you exercise."

"Who said this one took any time? Done in four minutes and ten seconds." She flaunted her puzzle. No erasures. All the same answers as I'd entered. "Once I saw the errors of my youthful ways," she went on, "my mother made sure I enhanced my education with puzzles, word games, and more."

"I would've expected her to make you knit."

"Um, no. I didn't have the knack. Knit, purl, drop two. I was a mess." She leaned in close. "Have you discovered anything in the Preston murder case?"

I gawked at her. She'd been serious earlier about me keeping her in the loop? No way. Couldn't be. She was goading me. "Not in the last two hours," I joked.

"Hi, Jenna, Bailey, and Chief Pritchett," the perky clerk at the register said as the line moved forward. "What do you three have there?"

We passed her our puzzles.

She surveyed the answers, studied our faces, and grinned. "You did it. Here you go." She gave each of us a blue raffle-style ticket. "You can sit at any available booth or wait by the counter for your potpies."

Cinnamon accepted her ticket and, after tipping the brim of her hat, moved to the right to view her cell phone again.

I scanned the diner. There was only one bright yellow stool available at the arced counter.

"You take it," Bailey said.

"Let's both stand."

I noticed Ulysses and Eva had found a booth. They might have come in for the completed crossword puzzle appetizers, but they were obviously staying for a meal. Both were perusing menus. He leaned forward and touched her hand fondly, then he pulled a packet of tissues from his satchel and offered it to her. Eva withdrew a tissue, blotted her eyes, and blew her nose. She was obviously grieving, and I got the distinct feeling that Ulysses was taking advantage of the moment to bond with her. Or was he? He'd made it clear when I'd spoken to him before that he had no interest in her. Had he been snowing me? Did he believe that Wesley had feelings for Eva, and by killing him, he could make a play for her himself?

And what about Eva? She seemed forlorn; however, if Flora was to be believed, and I had no reason to doubt her, Eva hadn't stayed in her room that night reading, as she'd claimed. I supposed she could've read for a while and then gone to Say Cheese Shoppe afterward. But why would she have? Say Cheese would have been closed by then. Charlene kept ten a.m. to seven p.m. hours. She was a one-woman operation. And if Eva had gone someplace that night where someone might have seen her, shouldn't she have mentioned it to my aunt and me to give herself a more substantial alibi?

When Bailey and I returned to the shop, it was abuzz with gossip. Gran said customers couldn't stop talking about Wesley Preston's death, and she'd sold out of nearly all of the crossword solver dictionaries. I said I would do a quick reorder of books — there was nothing I could do if we sold out of the cookie jars, salt shakers, and aprons — and excused myself to the storage room. Tigger hopped off his perch and joined me.

I sat at the desk with Tigger nestled in my lap, switched on the computer so I could view which cookbooks were in stock, and then dialed our distributor. She said she could provide the books I needed by tomorrow afternoon and asked if that would be soon enough. I told her she was a gem and signed off.

Staring at the computer screen, I thought of my aunt and how she'd tasked me with finding Wesley Preston's killer, and suddenly, I had the urge to do a deep dive into the people closest to him. Until his killer was apprehended, others in Crystal Cove might not be safe. I treasured our town. I wanted it to go back to normal. Granted, the police were conceivably doing a deep dive, too, but fresh eyes couldn't hurt.

After opening a search engine, I typed in Ulysses Huxley's name. In a matter of minutes, I ascertained he had grown up in the Midwest, had attended Ohio State, and had worked as a vehicle performance engineer for a major car company before moving to Crystal Cove to be an independent consultant to cruciverbalists. A couple of articles recapped public rows he'd had with Wesley about being his puzzle guinea pig. Why did he mind so much? He was responsible for hiring himself out as a consultant. He could stop at any time and go back to engineering, couldn't he?

I reached for a notepad with our Cookbook Nook logo imprinted on the top and, as I was prone to do when I'd worked on advertising accounts, began jotting notes. Ulysses was an avid amateur baker, as he'd said to Sunny earlier. He also coached at-risk youths in basketball whenever he could, telling a reporter that he'd had a huge temper as a kid and had barely stayed out of jail, but a Big Brother introduced him to basketball, and the game saved his life. I scrolled through photographs of Ulysses with Wesley and other puzzle solvers at various conventions. I paused when I landed on pictures of Ulysses with at-risk youths that he coached. Grins abounded. Overall, he struck me as a decent guy. On my notes, I scribbled the words *Motive: Disgruntled? In love with Eva? Jealous of Wesley? Angry about stolen puzzle?* and moved on to the next person.

Eva. There were plenty of photographs of her with puzzlers. She had aged well over the years, due to Botox injections, I speculated. She had no lines on her forehead and very few laugh lines around her eyes. According to one report, she managed the work of more than twenty constructors. She attended many conferences and had served as a judge at a handful of them. She was born in North Carolina, which accounted for her melodious drawl, and she'd attended the University of North Carolina Chapel Hill. In the *Gazette*, responding to interview questions as a new employee, she said she'd loved solving puzzles all her life. She was fond of other games, too, in particular card games. As a teen, she'd devoted her energies to learning magic tricks, and she was crazy about classic sports cars. She'd recently joined a Thunderbird car club. She'd never been married and contended that the notion of matrimony didn't appeal to her. Was my theory that she'd been interested in Wesley off base? Or was her answer about preferring singledom one that helped her avoid probing questions? I revisited my earlier theory about her and jotted *Motive: In love with Wesley? Did he reject her? Did that enrage her? Did they have a business dispute? Did he demand a heftier paycheck? Might that have threatened her career?*

Sunny Shore didn't have much of a presence on the Internet. I pulled up some photos of her and her daughters at a recent Make-A-Wish charity event. The girls were somewhere in their teens and as pretty as their mother. I couldn't believe it, but Sunny was wearing olive green in every shot. Her girls favored colorful, frilly florals. *In protest to their mother's monotone fashion sense,* I mused. I found a single photograph of Sunny in a black dress. It was from twenty-five years ago when she was playing her violin in the high school orchestra, seated as first chair. A couple of photos showed her at puzzle conventions over twenty years ago. Digging deeper, I discovered she'd attended UC Santa Barbara and had graduated with honors in mathematics. She'd also earned a PhD in mathematical sciences and, as she'd stated, had been hired by a computer company whose name I didn't recognize, but that didn't mean anything. I knew next to zilch about the tech world. I didn't find any mention of her inventions or patents. I didn't think she was lying about those. They simply weren't newsworthy yet. I was about to move on when I landed on an article in the Santa Barbara *News Press* about her and her husband, Samuel, a councilman. Six months ago, he'd filed for divorce and was now suing for custody of the girls. Why? Was Sunny an unfit mother? The article didn't elaborate. I figured the piece had been written because of the husband's career. I tried to learn more about Sunny's personal life but came up empty. There were no articles about her and Wesley Preston.

I leaned back in my chair to consider her predicament. Was Flora right? Had Wesley's refusal to pay Sunny destroyed her marriage and thrown her into a tailspin? I made notes on the pad, as I had for Ulysses and Eva, and then wrote *Motive: Money. Failed marriage.* I recalled the claim that Wesley had stolen one of her crossword puzzles, too, and added that to the list.

Finally, I turned to Noam Dixon. His online presence was quite extensive, mostly concerning his professorship at Berkeley and all the awards he'd received, a Distinguished Professor Award being one of them. His papers about Chaucer had turned up in numerous publications. He'd also published a book of tips for academic writing as well as a book about how to study Chaucer, including lessons with pronunciation for Chaucer's work as well as interlinear translations.

Above my pay grade, I decided.

A spirited editorial in the *Daily California*, a student-run newspaper for the university, addressed relationships between professors, citing Noam Dixon as a textbook example of why two brainiacs should not date. Apparently, Noam had been engaged to a fellow professor, a woman who taught physics, but he'd ended it a couple of months ago. There were no pictures of them. Could the woman be the one with the lustrous hair who had been looking for him? Had he broken her heart? The article didn't state why they'd split up, so I couldn't draw any further conclusions. According to his campus profile, Noam spent much of his time reading or doing research or creating crossword puzzles. He'd won ten crossword puzzle tournaments in the past twelve years. He hadn't written or published any works of fiction. I didn't see any photos of him with a woman named Yvette Simms, either. Did he miss her? Did he hold Wesley responsible for their breakup?

"What're you doing?" My aunt pushed through the drapes. She gazed at my notes and at the computer.

My cheeks flamed with heat. "You told me to investigate."

"I thought your father had put you off the notion."

"Dad is not the boss of me."

Aunt Vera peered at the most recent article I'd pulled up about Noam. "He is something else, isn't he? So brilliant. So accomplished. I remember Wesley and him going at it in debate club. Noam could run rings around Wesley in that regard. He was superb at drawing conclusions. Wesley was a bombast and never supported his suppositions with facts. Not unlike many politicians, come to think of it." She let out a bittersweet chuckle. "I often wondered why he didn't go into politics. He could have been a star. But I suppose a career involving words had always been his aim." She jutted a finger at my notepad. "Are you theorizing?"

"Yes. I did Internet searches on Sunny, Ulysses, and Eva, too."

"Find anything?"

"Nothing that proves anyone is a murderer." I tore off the notes I'd written, doubled them over, and slipped them into the outer pocket of my cross-body purse.

Lowering her voice, my aunt said, "You have my approval to dig as deeply as you need."

Chapter 19

Spiral puzzles: puzzles consisting of a grid of letters that corkscrew toward the center

Crystal Cove Community College was located to the north of the aquarium. The school offered hundreds of classes in about ninety academic disciplines and was known to have rigorous standards. If students maintained good grades, they could easily transfer to any of the University of California campuses. The grounds were landscaped with thousands of trees as well as a botanical garden and vineyard. The sports included tennis, swimming, and horseback riding. The facility was run entirely on solar energy. The Center, where the tournament was being held, featured a grand building with high ceilings and marble flooring and boasted a flawless layout for expositions.

Today, in the plaza outside the Center, dozens of food carts stood hawking cuisine from local restaurants like Taste of Heaven, BBQ, Seaside Bakery, Vines, and more. Through the plate glass windows, I could see more carts in the vestibule.

The event's registration table was positioned next to the Shredding food cart. I wondered how much the restaurant's owner had paid for that opportunity. She and I had spoken often about how important it was to get *eyes on the prize* to increase sales.

My aunt and I retrieved a schedule and our tournament badges and looped the badge lanyards around our necks. Neither of us was offered a tote bag as we were not participants. My lanyard entwined in the strap of my purse. As I untangled it, the notes I'd written during my deep dive fluttered from the outer pocket. I nabbed them as they hit the ground and stuffed them back in. We entered the building and came to a stop in the vestibule to survey the layout. Doors were opened leading into the main hall. Hundreds of visitors were moving in and out. The cacophony was incredible. Banners were strung around the perimeter welcoming contestants and guests. In honor of the foodie theme, pictures of appetizing dishes were posted everywhere. The enticing aroma of tacos, sausages, chicken wings, and more wafted to us. My mouth watered, and I found myself humming to the merry strains of "Walking on

Sunshine," which was playing through the overhead speakers.

Not far away, I spotted Tito Martinez holding his cell phone out to a woman in a yellow shirtwaist dress. I figured he was recording her response to a question he'd posed. To my surprise, I also saw Cinnamon and Officer Foster a few feet beyond Tito and the woman. Cinnamon had switched out of her uniform into casual clothes. Foster was dressed similarly. Were they trying to blend in so they could catch the killer? Was Officer Ford in the vicinity, as well, or had Cinnamon put him on notice for his indiscretion about the crime scene? I figured Appleby wasn't in attendance because Cinnamon had warned him off the case.

My aunt and I purchased two iced lattes from a vendor and moseyed into the noisy main hall, where a number of people were milling about.

A raised stage was set with a lectern, a microphone on a stand, and a long rectangular judging table. A large screen hung above the stage, but it was dark. Fifty tables for the puzzle solvers stood at the other end of the main hall, each about five feet apart. There were a plethora of chairs for the guests to observe the competition when it started. The table that stood along the rear wall was set with dozens of water pitchers and lots of tumblers.

The music stopped abruptly, mid-lyric. Everyone settled down.

Z.Z., in a neon blue suit, climbed the stairs to the stage, crossed to the microphone, and tapped on it. It reverberated, and she jumped back. "Whoa! It's live." She sniggered. "Welcome, everyone, to the tenth annual Crystal Cove Crossword Puzzle Contest."

The audience burst into applause. My aunt and I gravitated to the stage. She would greet everyone after Z.Z.

"For those who don't know me," our mayor went on, "I'm Zoey Zoeller—most folks call me Z.Z. I'm the mayor of this fine town, and I'm an avid puzzler." She drew attention to the various locations in the auditorium, like where the restrooms were as well as a bay of lockers. All contestants had to lock up their valuables, including cell phones, before competition so there would be no cheating. She also indicated a table at the foot of the stage holding freshly sharpened No. 2 pencils, erasers, and pencil sharpeners. "Firstly, could we all please honor Wesley Preston with a moment of silence. As you know, our dear friend, a creative genius, was taken sadly from this world on Wednesday night. We will be having a memorial for him on Sunday. Details to come. And now . . ."

"Oh, no," my aunt whispered under her breath.

"What's wrong?" I asked.

"Noam." She nodded to her left.

Noam Dixon had walked into the auditorium looking disheveled. His hair was mussed, he was unshaven, and his blue plaid shirt—the same shirt I'd seen him wearing yesterday—was halfway untucked.

"I hope he hasn't been drinking," she said.

"Does he have an alcohol problem?"

"I thought he'd put it behind him. Wesley's death must have really thrown him for a loop."

Or guilt had, I reflected. "Did Noam tell you where he was the night Wesley was killed?"

"I haven't questioned him, but he didn't do it. You saw him when he first heard the news. He was beside himself with grief."

I thought about the mysterious woman. Had she tracked him down? Was her sudden appearance the reason he'd fallen off the wagon?

Noam moved to a table near the water station and slumped into a chair.

"I'd go to him," Aunt Vera said, "but I'm needed on stage in a second." She looked bereft at not being able to help him.

After the minute of silence, Z.Z. thanked everyone, and said, "Let's go through the rules, shall we?" She read from a sheet of paper. "First and foremost, everything will be based on speed and accuracy. There will be three divisions, A through C, as well as age divisions and a rookie division. See the handout for the specifics. Division A is for everyone. Division B is for contestants who have never won the A division. Division C is for contestants who did not finish in the top twenty percent in last year's tournament."

I'd attended that event. There were a slew of new faces in this group.

Z.Z. continued to explain. The age divisions were for solvers under the age of forty and for solvers over the age of forty.

"That latter category includes you, my love," Z.Z. said and pointed at her husband, Jake, who was at the foot of the stage peering up at her. "Everyone, please meet my husband, Jake Chapman."

Jake, at ease at being the butt of her teasing, turned and waved to everyone in attendance. Not far from him, I saw Sunny and Ulysses. Eva was near the stairs leading to the stage. She seemed placid, but I could tell she was gritting her teeth by the way her jaw was twitching.

"Don't worry, folks," Z.Z. went on, "my better half will not get any insider knowledge from me. He hates doing crossword puzzles. He's a word search guy. Rookies, you are only competing in the rookie division. That should take the pressure off of you, right? There's a first time for everything. Now, all contestants may simultaneously compete in all events for which you are eligible, but if there's a question, see me. Last but not least . . ." She paused for effect. "If you didn't know, for the purpose of scoring, a word consists of any series of letters written between the black squares in the grid."

That drew jeers. A few commented that, of course, everyone knew that.

"Ten points will be awarded for every word you get correct, across and down. Twenty-five points for every minute you finish ahead of the recommended time to complete the puzzle. However" — Z.Z. raised a finger — "you will lose twenty-five points for each word you get wrong. Don't worry. You cannot go below zero. As a bonus, you can earn one hundred and fifty points for a perfectly completed puzzle. And now, please welcome Vera Hart."

The hem of my aunt's caftan swept the stairs as she climbed. When she reached the stage, she shook out the skirt, crossed to Z.Z., and accepted the microphone. "Hello, everyone. Most of you know me."

Many of the attendees cheered. My aunt had won the contest five years ago.

"Before we get down to serious business," she said, "we have a few fun activities to loosen you up." She crossed to the rectangular table and lifted a piece of yellow paper. "Complete this cryptogram in thirty minutes and turn it in. Or try your hand at" — she set down the yellow paper and lifted a piece of blue paper — "a spiral puzzle. They're my favorite. See how this one corkscrews around, almost like a snail's design? You'll find these puzzles at a table in the vestibule. You will have until two p.m. to complete them." She motioned to the entry area. "There will be modest cash prizes for the top solvers in each grouping."

Z.Z. checked her watch and took back the microphone. "Puzzle one will be distributed at three p.m. sharp. Be ready and clearheaded. Have fun! Oh, and don't forget, between puzzles two and three, we'll show a recording of a brief interview with Josh Wardle, a Welsh software engineer, more widely known as the inventor of Wordle."

Aha. That explained the reason for the screen above the stage.

"Hurrah!" dozens of attendees shouted.

"Following the third puzzle," Z.Z. said, "we'll have an evening reception on the plaza and, afterward, we'll announce the winners of today's fun rounds and puzzles. Keep your appetites. Vera's delicious Nook Café is catering the reception."

Katie had been working on a menu for the last two weeks. I couldn't wait to see what she'd come up with.

My aunt descended the steps and slipped her hand around my elbow. "Let's have fun and grab a cryptogram."

"You can't win. You're a judge."

"True, but I could use the diversion. Maybe, as we think outside the box, an idea of who killed Wesley will come to us." She guided me to the vestibule.

Out of the corner of my eye, I glimpsed the mysterious woman with the lustrous hair entering the women's restroom. She was carrying a duffel bag over her shoulder. It got caught as the door swung shut. She yanked it free and disappeared. Why had she brought it to the center? Had she obtained what she'd wanted from Noam and was prepared to leave town?

"Aunt Vera, did you see that woman—"

"Jenna! Vera!" Cinnamon weaved through the knot of attendees to us. "So nice to see you."

"Hello, Chief," my aunt said hastily. "Jenna, I'll meet you over there." She rushed away.

Snagglepuss, my all-time favorite cartoon character, couldn't have made a faster *exit stage left*. Was my aunt worried Cinnamon would snap cuffs on her despite the fact that she was in the clear?

136

Faith and the hotel maid had confirmed her alibi.

"Have you spoken to Charlene Grater?" I asked Cinnamon.

"Scheduled for tomorrow morning."

Rats. I wish she'd handled that today. "How did you like the mini potpie?"

"To die for." She let out a soft gasp. "Sorry. That was bad taste."

"I get it." I gave her a reassuring smile. "Slip of the tongue happens. Hey, I've been wondering who will be in charge of Wesley's estate." That was a fib. I hadn't been wondering, but seeing Sunny passing behind Cinnamon brought the thought to mind.

"His older brother."

"Has he come forward to claim the body?"

"He can't. We won't release it until after the autopsy. But he couldn't anyway. He's in Europe on business. He'll be arriving next week."

"What does he do?"

"He's a nuclear physicist."

I snorted. "No, really."

"Really," she said stoically. "Brains run in the family."

No kidding. "Have you reviewed Wesley's will? Is there a financial reason someone might have wanted him dead? A bequest or something?"

"We're on it. Nothing stands out. His brother inherits most. A few charities get some. Plus, as you posited yesterday —"

"Posited?"

"Theorized, speculated, conjectured."

"I know what it means. It's a fifty-cent word, rarely used in a sentence."

She smirked and continued. "You said he probably had creditors like the rest of us."

In particular, Sunny Shore, I thought.

"Chief." Foster slipped up beside Cinnamon and whispered something in her ear.

Cinnamon cut a look in the direction I'd seen the mysterious woman go. "Duty calls," she said to me. "Have fun."

I watched her hustle in the direction of the restrooms and was startled when someone flicked my arm.

Tito hiccupped out a laugh. "Sorry to frighten you, Jenna. Got a sec? I've received a tip."

"From whom?"

"See that woman in the yellow dress?" The one he had been questioning earlier.

"What about her?"

"She's one of the entrants, and she's staying at Crystal Cove Inn with a lot of the other participants. She's a newbie on the puzzle-solving circuit, but she's been a fan for years, and see, she knows Ulysses Huxley. By sight. He's sort of hard to miss."

I waited for more.

"It seems she was stunned to spy him at the inn Wednesday night because he's not staying there."

"He's local," I said.

"Right. Anyway, the woman—Martha—said she saw him lurking in the bushes not far from Wesley Preston's room around nine p.m."

Lurking? Like the killer might have been doing on the trail?

I said, "That sounds like odd behavior."

"That's what Martha thought. She presumed he hid when she opened the door. She wasn't sure how long he'd been out there. She'd been immersed in a rerun of *Jeopardy!*, but she heard two men yelling nearby and wanted to check it out to see if she needed to call management."

Was she talking about the same spat Ulysses overheard between Noam and Wesley? I said, "I'm not the one you should tell. Chief Pritchett is. Unless the woman—Martha—has told her."

"She hasn't."

"Is there any reason why not?"

"She didn't want to get Ulysses in any kind of trouble if he's innocent."

"Even so, Chief Pritchett should know. She's here with Officer Foster."

"I don't see them."

"I think they went in search of a mysterious woman."

Tito's eyebrows lifted.

"Don't get your hopes up," I chided. "I don't think there's a story there." I explained how she'd come to the shop inquiring about Noam Dixon. "I presume she's the professor he ended it with a few months ago, and she's come to town looking to make up or find resolution. Berkeley is less than two hours away. Hey, there's the chief." I pointed through the windows. Cinnamon and Foster were out in the plaza.

"Okay, I'm off to tell her everything I know. I don't keep anything from her nowadays."

Less than a year ago, Tito had been considered a suspect in a murder. Luckily, he had been exonerated, but he'd made it his policy, from that moment on, to be up front with the police about anything he discovered.

He pursed his lips, a small smile forming. "But I wanted to tell you about Huxley first," Tito said before leaving, "because a little birdie told me you were investigating on your aunt's behalf, seeing as the police think she's guilty."

"For your information, the birdie" —I grumbled *Bailey* under my breath—"is wrong. Aunt Vera isn't a suspect any longer. She's been exonerated."

Tito frowned. "That's not what I heard."

Chapter 20

Cryptogram: a message or code written in cypher; a puzzle where a phrase has been encoded

"What?" I bleated, and grabbed hold of Tito's arm. "No way. Cinnamon said my aunt was in the clear. Spill."

Tito splayed his hands. "Officer Ford said she continues to be a person of interest."

"Ford? Fiddlesticks. Where did you run into him?"

"At the station."

"Did he say why she's still a suspect? I mean, c'mon, two people confirmed her alibi."

"Ford said it's the word around the precinct. See, a cheese knife—"

"Is not the murder weapon. Not my aunt's cheese knife, anyway," I stated with authority, seething that Cinnamon hadn't put those rumors to rest.

"Let me finish."

Tito filled me in on Ford's account. He said the knife in question was with forensics, adding that whenever forensics held on to something, it was a surefire sign that the *thing* was significant. Tito contradicted him, stating that the lab would receive all sorts of evidence in the course of an investigation that had no bearing on the case, but Ford wouldn't be swayed.

"Rookie," I muttered.

Tito grinned. "Totally."

As he scurried away to talk to Cinnamon, I overheard Faith and Flora Fairchild shooting questions at each other.

"Nine-letter word meaning to cook or be cooked so as to develop the characteristic brown color and nutty flavor," Faith said.

"Caramelize," Flora answered. "Five-letter word meaning to injure with very hot liquid or steam."

"Scald," Faith replied. "Eight-letter word for a person who enjoys eating and often eats too much."

"Me!" Flora laughed. "Gourmand. Too easy. Okay, greasy, fatty. Four letters."

"Oily," Faith replied. "Four letter word for puree."

I spotted my aunt waiting in line to pick up one of the

cryptogram puzzles. As I hurried toward her, I glimpsed the mysterious woman again, slipping from the restroom and into the bay of lockers. Her head was bent forward, her hair forming a curtain around her face, and her duffel bag was, as before, slung over her shoulder. I wanted to pursue her, but my aunt called to me.

"Jenna, dear."

I went to join her and caught sight of Noam buying a hot beverage at the cart where we'd purchased our lattes earlier. Was he going to scarf down coffee so he could sober up, if he had, indeed, been drinking? My aunt could've been wrong about that. He might have awakened late and, not putting any thought into his grooming, threw on the same clothes he'd worn yesterday. He seemed better now, having changed into a green plaid shirt and brown corduroy jacket over khaki pants. He must've stowed an extra set of clothes in a locker, I decided.

My aunt handed me a piece of paper. "Here. Don't you love cryptograms? They're difficult but so rewarding once you solve them."

I stared at the paper and cringed. A *cryptogram* was a kind of secret code puzzle, but instead of finding definitions for words, a cryptogram provided the solver with the actual words of a quotation. The only problem was each letter was replaced with a different letter. For example, the letter *A* in the original text might be swapped with an *F*, or the letter *T* with an *O*. To be fair, the punctuation marks and the spaces between words were the same in the cryptogram as they were in the original text. Even so, I wasn't very good at cracking them.

"Did Cinnamon have anything to say?" she asked nonchalantly.

"Nothing much." I told her about Wesley's older brother being out of the country and his last will and testament not offering any clues as to who might have killed him. And then, knowing she'd find out anyway, I told her what Tito had said about the scuttlebutt with Officer Ford.

Her face paled. She fiddled with her amulet. "It's baloney."

"I know it, and you know it, but I suppose it's possible that the incision your knife makes matches the incision of the wound that . . ." I paused, realizing I was reiterating what Charlene Grater had said about various knives making similar slits. The police hadn't asked her about the set Eva Wainwright purchased, yet. Would tomorrow's testimony force the police to delve deeper? "I have to provide Cinnamon with other suspects, Aunt Vera. That's all there is to it." I filled her in on the woman in the yellow dress—Martha—who saw Ulysses Huxley lurking in the bushes outside Wesley's room.

"Heavens. Lurking? Is that the word she used?" My aunt released her amulet. "Such cloak-and-dagger—" She stumbled over the word *dagger* and choked back a gasp. "I didn't mean—"

"Relax. I'm on your side." I placed a reassuring hand on her arm. "Listen, I think Ulysses is the most likely suspect because of his size and his heated history with Wesley. On the other hand, he freely admitted to me that he went to the inn to talk to Wesley."

"He did?"

"Yes, I meant to tell you, but with Cinnamon plaguing you, I decided . . ." I twirled a hand. "He was whittling outside the café yesterday, and we got to talking, and after I told him about Wesley's death, he said he overheard Noam and Wesley arguing Wednesday night. He didn't lie about being at the inn, which means . . ."

My aunt turned pale. "Which means I'm not in the clear until you find another viable suspect." She screwed up her mouth. "Oh, Jenna."

"Don't worry." I offered a weak smile. "I'll figure this out. Promise. I'm going back to the shop."

"But you haven't done the cryptogram."

"I'll pass." I handed it back to her. "I'm no Alan Turing," I joked, referring to the famous cryptanalyst. "Besides, I've got enough to mull over. You stay. Try to have fun."

• • •

The Cookbook Nook was quiet when I returned, but aprons were hanging every which way, the display table looked like a tornado had struck it, and the jigsaw puzzle on the vintage table was helter-skelter. Bailey was moving between the shelves, carrying an armload of books and setting them, one by one, in their proper places. Gran was organizing items behind the sales counter. Tigger roused from his spot at the top of his kitty condo and thrust a paw in my direction. I scurried to him, gave his paw a shake, and told him to go back to sleep.

"Why is the place such a mess?" I accepted half of the books Bailey was carrying.

"Last-minute shoppers snatched whatever they could before they headed to the Center. Whewie!"

I peeked down the breezeway. The hot cross buns Katie had put out earlier had been devoured. "Think we need more treats?"

"Nah. The café is slammed right now with the dinner crowd as well as prepping for tonight's reception, and Katie is already on her way to the Center. Are you hungry?"

"No. The potpie filled me up. But I hate for the snack table to look empty."

"Believe me, whoever comes in before we close won't mind."

I slotted a copy of *Le Cordon Bleu Chocolate Bible: 180 Recipes from the Famous French Culinary School* between *Everything Chocolate: A Decadent Collection of Morning Pastries, Nostalgic Sweets, and Showstopping Desserts* and *Taste of Home Chocolate: 100 Cakes, Candies and Decadent Delights*. In my copy of the Cordon Bleu cookbook at home, I'd inserted more than fifty Post-it notes to tag recipes I wanted to make. Bailey raved about the *Taste of Home Chocolate* cookbook. The picture of the cake on the cover made me swoon.

"Remind me to order more of these books," I said.

"Already done."

"You're the best. Say, did you tell your sweet husband that I was investigating Wesley's murder?"

"I might have mentioned that you were, um, curious." She inserted her last book and then repositioned a few others. We preferred book spines to read right to left, top to bottom. "He texted that he'd unearthed a lead and had passed it along to you as well as to Cinnamon."

"He did."

"Good. I love what a law-abiding citizen he is." Bailey moved to the children's corner and started straightening what must have been a whirlwind of activities. "We made crossword puzzles today. Twelve children. All future cruciverbalists, if you ask me."

"My aunt tells me you can't start kids early enough on puzzle solving. It's like math. Puzzles stir the little gray cells." I brought over a recycle bin for the scrap paper.

"So, did you tell my husband who you suspect?" Bailey asked.

"No."

"Will you clue me in? I love how your brain works."

As I was telling her about the deep dive I'd done when I'd returned from Mum's the Word, I reached into the side pocket of my purse for the notes I'd jotted. They weren't there, which rattled me. Where had I lost them? Most likely in the restroom at the Center when I was washing my hands and I'd received a phone call from Rhett. They must have fluttered out and fallen into the garbage. By now, they were probably beneath a pile of used paper towels.

"Everything okay?" Bailey asked.

I shared my dismay. "But it's all right. I remember everything I wrote. First, Ulysses admittedly has a temper. He claims to have conquered it, but given the way he verbally assailed Wesley at the Q&A, I wouldn't put it past him to have lashed out on the trail. And if what Sunny Shore said is true, that Wesley stole one of Ulysses's puzzles, he had even more motive."

"A puzzle is worth killing for?"

"If it could thwart his career. He wants to be a premier cruciverbalist."

"C'mon. Do you think he could be at his age?"

"No one is too old to become a constructor," I said, reiterating Sunny's opinion. "Plus, I'm almost certain he's interested in Eva. Jealousy might have caused him to lash out if he thought Wesley was his competition."

"What about Sunny Shore?"

I recapped Sunny's marital problems and the fact that her husband was seeking custody of their girls.

"A shake-up of the family can't be easy," Bailey said. "Was there an explanation for why they split?"

"No. It was a very short article. I imagine a councilman would like his wife to be at his beck and call for events and such. If she spends too much time on her career instead of the family, that could cause a rift. Also, she might be in personal financial straits." I mentioned how Flora had seen Sunny at the bank and how Cinnamon had accidentally let slip about the bankruptcy. "If the marriage requires two incomes, and if Wesley didn't pay what he owed her—" I snapped my fingers.

"Wanting to get paid is a reason to keep him alive, don't you think? Let me check something." Bailey pulled her cell phone from the pocket of her aqua skirt and opened an Internet search. I peered over her shoulder. She typed in Sunny's name as well as her husband's and added a plus sign and the words *reason for divorce proceedings*. A couple of links materialized. She tapped on one and whistled. "Did you know about this? Samuel Shore was in an elevator accident. His car fell ten floors—nobody was hurt. Afterward, however, he put a restraining order on his wife. He claimed she rigged it."

"Was she prosecuted?"

Bailey read further and shook her head. "No. Her husband couldn't provide verifiable proof."

"Man, I feel bad for her if she isn't guilty. He obviously has it in for her."

She slipped the phone back into her skirt pocket. "What did you find out about Noam Dixon?"

I filled her in on his illustrious career, his failed engagement, and his lifelong rivalry with Wesley. "I can't put my finger on it, but there's something off about him. A woman, no name, came into the shop looking for him, and I'm trying to figure out who she is. I saw her again at the Center, but he and she weren't together. I was thinking it might be his ex-fiancée."

"*Ooh.* Intrigue."

"He was rumpled when he arrived at the event, which alarmed my aunt. He used to have a drinking problem, and she's worried he's fallen off the wagon."

"Because of this woman being in town?"

"Possibly. What if she tracked him down at the inn and had it out with him? Except why would she then show up at the event?"

"For another go-round?"

I scratched my ear. Something wasn't adding up.

"Jenna." Gran hailed me. "Telephone. It's Rhett."

Why was he using the landline to touch base? I pulled my cell phone from my pocket and saw I'd missed three calls from him in the last fifteen minutes. I dashed to the sales counter and answered. "Sorry, sweetheart. The vibrate-when-in-silent mode didn't alert me. Don't tell me you're canceling our dinner."

That was why he'd called me earlier, to set a date. We'd planned on having a quick bite before returning to the event together for the reception. We knew Katie's food would be amazing, but we wanted time to catch up. After finding the body and learning Aunt Vera was a suspect, I was desperate to drink in his calm.

"No, I'm not canceling. I'm just running late. We had a long staff meeting. The main entrée needed to be remade." Every afternoon at Intime, the waitstaff was required to sit down and taste all the entrées and appetizers to make sure they knew which ingredients were in each dish. That way they could answer diners' questions. "But Rook needs tending."

"Don't worry," I said. "I'm going to take Tigger home anyway. I'll walk Rook, feed him and Tigger, and meet you back here."

"What would I do without you?"

"Not survive."

"Got that right. I'd die."

His words jolted me.

Chapter 21

Crucadex: a grid and the full list of words to be entered in that grid, without explicit clues for where each answer goes

Rook was over the moon when Tigger and I entered the house. You'd think he didn't believe us whenever we said we'd be back soon. He danced around me, crouching and panting, ready to play. I set Tigger on the floor of the kitchen, told him to hang tight, attached a leash to the dog's collar, kicked off my sandals, and off we went.

The hazy orange sun hung low over the ocean. A lone sailing boat was cutting gracefully through the water. There was a gentle breeze, but it didn't chill me. I dug my toes in the sand as I walked, letting the soothing sound of the ocean clear my mind. Who had killed Wesley Preston? Were there suspects other than the ones I was considering? Eva contended she was in her room, but she'd been seen elsewhere. The woman in yellow had spied Ulysses in the bushes outside Wesley's room. Where did he go after that? Sunny had driven off in her car after her set-to with Wesley, but according to the concierge, she'd returned to the inn calm and collected. And Noam . . . where was he at the time of the murder? How could I wheedle an alibi out of him?

After I showered and changed into a simple forest green sheath and fed Rook and Tigger, I sped to the Nook Café. As I was parking in the lot, I saw Rhett entering. Excellent timing. I sneaked in behind him and kissed him on the neck. He startled, then smiled. Would I ever tire of seeing the way he drank me in with his eyes?

"Hello, husband," I said.

"Hello, wife. How are you holding up?"

"Still rattled. You?"

"Seeing a dead body isn't for the faint of heart."

"How's work?" I asked, changing the subject.

"Uh-uh. No shop talk."

"Okay. Let's be shallow for the evening," I said and winked.

"You're on." Fondly, he bussed my cheek.

The hostess, a cheerful, freckle-faced twenty-something, led us to a table by the window. The sky had turned dark since my walk with the pets. The moon, not yet visible from our viewpoint, was casting a golden glow on the ocean's inky-black surface.

"Here you go." She handed us two menus. "It's a limited selection tonight because so many of the staff are needed to help at the crossword event."

"No worries," I said. "How was Katie doing when she left?"

"On a high, as always." The hostess winked. "She loves big parties."

Our waiter appeared, and Rhett ordered us each a glass of white wine, butter lettuce salads with autumn vegetables, and striped bass meuniere. As we handed back our menus, the woman with the lustrous hair entered the restaurant. She didn't scan the café as if she was meeting anyone. She was still carrying her duffel. What was in it? A series of possibilities cycled through my mind. Had she witnessed Noam killing Wesley and was blackmailing him with a bag filled with damning photographs? Did she have equipment in the duffel that she could use to torture him into submission?

Get real, Jenna. Torture?

Casually, I lifted my cell phone and snapped a picture of her.

"What're you doing?" Rhett asked.

"See that woman in the wraparound burgundy dress following the hostess?"

Nonchalantly, he twisted his head to take a peek and turned back to me. "Who is she?"

"That's what I want to know." I told him how she'd inquired about Noam Dixon at the shop and how I'd glimpsed her again at the Center.

"Easy explanation," he said. "She's a puzzler here for the convention."

"Uh-uh. She'd be there now. And what's with that duffel bag? Why is she lugging it around?"

"Maybe her hotel room isn't ready."

I recapped my ludicrous theory about blackmail and torture.

"Darling, I have to give you kudos for your active imagination. Hey, I know, she's a flight attendant, and she carries the bag with her at all times."

"No. She's a midwife," I said, "ready for any birth."

"Wrong. She's a sun worshipper who takes her towel and lotions everywhere she goes."

We started giggling but continued our absurd litany. A yoga instructor — mat will travel. A jewel thief — camo clothing at the ready. A seamstress — making costumes at customers' homes for the upcoming Thanksgiving parade.

When our jesting ended, I held my cell phone out to him so he could study her face. She had large eyes, an aquiline nose, and full lips. Her phenomenal chain necklace made me think of the crest of a golden pheasant. I'd never encountered the bird in person, but I'd seen one on a nature watch television show. It was so regal.

Our waiter set our glasses of wine on the table and informed us our salads would be out shortly.

I thanked him and took a sip of the wine.

"Why don't you go over and ask the woman her name?" Rhett suggested.

I snorted, spewing wine onto the table. "C'mon. I know I'm curious, and at times I'm downright nosey, but I'm not that bold."

"Oh, yes, you are." He reached for my hand and gently rubbed his thumb across my knuckles. "That's what I adore about you. Granted, it makes me fear for your life, but I love you with all my heart, exactly as you are."

I narrowed my gaze. "Flattery will get you everywhere except to make me cross this restaurant and grill her."

"Okay." He gave me an eye roll. "Suit yourself."

When our salads and dinner came, we stopped talking. The dressing was savory, and the striped bass was melt-in-your-mouth perfect. As we were leaving, I scanned the café for the woman. She had gone.

Fifteen minutes later, we arrived at the Center. Katie and her staff were overseeing the tasting stations in the vestibule. She was clearly in her element, her chef's jacket spotless, her wild curls tamed beneath her toque. "Well, well. I hope you came with an appetite."

"We dined at the café, but we left room for dessert. This array looks great." I moved from station to station admiring the selections. Katie trailed me. "You've outdone yourself. Teriyaki shrimp kabobs, tandoori chicken on a stick, mini quiches, and everything presented in bento boxes. Lovely."

"I wanted it to be easy to pick up and move on."

"You are the best!"

Rhett echoed my praise. "Remind me, Katie, to have you do a seminar for my staff about catering large events."

She chortled. "Oh, don't stroke my ego any further, you two. My head will explode." She leaned into us. "Actually, I got the bento box idea from an Instagram that Lola posted. So clever. Yes, there's waste, but all the boxes are made from recycled materials."

I thought about Sunny's invention for edible popcorn bags. Had it been hard for her to follow through on her dream because of Wesley's nonpayments? Had she needed funds for prototypes?

Katie brandished a hand. "When those doors open, watch out. It'll be a stampede."

And it was. A mechanical switch threw open all the doors at once. The throng was clamorous as it exited the main hall. Voices rang off the ceiling. From the chatter, we gathered that the interview of Josh Wardle was amazing, puzzle two was the hardest of the three, and everyone's brains were, essentially, fried.

My aunt emerged through the far left door, radiant in an ecru knee-length dress and low nude heels. The hiking she'd been doing lately had really toned her calves. She'd mentioned the change to me a couple of weeks ago, but because she mostly wore caftans, I hadn't noticed. Z.Z. walked alongside her.

"See you in a bit," Rhett whispered, and kissed my cheek. He wanted to speak with a friend he'd seen heading for the coffee and dessert station.

I caught up to my aunt and Z.Z. "Where's Deputy Appleby? Isn't he planning on being here?" I couldn't see the faces of all three hundred in attendance, but he was so tall I could usually pick him out in a crowd.

"He's tending to a robbery at the north end of town," Aunt Vera said.

"Another one? What was stolen this time?"

"Plants."

I bit back a laugh. "As in someone dug up some plants? Were they rare orchids?" Orchids thrived in our climate.

"No. Remember that customer who loves to make fairy gardens? She was foolish enough to display one in her front yard. It was set in an antique wheelbarrow and featured an entire fairy village. Someone sneaked up and spirited it away. She's heartbroken without it. It took her two years to finish."

"Poor dear," Z.Z. said. "Let's tell Tito. He'll write an article for the *Courier*, shaming the thief, and the culprit will be so humiliated, he or she will return it."

Noam Dixon brushed by my aunt and gave her a quick pat on the shoulder. "Nice job in there, ladies. It's running like clockwork." His hair was combed, and his eyes were clear. Maybe he hadn't gone on a binge, or if he had slipped, he'd been able to get a grip.

"How'd you do on the puzzles?" Aunt Vera asked.

"All of them were a breeze. Speaking of which, I need some fresh air." He started for the exit.

"Noam," my aunt said.

He turned back. "Yes?"

"Earlier . . ." She hesitated. "You looked a little peaked."

That's a nice way of saying hungover, I mused.

"Are you feeling all right?" She slipped one hand into the other as if to prevent herself from reaching out to him.

"As good as I'll ever be." He headed out of the building.

"Oh, there's Jake." Z.Z. hurried outside, as well.

"Aunt Vera, look at this photograph." I pulled up the photos app on my cell phone and tapped on the mysterious woman's picture. "This is the lady who was at the shop this morning, after Katie's demo, asking about Noam. I saw her here in the vestibule, too. Remember when I asked you . . ." I paused. "No, I didn't. I never completed the question. Cinnamon interrupted me, and you darted away."

"I didn't dart."

"Yes, you did." I turned the phone so she could view it. "Do you have any idea who—"

My aunt gasped. "Yvette."

"Yvette Simms? As in the woman who left Noam for Wesley, and then when their relationship ended abruptly, fled the country?"

"The very same. She's older, but aren't we all? She was always elegant. Where did you take this picture?"

"At the Nook Café."

"That necklace she's got on is something else."

"It sure is." Her jewelry was what had made me equate her to a pheasant. Had I subconsciously done so because I'd sensed she had a connection to Wesley, the avid bird watcher? "I have this weird idea. What if she saw Noam kill Wesley and took a picture and is blackmailing him?"

My aunt laughed. "Impossible."

"Is it?"

My aunt gave me the side eye. "My adorable niece, you read too many suspense novels. I should tell Noam she's here, but if I do, I'm worried it could throw him off his game for tomorrow's puzzles, and he desperately wants to win this tournament. It's a matter of pride."

His way to one-up Wesley, even though he was dead, I supposed.

A new theory came to me, and I inhaled sharply.

"What's wrong?" my aunt asked.

"What if Yvette killed Wesley, and Noam saw her do it, and that's what drove him to drink?"

"Dear, no. Not Yvette. She's a good soul. Salt of the earth. That simply wouldn't make sense."

To be honest, nothing made sense. I felt like Ginny, who couldn't do a crossword puzzle to save her life because she didn't think in black and white. What was I missing? I mentally reviewed my list of suspects.

Noam, who despised Wesley for wooing Yvette away from him and throwing his career as an author into a tailspin. A lifelong hatred could drive an otherwise peaceful man to murder.

Yvette, dumped by Wesley, compelled to abandon the country of her birth.

Sunny, divorced and in need of money, furious that Wesley hadn't paid her what she was owed, but also angry that he'd poached her puzzle.

Ulysses, who might feel the same way about Wesley stealing his puzzle. Plus, I was certain he was interested in Eva. Again I wondered if he might have killed Wesley to get rid of the competition. And what about his dream to become a premier cruciverbalist? Had Wesley stood in his way?

Then there was *Eva*. Was she truly brokenhearted about Wesley's death or relieved? Had she been in love with him? Had he rejected her? And how was their business relationship? Had he demanded a larger salary than she could afford? Would that kind of pressure have cost her her job?

I felt like I was trying to solve a crucadex. I had lots of clues, and I could see the sixty-four-square grid, but I had no idea where each answer went.

Chapter 22

FITB: fill in the blank

"No," my aunt said. "I repeat, no way is Yvette a killer."

Rhett moseyed toward us carrying a plate filled with yummy-looking bite-sized pastries. He offered us each one. My aunt declined. Rhett said, "My favorite is the banana-date coffee cake. Katie has knocked it out of the park."

Even though I was pretty full from dinner, I couldn't resist. I took one and agreed. The bits of date and cacao nibs gave the cake a wonderfully chewy texture.

"Now, who isn't a killer?" Rhett asked as he plopped another square of cake into his mouth.

"Yvette Simms," my aunt said.

"The woman we saw at the café," I inserted. "Aunt Vera, you haven't seen Yvette in years. She might've changed."

"No. It's not her nature. Or Noam's nature. Or . . ." My aunt wrapped an arm around her torso, clearly upset that I would think people she'd grown up with were suspects in a murder.

"Jenna," Rhett said, "let's table any discussion of Wesley's murder for the time being and enjoy the rest of the evening."

Given the tender way he was looking at me and the way my aunt was shivering, I consented. I would reach out to Cinnamon about Yvette in the morning and let her follow up.

"Try the pumpkin cardamom tart," Rhett said.

I took one and ate it whole. "Yum! Superb!" I loved autumn flavors, and the cardamom added a nice touch, sweeter than cumin and more citrusy than fennel.

A few minutes later, a chime rang out. Everyone on the plaza disposed of their meals and desserts and headed into the hall. My aunt joined Z.Z. onstage. When the noise settled down, Z.Z. proceeded to announce the day's winners.

A man with salt-and-pepper hair won the cryptogram contest. Flora nailed the spiral puzzle. Both were allowed to give thirty-second speeches. The man thanked Sunny Shore, who took a mini bow. He said Sunny had given him all sorts of insider tips. Flora thanked her sister. Faith didn't look upset that her twin had beaten her, which made me happy. She could be quite the competitor. Not far from her, Ulysses was chatting up Martha. Was his intent to suss out exactly what she had seen at the inn or—I spied Eva standing morosely off to one side, her head buried in her cell phone—to make Eva jealous?

Next, Z.Z. announced the winner of all three event puzzles, which turned out to be Noam, to no one's surprise. He finger-combed his hair as he climbed to the stage to accept his awards. My aunt gave him a warm hug. He flinched beneath her grasp, but she didn't release him. When they did finally break apart, he smiled beseechingly at her.

A half hour later, Rhett and I called it a night and headed home. Sleep couldn't come fast enough. To my dismay, I dreamed about Noam, Yvette, Sunny, Eva, Ulysses, and Wesley, the six of them blending and merging into a big glob of muddled words, checkered boxes, spiral puzzles, and impossible-to-solve cryptograms.

• • •

At dawn on Saturday, when Rook pressed his damp nose against my arm, I was more than happy to scramble out of bed. I put on a pot of coffee, threw on leggings and a long-sleeved T-shirt, and took him on a mile-long walk. The moment we returned to the house, I smelled the aroma of bacon and hurried into the kitchen.

"You are the best man in the whole world," I said, kissing my husband firmly on the cheek. He was putting together an egg-cheese-and-bacon sandwich that would easily carry me through the day. "What's on your agenda?"

"I'll check in at Intime, make sure all the orders are filled, and meet you later at the convention."

"You're coming?"

"I wouldn't miss it." He slipped an arm around my waist, drawing me closer. "I want to see your aunt receive her award."

When he released me, I fed the animals, shrugged into an ecru linen skirt, chocolate-brown cropped sweater, and sandals, scarfed down my sandwich, and raced with Tigger to work. There was so much to do before I could attend the event, but I was determined not to miss a minute of it.

My aunt had arrived before me—I noticed her purse in the cubby beneath the sales register—but I didn't see her. She wasn't in the storage room, either. "Aunt Vera?" She didn't answer.

She must have gone to the café for a beverage. I set Tigger on the floor, and he scampered beneath the children's table, no doubt searching for scraps of paper left from yesterday's crossword puzzle session. My cell phone pinged in my purse. I pulled it out and scanned the screen. Bailey had sent a text that she was running late. Her daughter had spilled oatmeal cereal on the floor, making a sticky mess. She reminded me that Gran was taking the day off to visit with her granddaughters. I texted back that I hadn't forgotten. Yesterday, I'd asked Gran if she planned to bring the girls to the event at the Center. She did, but first she intended to bake with them to see if she could break their noxious video game habit. They would be making choc-o-monkey brownies. I begged her to bring some in when she came to work Monday. She said she wasn't sure they would last that long and suggested I ask Katie to make a batch. After all, it was her recipe.

Recalling that conversation, I texted Katie and entreated her to bring me brownies. She responded with a thumbs-up icon.

"Score!" I shouted, and was ready to dial Cinnamon regarding Yvette Simms when my aunt waltzed through the breezeway arch. She was wearing her favorite purple caftan. The gold filigree woven into the fabric sparkled in the sunlight that was spilling through the shop's windows.

"Good morning!" she trilled. "I needed tea, and we were all out in the storage room." She raised the paper cup she was carrying.

I made a mental note to buy more tea bags.

"Wasn't last night's event wonderful?" she asked.

"It was. I heard a lot of happy chatter."

"If only . . ." Her voice drifted off. "If only Wesley had been alive to see it. He would have enjoyed the festivities."

I nodded, commiserating.

"Marlon sends his love, by the way," she went on as she rounded the sales counter, set her tea to one side, and picked up a pen to review yesterday's receipts.

"You were able to see him before you went to sleep?"

"Yes. That issue about the fairy garden being missing? It's

resolved. The teenager next door, a budding artist, wanted to sketch the garden. She didn't think her neighbor — our customer — would let her, as there's bad blood between the families. She meant to wheel it back before dawn, but it was discovered missing before she could."

"Did our customer press charges?"

My aunt shook her head. "On the contrary. Her heart softened when she saw the teen's sketch and suggested the girl sit in her yard every day until she finished it. That did wonders for easing the tensions between the families."

"Does that mean Marlon can attend tonight's event when you receive your award?"

"I hope so. By the way" — she aimed her pen at the storage room curtain — "we received the order you put in yesterday."

"Great. I didn't expect it until this afternoon."

I slipped into the storage room and called the precinct. Cinnamon was out, so I left a message and texted her, too, giving her as much information as I could about Yvette Simms. Before signing off, I casually asked when my aunt's cheese knife might be returned. Then I fetched the new crossword solver dictionaries, returned to the main shop, and added them to the display table.

An hour later, as I was dusting shelves with a feather wand, I detected the aroma of something chocolate and hustled to the breezeway. Katie was setting a three-tiered tray with brownies on the table.

"You did it!" I exclaimed. "Bless you." I may have eaten an entire egg-cheese-and-bacon sandwich for breakfast, but I always had room for her brownies.

Katie grinned at me. "Enjoy!"

I took one and hummed. "They're still warm." The chunks of banana and chocolate gave the goodie precisely the right texture. "My new favorite."

"Every brownie is your new favorite," she teased, and pulled a recipe card from her pocket. "Here. You'll have no problem making these. Remember not to overbake them. Brownies are — "

"Better moist than dry," I finished. "You remind me every time."

"Jenna, dear, telephone," my aunt called from the shop.

I thanked Katie and zipped through the archway to the sales counter. I accepted the cordless phone from my aunt. "Who is it?

Cinnamon?"

"Ginny from Crystal Cove Inn."

"Hi, Ginny," I said into the receiver. "What's up?"

"A guest has some, um, sensitive information to share with you." She added in a whisper, "Information that might pertain to Wesley Preston's murder, but, um, see, she can't tell the police."

"Why not?"

"I can't say."

I snorted. "Yes, you can, but you don't want to." I happened to know Ginny was gifted at getting guests to confide in her.

"Could you swing by?" Ginny asked. "I know you've met with reluctant witnesses before. You'll figure out how to loop in Chief Pritchett on the DQ."

"On the down low," I corrected.

"Doesn't DQ stand for down quiet?"

"Uh, no, it means disqualified."

She chuckled. "For the life of me, that's why I can't ever solve a crossword puzzle. I get all the clues and answers mixed up. Will you come?"

"I can be there in an hour."

"How about sooner? Like now? She's ready to check out."

"Now?" I glanced at my aunt for her approval.

She waved a hand. "Go. Bailey will be here soon. I want you to find out what's up."

"Why don't you go?" I said to her.

"Me? No, dear. I may want justice for my friend, but I'm not nearly as good as you in the FITB department."

"FITB?" I tilted my head.

"Fill in the blank. They're used often in crossword clues and ideal when conducting interrogations."

To Ginny I said, "Twenty minutes."

The Crystal Cove Inn parking lots were fairly empty when I arrived. I assumed most everyone staying at the place had left to grab breakfast or brunch before heading to the Center. I entered the lobby and searched for Ginny. She wasn't around. The reception desk was empty, too. Sunny was standing nearby, polishing off a chocolate ice cream bar, her cell phone pressed to her ear. She didn't appear to be speaking to anyone.

Hoping I wasn't interrupting, I said, "Good morning. It's early for ice cream."

"I'm an ice cream fiend."

"Me, too. I'll eat it straight from the carton." I leaned in. "Sometimes right after I wake up."

She laughed. "Ditto."

I gestured to the empty desk. "Have you seen the concierge recently?"

"She'll be back in a sec." Sunny ended the call, tossed the ice cream stick in a trash can, and stuffed the phone into the pocket of her olive green fatigue jacket. I'd seen a similar one in a Banana Republic catalogue. Despite her penchant for wearing the same color, this sporty jacket-over-chinos look suited her.

"Trying to reach your kids?" I asked.

"I am." She hitched her oversized tote higher on her shoulder. "But they're not answering."

"Do you talk to them every day?"

"Not really. I mean, no. They've been busy."

Too busy to talk to their mother? "I'm sorry. How long has it been since you've spoken to them?"

"Late Wednesday night. My fourteen-year-old"—she gave an exaggerated eye roll—"won't deign to talk to me until after ten p.m. She has to chat with all her friends first. We must have talked for two hours straight. Since then, it's been hard to reach them. My husband . . . I mean my . . ." She stopped, and her cheek began ticking with tension. Plainly, she didn't want to call him her ex. "It's been a challenge."

Was the guy blocking access to her kids? Did his refusal to answer this morning's call irk her? Granted, he believed Sunny had deliberately caused the elevator car he was in to plummet, but he hadn't been able to provide proof. Couldn't he simply believe she was blameless and move on?

A guest toting a backpack passed by us. Another sporting a badge for the tournament followed. Each greeted Sunny, and she responded in kind.

I said, "What does your husband do, Sunny?"

"He's a councilman."

"Ooh," I said, as if it was news to me. "You must be very proud."

159

She smiled, but her smile didn't meet her eyes.

"He must have a demanding schedule," I said, eager to learn more. Had her miff with him made her combative with controlling men like Wesley? "Did you have to hire a sitter for your kids while you're away because he's so busy?"

"No. Their father juggles it all."

Their father, this time. Yes, definitely estranged.

Sunny checked her watch. "The concierge said she'd be right back. Why do you need to see her?"

"A woman wants to talk to me."

"About Wesley's death?" Sunny sucked in a breath, her eyes glistening with hope. "Do you know who did it? Does she? People say you've solved a few murders. It would be great if you could crack the case. It would put us all at ease, for sure."

"Whatever you've heard about me, it's highly inflated. Local lore, like the Loch Ness monster."

"Six-letter word for sea serpent legend . . . Nessie."

I aimed a right-you-are finger at her.

"I'd better get going." She started for the exit.

"Good luck today," I called after her.

"Thanks. I'll need it. Noam rocked it yesterday."

"Yes, he did."

Ginny rounded the corner rolling a large gray suitcase. She caught sight of me and waved. "Hold on a sec." She parked the luggage, hurried out of the building in the direction of the rooms, and returned with a petite woman about my age who was towing a smaller matching suitcase. Her chiffon floral dress was just the thing for an afternoon gathering or a day wedding. Her tawny hair was swooped into a messy bun with tendrils cupping her pretty face.

"Lois Lichtenstein," Ginny said, "this is Jenna Hart, the woman I told you about."

Chapter 23

Secret: clandestine, furtive, stealthy, hush-hush

Ginny steered Lois and me to the grouping of wing-backed armchairs by the oversized fireplace. A gas fire was lit and set on low. We each sat. The redheaded woman who worked the reception desk returned to her post and began manning the phones. A young man in a uniform similar to Ginny's sauntered into the room with a watering can and moved between the indoor plants, tending to each one. Two women chatting merrily passed by us, quizzing each other as Flora and Faith had done the day before. They exited through the front door without giving us a second glance.

"Are you going to the puzzle event, Lois?" I asked.

"Oh, no, I can't spell for the life of me. I'm a designer. Lois's Lovely Lines. I came to town to see if one of the boutiques would carry my dresses."

"Did you design the frock you're wearing?"

"Sure did."

"It's lovely. Very feminine."

"Oh, yay, you get me." She clapped silently. "That's it. I enjoy making clothes that enhance a woman's femininity. I think I landed an account with the shop in Artiste Arcade." She crossed her fingers. The arcade was a group of high-end dress and accessory shops not far from Fisherman's Village.

"Congrats."

"But we're not here to talk about me. It's about . . ." Lois toyed with a tendril of hair.

Noam Dixon scuttled into the lobby, his brown jacket tucked under one arm. He nodded in my direction and proceeded out the exit while straightening the collar of the green plaid shirt I'd seen him wearing last night.

Ginny said, "Go on, Lois, it's not gossip." To me she said, "It's about Eva Wainwright."

Lois said, "Do you know who we mean?"

"Yes," I replied.

"She's stylish but too bony, if you ask me," Lois said. "My room was next door to hers. Mine was a regular room, on the corner. Hers is a cabana. Anyway, she—"

I pressed a finger to my lips to quiet Lois as I spied Eva striding beneath the archway that Lois and Ginny had come through. She was studying her cell phone as she headed toward the front door.

"See what I mean?" Lois whispered. "She's got class, but *oof.* She's way too thin."

Eva did look chic but skinny in a black-and-white suit, a large black patent leather purse slung over her shoulder. She halted and stared at us. The way her eyes narrowed unnerved me. Had she sensed we were talking about her? After a moment, she shook her head and returned to studying her phone. Deciding that she'd glanced away from her cell to mull over whatever it was she was reading, I exhaled the breath I was holding.

When she exited the hotel, I twirled a finger for Lois to continue.

"Anyway, through the wall of my room, I heard him and her talking."

"Him?"

"Wesley," Ginny said. "On Wednesday night."

"Yes," Lois went on. "Wednesday. He said, 'Give me more, or else.'"

"More what?" I asked.

"I don't know."

More could refer to anything. Maybe Wesley had met Eva for a glass of wine, and he'd wanted her to refill his glass, or they'd been snacking on something and she'd hogged the bag or bowl.

"His voice had an edge," Lois said. "He sounded upset. Like he was negotiating with her. *More,* he repeated, like she wasn't giving him enough."

"Could he have been asking for a bigger paycheck?" I asked, wondering again about his and Eva's business relationship.

"I suppose. I couldn't hear everything because Eva's television was on. I think it was tuned to a rerun of an action movie. There were lots of explosions." Her cheeks tinged pink. "The sole reason I was listening was because I was trying to figure out which movie. See, I was bored and wanted something to watch. I love movies like *Mission: Impossible* and anything James Bond. My husband, may he rest in peace, was a nut for those kinds of movies and got me hooked."

Ginny checked her watch. "Your ride to the airport will be here in a few, Lois."

"Right. Speed up the story. I can take forever to tell one." Lois offered a self-deprecating laugh. "Good for chatting up customers, but not for something like this." She motioned between us. "Anyway, around nine fifteen, I went to knock on Miss Wainwright's door, intending to ask her what she was watching, but I spied a man hiding in the bushes, and I got scared, so I quickly retreated to my room and bolted the door."

Eva's cabana was two away from Wesley's. Had Lois seen Ulysses Huxley outside Wesley's room like Martha had?

"What did the man look like?" I asked.

"He had whitish blond hair, like the villain in *Skyfall*. He even resembled him with his square jaw and big face. Did you see that Bond flick? Javier Bardem played him."

I had seen the movie. Bardem was typically dark-haired, but the wild bleach job he'd sported in *Skyfall* had made him look extra sinister.

"I checked a few minutes later, through the peephole," Lois went on, "and seeing as he was gone, I slipped out and knocked on Miss Wainwright's cabana, but she didn't answer. Concerned, because, well, I'd heard a door slam after I retreated to my room, and worried that she and the man—"

"Wesley," Ginny inserted.

"Might have had a fight, I stopped a housekeeper who was taking fresh towels to another room and asked if she would open the door to make sure Miss Wainwright was okay. She did, and we called out for her, but again, she didn't answer. So we tiptoed inside. And she wasn't there!"

Whoa! Flora was right. Eva had given me and my aunt a phony alibi when she'd told us she was in her room reading.

"But guess what was?" Lois continued. "A black canvas bag. It was open on the bed, and inside was a strong box filled with cash. Lots and lots of it. Mostly hundred-dollar bills."

I recalled seeing the canvas bag when I'd visited Eva's room and ordered her coffee. The bag had been zipped, but when she'd tossed it onto the floor, it had landed with a metallic *thud*.

"The TV was on," Lois added.

Was that about the time Eva went to Say Cheese Shoppe? Did she idle there in her T-Bird, waiting to follow Wesley when he passed by? How would she have known where he was headed? I supposed he could have told her his plan to go birding on the North and South trails. I revisited the mention of the cash on her bed. Had she obtained it illegally? Did Wesley see it and figure out how she'd gotten it and demand hush money? After she paid him, did he want *more*?

I stared at the inn's front door as another scenario came to me. After Lois fled into her room and Wesley stormed out of Eva's cabana, was it possible that Ulysses followed him? Or Sunny? Or Noam?

A driver in a black suit, polished-to-a-shine shoes, and black cap, entered the foyer and made a beeline for us. "Lois" — he referred to his cell phone — "Lichtenstein?"

Lois popped to her feet. "Ready. Thanks for listening, Jenna."

"Lois, one last question. Why didn't you tell the police?"

Lois ran her lower lip between her teeth. "I have dozens of unpaid parking tickets, and I can't afford to pay them or the fines I've accrued."

"But you're staying at the inn. Rooms aren't cheap."

"About that. I've nearly maxed out my credit card." She bobbed her head. "I know. I know. I must learn to balance my budget better, and I will, but this week . . . coming here . . . It meant everything to my business so I splurged. Bye."

The driver attended to her luggage and followed her out of the building. I studied her, weighing her explanation. She'd arranged for a driver and a room but couldn't pay her parking tickets? I supposed appearances did need to be maintained. I'd never been so cavalier about using a credit card, but then my father and mother had given me warning upon warning about never building up debt. Had Sunny Shore, like Lois, lacked the discipline to balance her budget?

I thanked Ginny for reaching out to me and hopped into my VW, adjusting my purse to the right so I could hook the seat belt. Windows down, I drove along Seaview Road toward Main Street. The fresh air felt good on my face as I reviewed Lois's statement. Ulysses was there not merely when Martha caught sight of him outside Wesley's room—when he overheard Wesley arguing with Noam—but he was also there a few minutes later, when Lois spied him outside Eva's room. Therefore, he hadn't gone home when he'd said.

I turned into the first curve and tapped on the brakes as I normally would. The car didn't slow. I hit the brakes again, but the VW was picking up speed. A frisson of fear zipped up my spine. I tried the brakes again. Nothing. Not even a hitch.

"Stop!" I ordered the car, like that would help. Two sedans were ahead of me. "Stop, stop, stop!"

Negotiating the next curve, with the car picking up speed, I tried to remember what my father had drummed into me and my siblings when he'd taught each of us to drive. *If the brakes ever go out,* he said . . .

"What do I do, Dad?" I shouted, not remembering the rest. "What do I do?"

I wasn't supposed to pull on the hand brake. That was designed to stop a car from a standing position. Then my father's words came to me. *Stand on the brakes and throw the car into neutral.* I did, but the VW wouldn't slow.

Panic scudded through me. I was nearing the vehicles in front of me.

Ahead, in front of Enchanted Garden on the opposite side of the road, I spotted a big truck filled with plants. It was parked. A deliveryman was standing to one side, rearranging a cart filled with bags of dirt. A car coming up the hill was way off in the distance.

I only had seconds to make a decision. I beeped my horn and yelled out the window, "Watch out! Move! Move!" and then I deliberately veered the VW into the truck. I struck it at thirty miles an hour. The truck didn't budge.

The man with the dirt squawked.

The VW's airbag activated, and I face-planted into it. The seat belt pinned me in place. My breathing was ragged, but I was alive.

In less than a minute, I heard a siren, the screech of tires, and slamming doors.

"Jenna?" a man said.

Not sure if I'd injured my neck in the impact, I turned my head to the left very slowly. It felt okay. No spasming.

Bucky Winston, Cinnamon's husband, peered at me through my open window, looking as handsome as ever in his crisp fireman's uniform. "Hey, there. How are you doing?"

"Okay, I think. You got here fast."

"The station's right around the corner." He smelled of suntan lotion and peppermint gum. "Do you need an ambulance?"

"I don't think so." I opened my jaw. Wiggled my fingers and toes. Everything seemed in working order. I moved my head back to center. My spine felt okay, not like the time in high school when I'd attempted a flip in gymnastics, landed on my head, and jolted my back. My right leg was aching from jamming on the brakes, but I could bend my knee. "Can you help me out?"

Gallantly, he opened the door, squeezed between the airbag and me, and released my seat belt. Then he offered me a hand and guided me out of the car. "You look shaken up. Let me get you a chair. You okay to stand for a sec?"

"Yes." I held on to the VW's door for balance.

Bucky fetched a director's chair from a cabinet on the fire truck and opened it. Gently, he guided me to it and lowered me into it. "Don't lean your head back. Keep your head upright."

"To prevent whiplash," I said.

"Exactly." He crouched in front of me and checked my eyes. Felt for my pulse. Palpated my neck. "You seem intact. Can you tell me what happened?"

I did, replaying it second by second. The first curve. The brakes not working. Standing on the pedal while thrusting the gear into neutral. Veering the car into the delivery truck. "It was the only way I could think to stop."

"Fast reflexes."

I glimpsed a cluster of children peering around the truck that I'd slammed into, and my stomach did a flip-flop. If they'd materialized any sooner, like when I'd swerved . . . No, I didn't want to think about the possibility.

"I'll be right back," Bucky said, and dashed to my car. He inspected underneath the carriage and returned. "Looks like your brake line burst."

"How?"

"Not sure. It's broken in half. Wear and tear is a possibility. Or it might have been cut."

My insides snarled. "Intentionally?"

"Hard to know without further investigation." He gazed up Seaview. "You left a stream of fluid on the road."

I pulled my cell phone from my purse and started dialing my aunt when I heard someone call, "Jenna!"

Tito Martinez was jogging toward me. "You okay?"

"Yes." I was, wasn't I? I could see straight. I didn't have any noticeable aches other than my right leg.

He strode to Bucky. "What happened?"

They began talking, and my mind cycled through possible scenarios. When Noam Dixon hurried through the lobby, he'd seen me and had nodded in acknowledgment. Did he know how to disable a brake line? Did he think I knew something that would incriminate him in Wesley's murder? Had he cut the line on the off chance I'd crash and die?

Seconds later, Eva Wainwright had passed through the lobby, also spotting me. Had she overheard Lois and me talking about her? She was crazy about classic cars, if I recalled. She'd know where to find a brake line. Was there a cutting tool in the large purse she was carrying?

And I couldn't forget Sunny. She'd seemed delighted to hear that I was looking into Wesley's murder, but that could have been a cover. She was an inventor. Her husband thought she'd rigged an elevator to take a nosedive. Could she have tampered with my VW?

Tito returned to me with a bottle of water. "Police are on their way."

I groaned.

"FYI," he went on, "last night after you left, I found out something. Martha, the woman in the—"

"Yellow shirtwaist dress."

"Right. She turned out to be a good little gossip. It seems Ulysses Huxley gave a puzzle he created to Wesley Preston to get his opinion. In particular, a nocturnal bird puzzle, but, lo and behold, Wesley purloined it and published it with *his* name as the constructor."

Whoa. Sunny hadn't been lying about Wesley stealing puzzles.

It dawned on me that killing Wesley might not have been a spurof-the-moment decision for Ulysses. After all, he had asked Wesley about his penchant for birding at the Q&A. Had he done so in order to claim he wasn't the only person who knew where Wesley might go that night?

Chapter 24

Gastronome: epicure, connoisseur, gourmand

A patrolman arrived and wrote up an incident report. After that, I exchanged insurance information with the owner of the delivery truck that I'd slammed into. The guy was so forgiving, visibly more concerned about my health than his vehicle, and I promised I'd make him whole.

When I returned to the Cookbook Nook in the rental Honda Civic Tito had arranged for me—my VW would need a major overhaul—Bailey was waiting in the parking lot for me.

"Are you okay?" She braced my elbow like I was feeble. "Tito texted me."

"I'm shaken but not stirred," I joked. "That's a James Bond reference."

"I know all about Mr. Bond. Tito is a huge fan. We've watched every movie at least twice."

"Us, too."

I entered the shop and was immediately greeted by my aunt—who was worried to distraction—and Katie, who had brought coffee lattes and blueberry scones for all of us.

The scones, she said, were to mend my freaked out heart. "Comfort food always does the trick."

I thanked her and promised to try a scone soon. For the moment, my appetite was nil. I shuffled to Tigger to pet his head. He was nestled on the middle floor of his kitty condo and purred his concern. "I'm fine, buddy." I kissed his nose.

Bailey handed me one of the lattes. "Tito said your brake line was cut."

"It might have been, although Bucky said it could've been wear and tear." I doubted that, though. Three months ago, I'd taken the car in for its regular service. Nothing had been amiss.

"Who would have cut it?" Aunt Vera asked.

I told them how I'd seen Eva at the inn when talking to Lois and wondered whether she'd cut the brake line because she was worried that I was nearing the truth—that she'd killed Wesley. I recapped the exchange with Lois, how she'd heard Eva and Wesley arguing,

Wesley demanding *more*, the door slamming. "She checked on Eva to make sure she was okay but found her gone." I added the tidbits about them seeing the cash in the canvas bag and the fact that Eva was into cars.

"She lied to us about her alibi," my aunt murmured.

"Yep."

"Follow the money," Bailey said.

"However," I continued, "Sunny Shore was also at the inn. Given her talent for creating inventions, she might have known her way around a car."

"And what's her motive?" my aunt asked.

Bailey replayed the deep dive info I'd gleaned on Sunny, her tenuous financial situation, her estranged marriage, and the possible rigged elevator incident.

My aunt looked stunned.

"Lois also mentioned that she saw Ulysses Huxley lurking outside Eva's room," I said. "I didn't see him at the hotel, but what if he was there, and he spotted me? He used to be a vehicle per-formance engineer. I imagine he would know how to—" I couldn't finish the sentence, the memory of the accident too fresh in my mind.

"Tito told me about Ulysses's beef with Wesley," Bailey said. "Is it true he stole one of the guy's puzzles?"

"Yep," I said. "He stole one of Sunny's, too."

"Why on earth would Wesley do that?" my aunt asked, astounded. "He was masterful in his own right. He didn't need to filch anyone else's work."

"Sunny hinted that he'd lost his mojo." I sipped my latte. "Look, two witnesses have now spied Ulysses hiding outside or near Wesley's room on the night of the murder, and Ulysses admitted to being there, but not lying in wait in the bushes."

Bailey said, "Jenna also thinks Ulysses might have a thing for Eva and was in competition with Wesley for her affections."

"Heavens." Aunt Vera sighed. "Wesley had no interest in Eva whatsoever. Theirs was a business relationship, pure and simple."

"So you've said, but if Ulysses suspected otherwise . . ." I paused. "Jealousy is a hard thing to tame. He might have waited until Wesley left Eva's room and followed him to the trail." I took a long beat, knowing how my aunt was going to react to my next theory. "And then there's Noam."

"He's not guilty," she said.

"Hear me out." I replayed how Ulysses had eavesdropped on Noam arguing with Wesley at the inn. "Martha caught it, too. And he, Noam, saw me talking to Lois."

"No, no, no," my aunt cried.

"You've told me how smart he is. I'm sure he'd know how to tamper with brakes."

My aunt's face pinched with concern.

"Did you tell your suspicions to the officer who arrived at the scene?" Bailey removed the lid of her cup.

"No. He had enough on his plate." I pulled my cell phone from my purse. "I was getting ready to contact Cinnamon again. I left her a message and sent a text earlier, but she could use an update."

"So could we. From her." My aunt folded her arms. "We deserve to know everything she does about Wesley's murder."

"She won't tell us," I countered.

"But she should. I was his friend. I've been exonerated."

"No, Aunt Vera. Not if Officer Ford—"

"Tosh!" She flipped a hand. "I told you that's utter nonsense."

Swayed by her conviction, I said, "I'll call Cinnamon now."

"Wait. Hold the phone." Bailey giggled and smacked her thigh. "I've always wanted to say that."

I threw her a snarky look. This was no laughing matter.

"A bit ago," Bailey continued, "I was at the Center searching for Tito's lucky pen. He lost it last night. I found it, but that's not the point. I happened to see Ulysses"—she sipped her drink—"entering the gym across the plaza from the Center."

I knew the gym well. Rhett and Bucky often went there to instruct disadvantaged kids. I'd watched a few scrimmages.

"Ulysses was decked out like he planned to play some hoops," Bailey added. "Therefore, he couldn't have tampered with your brakes."

"Sure he could've," I countered. "He could have been at the inn, seen me, done the deed, and driven to the gym in a matter of minutes to establish an alibi."

"You should have a chat with him, Jenna," Aunt Vera said.

"Me?"

"Your aunt is right. I'll go with you." Bailey elbowed me. "Let's give him the chance to tell us what's what before we sic the police on him."

"But—"

"You know how Cinnamon hates to follow bad leads," Aunt Vera added coyly. "He's in a public place. It'll be safe."

"By the way, Rhett called," Bailey said.

Rhett. Oh, my. I hadn't touched base after the accident. I hadn't wanted to worry him.

"He heard from Tito and tried to reach you"—Bailey mimed taking a phone call—"but you didn't answer, so he contacted me."

I viewed my cell phone and saw I'd missed two messages. I called him using FaceTime.

He answered, his brow puckered with worry. "Hey, are you okay?"

"I'm fine."

Bailey crowded me so she could be in the picture. "We're going to the gym by the Center to talk to Ulysses Huxley. He has to explain where he was right before the incident."

"I'll meet you there," Rhett said.

"No," I said. "You don't need—"

He ended the call.

"Bailey," I groused. "We can't leave. Aunt Vera has to be at the tournament in an hour. With Gran off today—"

"I've got it covered." Bailey texted a message, read a reply, and sent a second. "Tina is coming in. Traffic is slow right now. She can handle the shop on her own." Tina Gump used to clerk for us while attending culinary school and serving as the nanny to Bailey's daughter.

"But she's working at the Pelican Brief," I countered. Now that she was a full-fledged sous chef, being trained by none other than Bailey's mom, Tina had given up all other part-time work.

"She has today off," Bailey said, "and said she'd be happy to help out. Let's go. I'll drive. Keys." She held out her hand.

I gave her the rental car set. I wasn't usually so passive, but the near-death experience had thrown me for a loop, and I had to admit I was eager to question Ulysses about why he'd been lurking in the bushes if his intent had been to talk openly with Wesley.

Minutes later, we met Rhett in front of the gym. He looked like he'd recently completed a long run, his hair moist and tousled, his jogging clothes sweat-stained. He kissed me and then cupped my chin and checked my eyes.

I wriggled free. "No head trauma. Don't baby me."

He chuckled. "Just making sure your feistiness is intact." He swung open the gym door.

The sound of basketballs and tennis shoes slapping the maple floor echoed as we entered. Eight high school–aged youths, seven boys and one girl, were racing to the far end of the gym, four on offense, four on defense. I didn't recognize any of them. None had come into the shop with a parent. None were any of the kids I'd seen working with Rhett and Bucky.

Ulysses, outfitted in navy gym shorts and a T-shirt that clung to his muscular frame, was taking a video of the practice. He lowered his cell phone and blew a whistle. "Hustle in. Hustle in. Balls in the bin." He motioned to a wire basket.

The teens obeyed, the equipment thudding against the metal.

Ulysses referred to a sheet on the clipboard he was holding and pointed at the kids as he singled them out. "Stu, you missed a layup. Mick, you gotta make sure you're signaling what you're up to. And Ainsley"—he stared at the girl—"we don't need anyone to grandstand."

The girl pouted and flipped her braid over her shoulder.

"I know, young lady. You're the next Steph Curry," Ulysses said. "You make every three-pointer you throw, but for now, we're playing as a team. Let everyone have a turn." He saw us and held up a hand. "Kids, take five. Hydrate."

He walked toward us with long, loping strides, his grin broad. "Hey, have you had your fill of crossword puzzles and come to watch practice?"

"Yes." I observed the teens from afar, taking in the state of their tennis shoes. All appeared to be well-worn. None were high-end.

Rhett motioned to the teens. "They move well."

"They're good," Ulysses said, "but rough around the edges. Their parents are struggling to make ends meet, so the kids don't get the private coaching others do."

"Rhett works with disadvantaged kids, too," I said.

Ulysses swept a meaty hand along the side of his hair. "Observing isn't really why you're here, is it? Wait, let me guess." He aimed a finger at Bailey. "Your husband, that reporter, was asking questions last night. He learned something, but he doesn't want to come right out and ask me, so he sent you three to grill me, all nice and friendly like. Am I close?" His tone had an edge.

"Can't put anything over on you," Rhett said, and folded his arms across his chest, not to look formidable, more likely to appear casual and to set Ulysses at ease.

Ulysses mirrored Rhett's stance and said to Bailey, "What's your husband's name?"

"Tito Martinez."

"Right. I remember now. What did he discover? I already told the police what I told you, Jenna, that I went to the inn that night and heard Noam and Wesley arguing, so I decided to go home and wait for a better opportunity."

I said, "But did you tell them you were hiding in the bushes?"

Ulysses whistled. "Well, that's to the point. No pussyfooting around for you. None of you are cops, so why do you care where I was?"

"My aunt loved Wesley Preston like a brother," I said. "She wants to see his killer brought to justice."

"*Ahh.*" Ulysses loosened his jaw. "Well, I'm the wrong guy. And I wasn't hiding—"

"Don't lie," I said.

"I'm not lying—"

"A second witness saw you, too. When Wesley and Eva were having a spat. He stormed out of her cabana, and—"

"What I meant was, I wasn't hiding." He cleared his throat. "Okay, yes, I was out of sight, but only because I didn't want to get caught. Wait. That came out wrong. See . . ." He scratched the back of his neck. "I go around town to restaurants and collect leftover food from the kitchens. For my kids." He gestured to the teens who were across the gym knocking back the bottles of water. "I do my best to make sure they're fed. In the interest of full disclosure, the inn wasn't on my usual rotation, but the sous chef at Petito's—that's the upscale restaurant at the inn beyond the cabanas—he texted me and said they had a lot of salmon left over from the night because of the tournament reception."

I knew Pepito's well. Rhett and I had gone there on our second date.

Ulysses said, "It dawned on me if I swung by the inn to pick it up, I could get a word with Wesley. You know, clear the air."

"About the puzzle he stole from you?" Bailey asked.

He cocked his head. "How do you know—"

"We have our sources," I said.

He jammed his lips together. "Yes, he was a puzzle stealer. Not purely from me, either."

By admitting it, did it mean he wasn't guilty?

"I started for his room first," Ulysses went on, "but someone was coming, so I ducked into bushes."

"Sounds pretty shady," Bailey said.

"It was a knee-jerk reaction," Ulysses said, "but I didn't want Eva to see me there because . . ."

"Because you like her and thought she'd think less of you," I inserted.

He blushed. "It turned out it was Noam. Like I said, I waited while they argued. When it went on for so long, I decided to pack it in and hustled to Petito's for the food. On my way back, I saw Wesley entering Eva's room. I made another snap decision to wait. How long could he remain there? When he surfaced ten minutes later, he was hopping mad. In fact, he slammed the door so hard it rattled. Trust me, that is *not* the best time to talk to someone. I know because I've got a temper." He paused. "I *had* a temper."

"Had?" Rhett repeated.

"I've worked through that, for the most part, but every once in a blue moon, anger can rear its ugly head. And, honestly, while waiting for Wesley to show his stupid mug, I realized I should apologize publicly, not privately, so people could hear what we said, and nothing would be *he said/he said*, you know? When he strode back to his room, I headed home."

"Did you see Eva leave?" I asked.

"No."

"What was Wesley wearing?"

"He'd changed into a camouflage shirt, cargo pants, and hiking boots."

"Will the sous chef corroborate you picked up the salmon?" Rhett asked.

"Yep."

I said, "And what about when you got home? Can someone confirm that?"

"I didn't see a soul, and I'm not sure anyone saw me. I live in a quiet neighborhood." He rubbed the underside of his chin. "Around ten, I started baking. A neighbor might have smelled the aroma."

"What were you baking?" I asked. "Sourdough bread?"

Rhett and Bailey regarded me.

I shrugged. "Sunny told me he's an amateur baker, partial to sourdough."

The teens drew near. Each appeared eager to get back to the scrimmage. Two reached into the basketball bin and plucked out balls.

Ulysses said, "She's right. I enjoy making bread, but, like I told you, I took home a bunch of salmon, and the kids weren't going to eat all of it. It's an acquired taste. So, I decided to use some of it to make salmon cat biscuits. My cats can't verify my whereabouts." He pulled his cell phone from his pocket, tapped his photo app, and showed us a picture of his critters. Three of them, all beauties. "They loved the treats so much, I'm thinking of opening my own business and selling to pet stores."

I narrowed my gaze. How many talents could one man have? Did baking for cats earn him a pass as a killer?

"I could use the extra bucks," he went on, "because, let's face it, I can't make a living hiring myself out to solve puzzles, and the world of engineering has chewed me up and spit me out. Each job in the past ten years has been eliminated."

"I heard you want to become a premier cruciverbalist," I said.

"Everybody can dream, but I have a better chance of becoming an entrepreneur."

The girl—Ainsley—said, "The cat biscuits smelled good, Coach."

Ulysses gave her a questioning glance. "How would you know?"

"Um . . ." She screwed up her mouth. "I was near your house."

"On Wednesday?" Bailey asked.

"Yeah, Wednesday," Ainsley replied.

Rhett said, "And you caught the scent of him baking?"

"Uh-huh. I mean, the biscuits might be for cats, but they smelled incredible. Real gourmet. Coach is a gourmand."

Ulysses's mouth twitched at the corners, pleased with her assessment. "It was late by then, Ainsley. What were you doing in the area?"

She threw her arms wide. "I wanted to ask if you'd teach me privately. I didn't want to beg in front of the others, and I know my mom and me don't have the money, but I was thinking I could offer to clean your house once a month in exchange." Her cheeks had tinged pink. She seemed close to tears.

"Okay. Okay." He held up his hand. "We'll talk. All of you, on the court. Ainsley, practice sharing the ball."

"You should have seen the cats lining up outside his place hoping for a handout," Ainsley added over her shoulder. "There were, like, a dozen of them."

Ulysses smiled self-consciously. "I have three cats, but I feed a family of six feral cats."

"That's a lot of cats," I said.

"I'm a sucker for furballs."

Chapter 25

Split Decisions: a puzzle that asks the solver to finds pairs of words that share letter strings

Outside the gym, the autumn sun blazed down on us. Rhett suggested I give Cinnamon an update, and then he kissed my cheek and told me he'd check on me later. He needed to stop in at Intime.

I pulled my cell phone from my purse.

Bailey said, "Uh-uh. Cinnamon can wait. You've left messages, and she hasn't called you back. C'mon. I'm starved. It's nearly one o'clock." She looped her arm through mine. "I finished the daily puzzle, no mistakes, and I want to pick up my treat from Pelican Brief. Mom is offering spicy crab cake appetizers to all successful puzzle solvers."

"I didn't finish."

"I'll share."

"Okay, but first, let's see if Aunt Vera is at the Center."

The food carts on the plaza were overrun with customers. The carts in the vestibule were, as well. The hall was crammed with attendees. The chatter was merry and loud. I spotted my aunt near the stage conversing with Z.Z. As I weaved through the throng to join her, a chime pealed through the hall's speakers.

Z.Z. viewed her watch, said something to my aunt, and took to the stage. A spotlight followed her. Dressed in a bright orange suit, her hair gelled into spikes, she reminded me of a firecracker. Words sizzled out of her as she greeted the attendees. "Everyone, puzzle four will begin promptly at three p.m. Puzzles five and six will follow with short breaks between each. In the meantime, the event planners have provided two more games with cash prizes. We'll start with puns and anagrams and then do Split Decisions. If you've never done a Split Decision puzzle, here's how it works."

An image materialized on the screen behind her.

"Split Decisions asks the solver to find words that share a pair of letters. For example, blank blank blank *er* slash *ol* blank blank . . ." — she gestured with a pointer to the image on the screen, *er/ol* — "would have the answers *reserve* and *resolve*. Therefore, you would write *res* in front of *er* and *ve* after *ol*. Get it?"

There were groans from the crowd and grumblings from some who hated Split Decisions. If I was honest, those were tough puzzles for me, too. My mind didn't think that way. And, yet, wasn't that what problem solving was about? Finding clues that intersected with others?

"After puzzles five and six," Z.Z. went on, "we'll be showing a short film previewing a new musical coming to Broadway entitled *Cross Words.* Following that, we'll present a lifetime achievement award to my very dear friend Vera Hart."

The spotlight on Z.Z. swung to highlight my aunt, but she was making haste for the exit.

"Uh-oh." I tagged Bailey. "Something's wrong. Come with me." We caught up to my aunt in the vestibule near the hallway leading to the bay of lockers. "Where're you running to?"

"Yvette . . ." My aunt hustled around the corner and stopped abruptly.

I bumped into her, and Bailey collided with me.

"Where'd she go?" my aunt asked.

"Got me," I said.

The hallway was empty.

Aunt Vera made an abrupt U-turn and bustled to the women's restroom. She stepped inside and returned to us, frustrated. "I know I saw her head this way."

"Maybe she's a phantom," I joked.

My aunt threw me a withering look.

"There's a fire exit at the end of this hall." I pointed. "She probably went through that."

"Why is she in town?" my aunt asked, her concern intense.

"You refuse to believe Noam is a killer, so instead, maybe Yvette is here to support Noam in his time of grief," I suggested.

Bailey said, "What if she went to the Pelican Brief to get her free appetizer? Hint, hint." She elbowed me. At the same time her stomach grumbled like a freight train.

"Good idea. Let's try there," I said.

We left my aunt's Mustang in the parking lot, and the three of us piled into my rental car. We found a spot on the street, fed the meter, and trooped into the Pelican Brief. The aroma of delicious fried fish wafted to us, and my stomach started making the same noises

Bailey's was making.

Lola, as sprightly as ever, approached us with menus. "Three for lunch?"

"One for your appetizer," Bailey said, producing her crossword puzzle. "No erasures."

Lola took it from her, scanned the answers, and smiled. "Like mother like daughter. Perfect." She petted her daughter's cheek and told us to go to the bar to wait, adding, "I'll bring enough for all of you."

"Hey, Mom, hold on. Have you seen—" Bailey eyeballed me. "What does Yvette look like?"

I described her.

Lola shook her head. "But I haven't personally seated everyone. Feel free to roam."

The place was packed. Every table was filled. As we strolled to the bar, I didn't see Yvette anywhere, but I caught sight of Eva Wainwright sitting in a booth with Charlene Grater. Both were leaning forward on their elbows as if sharing a huge secret.

"Jenna," my aunt said, "do you see Eva over there?"

"Yes." I tapped Bailey's elbow. "We'll meet you at the bar in a sec."

My aunt and I strode to Eva and Charlene's table.

"Hi, ladies," I said. "Enjoying yourselves?"

"Hey, Jenna, Vera." Charlene smiled. "We ate the most incredible meal. Mahi-mahi with an arugula and spinach salad. Divine." She'd scraped her plate clean. Eva's plate held remnants of spinach and tangerines.

"No cheese involved, Charlene?" I joked.

"I'm not that obsessed," she said. "Okay, I am, but I have to watch my weight if I intend to run that marathon. Faith is really applying the pressure."

My aunt said, "Yes, she can be a taskmaster when she sets her mind to it."

"Charlene, did you talk to the police this morning?" I asked.

"I did. I confirmed Faith's account."

My aunt released a relieved sigh.

With Eva sitting right there, I didn't want to ask Charlene if the police had questioned her about the cheese knife set Eva had purchased. Instead, I said to Eva, "I thought you'd be at the convention hall by now."

"I needed a breather." She fanned herself comically. "Talking puzzles all day makes me feel like I'm at the office. This was supposed to be a relaxing getaway." She stopped abruptly. The corners of her mouth turned down. "I'm sorry. That was insensitive," she murmured, plainly realizing Wesley's murder had made the getaway anything but relaxing.

"Eva," my aunt said, "Jenna told me she saw you earlier today at the inn."

"Oh?" Eva's eyes widened. "You were there? I didn't see you."

I had wondered at the time if she'd been mulling over whatever she was reading on her cell phone.

"She was there to meet a woman who was staying in the room next to yours," Aunt Vera added.

"What a coincidence." Eva's voice riffed higher with a girlish pitch.

Aunt Vera folded her hands in front of her. "As a matter of fact, the woman said she heard Wesley in your room on the night he died."

"In my room?" Eva glanced between us.

"The woman wasn't prying," I said. "She was trying to figure out what movie you were watching. She said Wesley sounded angry. She heard him ask you for more of something."

Eva blinked.

"Was he demanding a bigger salary?" I asked.

"That's an odd conclusion to jump to," Eva said. "He was always paid handsomely."

"A bit later, the woman heard your door slam," I went on. "She waited for a bit, and then believing Wesley had left, went to your room and knocked. When you didn't answer, she requested the housekeeper allow her to peek inside."

Eva huffed. "The nerve!"

"She was worried that Wesley might have hurt you. She wanted to make sure you were okay."

Eva carefully lifted the napkin from her lap, folded it into a triangle, and set it on the table.

"You weren't in the room," I added.

"Your point?" Eva stared daggers at me.

My aunt said, "You told me and Jenna that you went back to your room after the reception at Intime and read a historical novel."

"I did. Later. After Wesley left."

"After he stormed out," I revised.

"*Left,*" she reiterated, her jaw tight. "First, I took a walk."

Oh, man. Nobody had a solid alibi. Sunny talked to her daughters that night. Eva went on a walk. Ulysses made cat food. And Noam? What was his alibi?

"Did you take a walk because of your altercation with Wesley?" I asked.

"We didn't have an altercation."

"Did your conversation have to do with the cash you keep in the canvas bag?"

"I don't know what you're talking about." She raised her chin defiantly.

I said, "Thursday, when I drove you back to the inn and ordered coffee, you tossed your bag off the bed. It landed with a thud. It so happens it was wide open in your room when the neighbor and the housekeeper entered. They saw what was inside it. Cash in a metal box. Lots of cash. Mainly hundred-dollar bills."

"Where did you get it?" my aunt asked, surprising me with her brazenness.

"What are you implying? I'd like you to leave." Eva twisted in her seat as if looking for management.

Charlene said softly, "Tell them the truth, Eva."

"No."

Charlene reached across the table and stroked Eva's hand. "It's okay. Jenna and Vera will be discreet."

Ridiculous reasons for why she'd have so much money ran roughshod through my mind. She was a high-priced hooker. An arms dealer. A money launderer for the Mafia.

After a long moment, Eva heaved a sigh and began. "Wesley barged in. He'd had too much to drink, but he wouldn't be deterred. When he saw the cash, he demanded to know where I'd gotten it. He asked if I'd stolen it or robbed a bank. I told him it was mine. From savings. And then I divulged that I was on my way to a private poker game."

"Poker," my aunt and I said in unison.

"He didn't believe me at first, but it was true. I always carry a large sum of cash when I travel. The games in which I play are high stakes."

"Why didn't you store the cash in the inn's safe?" I asked.

"My room was secure, as far as I knew. I never asked house-keeping to turn down the bed. I needed accessibility." She drummed the table with her fingertips. "Anyway, Wesley pressed me and asked if I was addicted to gambling. I told him that was none of his business. He said it was, and he threatened to tell my employer, adding that he knew I was on thin ice after—" She drew in a sharp breath. A pained expression crossed her face.

"After?" my aunt coaxed.

"After I messed up last year."

Aunt Vera tilted her head, waiting.

"I padded an expense account on a trip to Europe," Eva said. "It wasn't the first time. My boss found out and put me on probation. One more slipup and I was out for good, he warned. I'd never work in publishing again. Wesley knew the situation. He and my boss were friendly. He demanded I give him a chunk of cash to keep quiet, so I did, but then he demanded more."

More, I thought. That was what Lois had heard.

"I did as he asked. I knew he'd hound me, otherwise."

"When he left," Aunt Vera continued, "you followed him and killed him."

"No!" Eva jammed her lips together. "No," she said more softly. "I went to the poker game."

"Who can corroborate that? You?" My aunt eyed Charlene.

She shook her head. "Usually, I go to the game."

"But you didn't this time," I cut in, "because you were running on the beach with Faith."

"Right."

"Who else attends?" Aunt Vera asked.

"It's a private game," Charlene replied.

"You mean a secret," my aunt said. "All identities protected."

Charlene nodded.

"Don't ask me who's in it, either." Eva sat taller and squared her shoulders. "I won't reveal the names. If I did, I could ruin reputations."

I scoffed. "For playing poker?" In my twenties, I'd participated in penny-ante games with female friends. No one lost more than ten dollars.

"She's not wrong, dear," Aunt Vera said. "There are a few morally righteous people in town who frown upon such things. The pastor of the congregational church comes to mind."

Charlene cleared her throat. Eva threw her a cautionary look.

"Eva," I continued, "someone saw you loitering outside Say Cheese Shoppe on the night of the murder. Is that true?"

"Yes, Jenna," Charlene cut in. "She was there. To catch a ride with a friend of mine to the game." She scooched over on the banquette and patted it. "Sit, ladies. Hear Eva out." To Eva she said, "Tell them everything, including names."

After taking a cleansing breath, Eva began her account. She'd heard about the game from Charlene when they were chatting about cheese. She had her own private high-stakes poker game in San Francisco. Charlene offered her seat to Eva. The women played stud poker, drank wine, and had fun until two a.m.

"And the players?" Aunt Vera coaxed.

Eva complied. A school administrator, banker, and restaurateur. All were women. "Posey Parker took part, too," she said. "She owns—"

"Crystal Cove Florists," I said. "I know her well." Posey was the wife of the aforementioned pastor.

My aunt let out a low whistle.

"Posey's husband hasn't a clue," Charlene added.

That could explain why Charlene and Posey had ended their secretive conversation at Say Cheese so abruptly the other night. "He won't hear it from us," I promised.

My aunt said, "Tell us about Wesley, Eva. He didn't know about the cash until he entered the room. Why did he barge in? To hurt you? To have his way with you?"

"No, he wanted ultimate approval over any new cruciverbalists featured in the *Gazette*." Eva sipped her water and pushed her glass away with a fingertip. "If I didn't vow to do that and pay the hush money, he said my career . . ." She shuddered. "I knew he'd follow through. He could be so cold."

Cold didn't quite capture it. I thought of how he'd hurt Noam by wooing Yvette and how he'd ended it with Yvette three years later. How he'd stolen puzzles from Sunny as well as Ulysses. The man had been merciless.

"I paid him ten thousand dollars and said I'd give him ten more at the end of the tournament," Eva went on. "Then I went to the poker game, but I brooded over my situation all night. The women listened. They gave advice." She regarded Charlene fondly. "When I got back to the inn, I decided to quit gambling forever."

Charlene said, "The other girls will vouch for her, but only if absolutely necessary."

Eva ran a finger along the edge of her plate. "If you ask me, the one person who really had it in for Wesley was Ulysses."

Hoo-boy, as Katie would say. I guessed Eva didn't return his affection after all. "Why's that?" I asked. "Because he wanted to be as famous as Wesley?"

"Because Wesley poached a puzzle Ulysses created."

I said, "Yes, I heard. The puzzle with the nocturnal bird theme."

"No. This one was about witticism, with words like *quipster, pundit, wisecracker, badinage, persiflage,* and *repartee.*"

"Badinage and persiflage?" Charlene quirked an eyebrow. "I don't know those words."

"Both mean banter," Eva said.

Oh, my. Wesley had stolen two puzzles from Ulysses?

"Ulysses had dedicated the puzzle to George Bernard Shaw," Eva added.

"How did you hear about it?" I asked.

"We had coffee. He shared the story. He wanted me to consider other puzzles he'd created, but he was very bitter about how Wesley had snookered him and claimed that particular puzzle as his own."

I flashed on Wesley joking at the Q&A that he was feeling rather *witty*, and later, at the reception at Intime, hearing Ulysses warn, *It's the last time.* Had Wesley's theft of the second puzzle pushed Ulysses over the edge? Had Wesley taken more than two? Had Ulysses duped Bailey, Rhett, and me with the cat biscuit story? Had he promised to coach Ainsley for free if she'd back up his alibi?

I thanked Eva and Charlene and slid off the banquette. As I stood, I eyed Eva's large purse. White paper was jutting from an external pocket, doubled over the way I'd folded the notes I'd taken when I did the deep dive. Had she found them at the Center after I lost them? Did she know that I had been ruminating about suspects' motives?

"What's wrong?" Eva glanced in the direction I was looking.

"What's on the paper?" I asked.

"This?" She plucked it and unfurled it. "My to-do list of phone calls to clients on Monday. Why?"

I could see it was notepaper from the inn and felt my cheeks warm. But then I glanced at her purse again and the size of it gave me pause. It appeared to be stuffed to the gills, and for a second time, my mind flew to the notion that she might have fiddled with my brake line. Had she, when she'd passed through the inn's lobby, figured out what Lois Lichtenstein had been telling me? Had she expected me to die in the crash so I couldn't clue in the police about her altercation with Wesley or about the cash that was in the canvas bag in her room? She was savvy with cars. She belonged to a classic Thunderbird car club. She could be lying about the real reason she'd argued with Wesley.

"Now what are you staring at?" Eva's forehead pinched with frown lines.

I said, "Your bag looks crammed with more than crossword puzzles. I was wondering what you carry in there?"

"Take a look." She unzipped it and pried it open. Within were stacks of red and blue poker chips. "My winnings from Wednesday. I thought I'd take in another game while I was here until I made the decision to give it all up. Charlene has offered to cash them in for me."

Chapter 26

Clarify: (verb) explain, illuminate, clear up; (verb) refine, cleanse, filter

Bailey joined my aunt and me near the exit. She was holding a Pelican Brief bento box. "Score!" She lifted the lid. "Three crab cakes. One for each of us. Don't they smell divine? Now, before I go back to the shop, I want to swing by California Catch and snag a free spicy fish kebab."

"But Tina is on her own," I said.

"Don't stew. She'll hold down the fort. I'll even buy her that avocado roll she adores. Pretty please?" She batted her eyelashes.

My aunt chuckled. "Does that ploy work with Tito?"

"Every time." Bailey giggled. "I'm teaching Brianna the trick, too."

I groaned. "Heaven help her father."

California Catch was an upscale fish restaurant painted in soothing ocean tones with accents of marble and glass. The twenty-foot-long aquarium filled with blue- and aqua-colored fish always drew my attention. The aroma of butter and garlic permeated the air, making me salivate. A line of four was standing at the register. I spotted Cinnamon in full uniform, off to one side. She was reading something on her cell phone.

I strode to her. "Did you complete today's puzzle? Are you here to pick up your free appetizer?"

"You bet I am. You?"

I hitched a thumb at Bailey. "She finished. I haven't had time."

Cinnamon's mouth turned up at the corners. "Because you've been too busy sleuthing?"

"Because I was in a car crash."

"I heard. Bucky gave me the lowdown." Her gaze warmed. "How are you feeling?"

"I'll live." I gestured to her phone. "Did you get my message?"

"Message and text. Yes."

"Why didn't you respond?"

"Because I thought you should take the day off and heal. Relax, Jenna, I've got this."

I scowled. "Hey, don't be like that. You told me to keep you in the loop."

She threw me the side-eye. "What am I going to do with you?"

My aunt moseyed to us. "You could start by acknowledging my niece's magnificent brain. It runs in the family."

I said, "And by telling my aunt that, after questioning Charlene Grater, you no longer consider her a suspect."

Cinnamon smiled. "Her statement holds up. Vera, you're exonerated."

The relief on my aunt's face was palpable. I looped an arm around her waist and squeezed with joy.

"How are you, otherwise, Jenna?" Cinnamon asked. "Did you suffer any injuries?"

"My leg hurts from jamming brakes that didn't work, but that's all."

A waitress approached Cinnamon and passed her a to-go bag. "Here you go, Chief. Wet wipes are inside, too."

Cinnamon thanked her and started for the exit.

"Wait, Cinnamon," I said, "can you tell us if you followed up with Yvette Simms? I agreed to tell you everything I learned."

Cinnamon cracked a smile. "Yes, but I never agreed to tell *you* anything."

"C'mon. Share. Tit for tat."

"Fine." Cinnamon switched the to-go bag to her other hand. "I've found out where Miss Simms is staying, and I've left messages for her there as well as on her cell phone."

"Don't you think it's interesting that she shows up in Crystal Cove right when her former flame is murdered?" I asked.

"It's interesting but not impactful." She turned to go.

My aunt prodded me. "Tell her about Ulysses Huxley, Jenna."

"One more thing, Chief," I said, realizing Bailey's craving for appetizers had delayed me from contacting Cinnamon after our chat with Ulysses at the gym.

"Chief," Cinnamon repeated. "Wow. I must rate." She cocked a hip.

"I always call you Chief."

"Seconds ago you called me by my first name."

I scrunched up my nose at her snipe, but let it go. The more I reacted in the negative, the more power I relinquished. "Ulysses Huxley's motive is much stronger than I believed. We"—I gestured between me and my aunt—"learned from Eva Wainwright that Wesley Preston poached a second puzzle from Ulysses. I could understand him forgiving Wesley for stealing one puzzle, but two? And what if he appropriated more?"

Cinnamon coughed out a laugh. "You think stealing a puzzle—"

"Puzzles. Plural."

"You think that's a motive for murder?"

"It is if you want to be the leading crossword puzzle constructor in the world but the most well-known cruciverbalist is the person filching them. And get this. Ulysses's alibi—"

"I know his alibi. He and I have spoken."

"Between you and me, it's iffy."

Her gaze narrowed. "Don't tell me you've grilled him, too."

"Not grilled. Chatted. My aunt suggested—"

"Jenna!" Cinnamon lasered me with a hard look. "Now you're bamboozling friends and family into investigating?"

"Bamboozling? I've never bamboozled Bailey or my aunt or anyone into doing something."

"Vera, whatever you do"—Cinnamon eyed my aunt—"don't go off half-cocked like you know who."

Half-cocked. Is that how she thought I delved into things? She was really starting to irk me. If I was a cartoon character, steam would be shooting out my ears right about now.

"*Pfft.*" My aunt lifted her chin. "I would never go off half-cocked. And for your information, I am involved of my own accord. Wesley was my dear friend."

Her dear friend that we recently found out was a total scoundrel, I mused.

"I'd like to make sure that the real culprit is brought to justice," my aunt continued. "What Jenna intended to tell you, before you cut her off, was two witnesses informed her that they saw Ulysses Huxley at the Crystal Cove Inn on the night Wesley was killed."

"Two?" Cinnamon's mouth dropped open. "He told me one."

"Two," my aunt said. "At different times. By the way, Ulysses isn't staying there. He lives—"

"I know where he lives, Vera," Cinnamon interrupted, and twirled a hand. "Go on. Jenna, the alibi."

"Earlier, Bailey, Rhett, and I chatted with Ulysses at the gym." I told her how he was coaching some at-risk teens in basketball. "When we pressed him about the two witnesses, he claimed he went to the inn because he wanted to hash over something with Wesley, but when he heard Wesley and Noam arguing, he thought better of it, believing he should carry out the discussion publicly the next day."

"Publicly, like he did at the Q&A?" Cinnamon clicked her tongue. "That went over like a lead balloon, if gossip is any indication."

"He said he then collected the surplus salmon from Pepito's—"

"Surplus salmon?" She squinted.

"Yes." I explained about him asking for leftovers from kitchens so he could feed the at-risk youths. "He said he received the salmon, and as he drew near to Wesley's cabana, he reconsidered chatting with him, but at that time Wesley was going at it with Eva Wainwright—"

"Going at it?"

"Yes, they argued, too, but she's not guilty." I quickly explained the disagreement, Wesley's blackmail attempt, and Eva's poker game alibi, confirmed by Charlene Grater.

"Okay, let's table her possible culpability for the moment," Cinnamon said. "Go on about Ulysses Huxley."

"When he heard them quarreling, he again felt it would be better if he engaged Wesley the next day, so he went home and baked biscuits for his cats."

"His cats."

"*Mm-hm.* One of his basketball teens, Ainsley something, maintained she went to his house that night to ask about private coaching, and she smelled the biscuits."

"What's so iffy about that?" Cinnamon asked.

"It seems, I don't know . . ." I twirled a hand. "What if he told Ainsley he'd coach her for free if she backed him up about the biscuits alibi?"

She mulled that over. "Okay. Thanks. I'll take it under consideration."

"The neighbors might know more," I suggested.

"Have a nice day." She tipped the brim of her hat and left the restaurant.

Bailey joined my aunt and me with her reward and Tina's avocado roll tucked into a to-go box. "What did Cinnamon—"

"Vera. Jenna. Bailey." Gran hustled to us, her trio of grand-daughters trailing her. The girls were clad in adorable matching dresses. "Sweethearts, show the ladies what you've accomplished."

Each of her granddaughters held up completed crossword puzzles.

The youngest was beaming with pride. "Gran gave me a few of the answers."

"That's a good way to learn," my aunt said. "Congratulations."

"Gran bought us lunch, too," the youngest said, "and we're taking the appetizers we won home with us."

"For Mom," the oldest girl said. Gran's son had died a number of years ago. That was the reason why she'd moved to California, to help her daughter-in-law raise the girls.

"You three, head outside to the car," Gran said. "I'll be right there." As they trotted off with the tween leading the group, she held back. "Vera, I've been thinking about you all morning."

"Why?"

"I know how much you cared for Wesley, and, well, after the girls went to bed last night, I was watching a movie. I couldn't sleep. You know how I struggle. What was the name of it?" She drummed her fingertips on her chin. "It was a spy movie with that handsome Colin somebody."

"Colin Firth," I said.

"Not him. The other Colin." Gran flapped a hand. "Anyway, I was flabbergasted when he used a knife to kill his enemy. I always thought a knife was a woman's weapon. He'd hidden the knife cleverly . . . in plain sight. It had been fashioned from a pen, and he kept it in his jacket front pocket along with a silk handkerchief. I squealed when he whipped it out and slit his enemy's throat. The whole affair made me think of poor Wesley Preston." She shook her head. "What a horrible, horrible way to die."

• • •

I drove my aunt back to her car at the Center, then we all headed to the shop so Bailey could relieve Tina. When my aunt and I returned to the Center, Z.Z. was collecting the latest puzzles and congratulating everyone on their fine efforts.

The happy noise in the hall was infectious as people rose from their chairs. Flora and Faith, dressed in black-and-white outfits to celebrate the tournament, I guessed, were gushing about how they'd figured out all of the Split Decisions. Martha, who was wearing a honey-toned floral shirtwaist dress, was bragging to a friend that she'd conquered the anagrams.

Tito, who was moving among the contestants, moseyed to me and inquired how I was feeling.

"Fine."

"Your accident is the talk of the town." He winked.

"I'll bet it is. Crazy female driver."

He laid a hand on my shoulder. "Far from it. You're a hero for figuring out where to turn to keep from wiping out the other drivers. Plus, you're a bit of a medical wonder for coming out of it unscathed."

"If one of those children had skirted the truck," I began, and shuddered as the memory of the impact replayed in my mind.

"But they didn't," my aunt said. "Let it go."

Could I? Had someone intentionally tampered with my brake line? After speaking with Eva, I doubted she had. But what about Ulysses or Sunny or Noam? "Tito, any news to report? Any more purloined puzzles?"

"I've got my ear to the ground."

"FYI, Chief Pritchett will be looking into Ulysses Huxley."

"Good to know," Tito said. "Everyone is a suspect until proven innocent."

He'd reversed the adage, but I didn't correct him.

Aunt Vera turned her head right and left, scanning the crowd.

"Is something wrong?" I asked.

"I don't see Noam."

Out of the corner of my eye, I caught sight of Yvette Simms wearing another preppy outfit slipping out of the hall. "Aunt Vera," I whispered. "Look. There."

We hurried after Yvette. As she had earlier, she evaded us. We peeked into the hallway of lockers. She wasn't there.

"Bother," my aunt grumbled. "She must have used the fire exit again."

"Wait. I see her," I said. "Outside on the plaza, heading right."

Like the other day, her duffel bag was slung over one shoulder.

We rushed from the vestibule and tailed her. A minute later, when we caught up to her on the far side of the building, we lurched to a stop. Yvette was in a passionate embrace with Noam, her duffel by her feet. Her lustrous hair was draped over his arms, her hips pressed against his, her lips locked on his mouth.

Ooh la la, I thought.

Aunt Vera cleared her throat. "Noam!"

Noam pushed away from Yvette and jerkily pulled the cuffs of his rumpled green plaid shirt lower on his wrists so the cuffs would appear from beneath the arms of his brown blazer.

Yvette smoothed her hair, swiped a finger beneath her lower lip to remove smeared lipstick, and hoisted the duffel bag. She pressed it against her chest like a shield.

"Vera, Jenna," Noam said. "Um, what are you doing here?"

"I'd ask you the same thing," my aunt said. A schoolmarm couldn't have sounded more exacting.

"You remember Yvette." Noam acknowledged her with a nod. "We were just catching up."

"Is that what you call it?" My aunt's gaze narrowed. "Hello, Yvette."

"Hi, Vera. Long time no see."

"Why are you in town?"

"I . . ." Yvette squinted at Noam. "I heard about Wesley's death, and I thought Noam might need me. I was on a well-deserved hiatus in the Bahamas after the last *NatGeo* assignment."

"And you thought coming here while a murder investigation was underway was a good place to vacation?"

"N-no," Yvette sputtered. "I felt it was time I checked in on Noam. He's been calling me for months."

My aunt regarded Noam.

He nodded. "Ever since my ex broke up with me."

"She broke up with you?" I asked. "I read an article that said you ended it."

"No, vice versa. With reason. You see . . ." He hesitated and gnawed the inside of his cheek. "A few months ago, I fell off the wagon and lost my anchor. She wanted nothing to do with me. I tried to patch things up, but she refused. That's when I started calling Yvette, hopeful she'd answer. She could always talk me out of drinking. She'd tell me I wasn't an addict and that I could beat this. But she didn't pick up," Noam went on. "Why would she? I was drunk every time I left a message. I hated myself for falling into an old habit. I felt so weak."

"It was my fault," Yvette said. "You never would have turned to alcohol if I hadn't—"

He fanned the air. "Stop. It was not your fault."

"But—"

"No." He touched her lips with his fingertip. "Anyway, three weeks ago, I finally found the courage to go back to AA."

Yvette offered him a supportive smile.

"I attend meetings twice a day. Either morning or midday, and every night at ten."

"You're not drinking?" Aunt Vera asked. "Because yesterday, I could've sworn—"

"I know, I know." His smile was weak. "I looked a wreck, but that's because I've been staying up nights, practicing and cramming for the tournament. You know how obsessive I can be."

"Where are your meetings located?" Aunt Vera asked. "The Y? The Congregational church?"

"Oh, they're not at a place. They're on Zoom."

"Zoom?" My aunt frowned.

"Uh-huh. There are twelve of us. We all travel or have busy schedules, making it impossible for us to meet in person, but our sponsors wanted a safe space for us to talk and find support, so they recommended Zoom. It's been incredible." He scrubbed his chin. "Anyway, back to . . ." He motioned to Yvette. "A week ago, I left her a message telling her I was winning the battle. She showed up yesterday to surprise me."

Yvette nodded.

"That's where I was," Noam went on, "an hour ago, before coming here. I was in my room. At the inn. On Zoom." He studied his clothes. "And that's why I look like this. I was running late. I didn't have time to shower."

"I brought him a change of clothes," Yvette said, loosening the grip on her duffel.

"You brought him clothes yesterday, too, didn't you?" I said, now realizing why she'd been traveling with the bag.

She seemed stunned that I'd figured it out.

"Noam—" I halted when I spotted the top of his ballpoint pen peeking from the pocket of his jacket and flashed on Gran's tale of the weapon used in the spy movie. Was Noam's pen the murder weapon? Had he been carrying it around *in plain sight* all this time? "Your pen."

"What about it?"

"You click it all the time. Is it like a fidget spinner? To ease anxiety?"

"Sort of. I click it to . . ." He moistened his lips. "To distract me from wanting a drink."

"May I see it?" I held out a hand.

He met my gaze. "W-why?"

"I love retro things."

My aunt eyed me curiously.

After a long moment, Noam removed the pen and presented it to me. I studied it, twisting the top as he'd done at the Nook Café. The nib of the pen protruded and receded, in and out, in normal fashion. Noam held out his hand, eager for me to return it.

I stepped away and tugged on the top of the pen. It remained fixed. Then I twisted it in the opposite direction, and the top popped off, revealing a sharp knife about the size of a nail file tucked into the base of the pen.

Yvette gasped. My aunt, too.

"Where'd you get this, Noam?" I asked.

"Give it back," he demanded.

It looked handcrafted, which made me think of the knife Ulysses had been using while waiting on the bench outside the Nook Café. "Did Sunny Shore make it for you?"

"Sunny? She doesn't make penknives."

"Actually, she made a knife for Ulysses."

Noam's face scrunched up. "Really?"

"A whittling knife."

"Yeah," Noam said. "He loves to whittle. He's lousy at it, but who am I to judge?" He coughed out a ragged laugh. "Nah, I found this one online."

"Why do you have it?" my aunt asked.

"For protection. I was mugged once in New York."

I said, "Have you shown this to the police?"

"Why would I?"

"Because Wesley was killed with a knife."

Noam shook his head. "Not with mine. I was nowhere near Wesley the night he was murdered."

"Wrong," I countered. "You were heard arguing with him around nine fifteen on Wednesday night."

"Who says?"

"Ulysses."

"That guy doesn't know his head from his—"

"Noam!" Yvette said sharply.

He blanched.

I turned to Yvette. "When did you arrive in town?"

Her eyes widened. "You can't possibly think I had anything to do with Wesley's death."

My aunt said, "No, dear. Jenna simply likes to get facts straight. The police have told her to fill them in on anything she learns. In fact, Chief Pritchett has left you messages. Have you spoken with her?"

"Not yet."

"When did you arrive?" my aunt tried again.

"Thursday, around midnight," Yvette said. "I booked a room at Nature's Retreat and decided I'd search for Noam the next morning."

If she could prove she was on a plane Thursday from the Bahamas, she was not a suspect.

"Why did you come?" my aunt asked.

Yvette gazed at Noam. "Noam's phone calls broke my heart. I didn't care about Wesley any longer, but I did love Noam. I . . . ." She released my aunt's hands and turned to him. "I never stopped loving you. I know we went our separate ways, but I always held you close in my heart."

He swooped an arm around her and pecked her cheek, then he eyed me. "I didn't kill Wesley. Yes, we quarreled that night."

"He called you names," I said. "User—"

"And loser."

Suddenly, I understood the terms. *User* because he was an

alcoholic. *Loser* for much the same reason. "Those taunts had to have made you feel pitiful and resentful," I said.

"They stung," Noam admitted, "but I knew he had a mouth on him, so I disregarded the insults and went to my room for my AA meeting."

Aunt Vera said, "Can someone corroborate that you were on the call that night?"

"Well . . ." Noam scuffed the toe of his shoe on the pavement. "No, not really. The meetings are anonymous. I mean, we know what each other looks like, but we don't share personal information."

"Doesn't your Zoom account post your name?" I asked.

"It would, if I was using my real name."

My aunt placed a hand on his shoulder. "You need to find someone who will back you up."

Chapter 27

Zest: tang, keenness, gusto; piquancy, bite

When my aunt and I returned inside the vestibule, Flora, Faith, and Sunny were huddling by the hallway leading to the lockers. Each was holding a white sheet of paper. Puzzle five wouldn't have been distributed yet, so what were they looking at?

"Your puzzle is super clever," Faith said to Sunny.

Aha. Sunny was showing them one of her creations.

"I love the clues for boxed sets," Faith went on. "Juries, DVDs, the title of Tori Amos's boxed set, *A Piano.*" She fanned herself with her paper. "Brilliant."

"Jenna, Vera." Flora waved us closer. "Look at the puzzle Sunny created."

"I don't get the clue *ears*," Faith said.

Sunny mimed punching her own ears.

"Oh. Ha-ha. Two ears. A *boxed* set."

Flora said, "She's submitting it to the *New York Times.* Sunny, how do you dream these up?"

"Sometimes my daughters help," she replied. "They're really smart girls. I think TikTok sharpens their minds, you know? They have to think in snippets that entertain their friends. Speaking of which, I should touch base with them. Excuse me." She pulled her cell phone from the pocket of her jacket.

"Sure thing," Flora said. "Good luck tomorrow."

Faith whacked Flora on the arm. "Don't wish her good luck. Wish me good luck."

"Yes, good luck to both of you," Sunny said, and stepping away from the women, tapped an image on her phone. After a moment, she said, "Hi, it's me. I want to talk to Skylar." She listened for a sec. "C'mon, Sam, you know I didn't—" She squinted at the cell phone screen and moaned, her cheeks blazing red with frustration. Had her ex-husband hung up on her? What a jerk.

"Oh, there's Marlon," my aunt said. "I'll be right back, Jenna."

"Take your time. It's nice that he's here to support you."

"I doubt he can stay." She rushed to him, and they embraced.

Sunny joined me. "They sure look happy, don't they?"

"They are." I motioned to her cell phone. "No luck reaching your daughters?"

"No. They're super busy."

The microphone crackled through the loudspeaker, followed by Z.Z.'s voice. "Testing. Ah, there we are. Sound." She chortled. "I forgot to switch it on. Hello again, everyone. If you'll make your way into the convention hall, we'll get started on the next puzzle."

Sunny dropped her phone into her jacket pocket, and she and I trailed the crowd.

"Here's an update," Z.Z. said, standing center stage. "Sunny Shore was the first to turn in puzzle four, and it was perfection."

The audience applauded, and Sunny raised a hand.

"How do you do it?" I asked her as the applause died down.

"Do what? Solve puzzles in a matter of minutes?"

"Balance your family and career."

She tucked her hair behind her ears. "It's definitely a challenge. Do you plan on having a family?"

"Rhett and I are discussing our options." Lately, he and I had been realizing how much energy it took for our friends to raise their children. We weren't sure we were ready to juggle schedules and often questioned whether we were parent material.

"By the way, I've been meaning to tell you, your aunt is so wonderful to offer the prize for the cruciverbalist challenge." She leaned into me. "I hope I win, of course. Actually, I want to win the whole shebang. I'm way behind Noam, but if I can nail all three today—"

"Jenna," my aunt said, returning with Deputy Appleby in tow, "we're catching an early dinner."

I consulted my watch. *Super* early.

"Want to join us?" she asked.

"I should check on Bailey."

"I did. She's doing fine. Tina was having such a good time, she decided to stick around."

"Then I'm in. Let's go to Intime. They'll be able to accommodate us." I glanced at Sunny. "Good luck with the next two puzzles."

"Thanks. I'll need all the luck I can get."

We arrived at Intime in minutes, and Rhett set us up at the captain's table in the kitchen. It was rectangular with a banquette and four chairs. We had a similar setup at the Nook Café. On occasion, like Katie, Rhett would advise his executive chef to wine and dine special customers, preparing items that weren't on the menu.

Rhett served us iced tea and sat beside me on the banquette. As much as we'd all have loved a glass of wine, we knew we needed to keep clear heads for the evening's activities. The chef was making us sautéed sole on a bed of asparagus.

We were telling Rhett about the tournament, Appleby marveling at the crowd size, when my aunt turned the conversation to what was obviously preying on her mind.

"My darling husband" — she sipped her tea while gazing lovingly at Appleby — "is there anything you can share with us about the investigation into Wesley's murder?"

He opened his hands. "C'mon, sweetheart, we're not going to spoil dinner with talk about that, are we?"

"But, *sweetheart*" — she smiled — "I need answers."

"We all do," he cooed.

Man, they were cute.

"But, if you'll recall, I am no longer on the case," he added.

She harrumphed. "Marlon, don't lie to me. You know as well as I do that I'm no longer a suspect, so of course you're on the case. For your information, Jenna has been asking a few questions. Cinnamon specifically told her to keep her in the loop."

"Did she now?" Appleby skewered me with a look. "And did she say we'd keep you in our loop, Jenna? No, she did not." He snorted.

I flicked salt at him. He roared. So did Rhett.

My aunt patted the table. "Be serious."

"I'm deadly serious," Appleby retorted.

The waiter tending to our meals set down a plate of warm brie-leek tart appetizers and four sampling portions of lobster bisque. "Your dinner will be up shortly."

My aunt thanked him, then said, "Who do you think did it, Jenna?"

Appleby harrumphed, took a tart, and downed it in one bite. "These brie things are good."

"Our specialty," Rhett said.

"So special he won't give me the recipe," I said. "I'd make a mess of them."

Rhett poked me in the ribs. "You know that's not the reason. All restaurants have proprietary secrets. This recipe is ours."

"Nutmeg," I said, taking in the aroma. "You've added nutmeg."

He held a finger to his lips and moved a serving of the bisque in front of me. "Taste this."

I did and hummed my approval as I discovered hearty chunks of lobster in each spoonful.

"Jenna" — my aunt plucked an appetizer for herself — "answer my question."

"Okay, I suspect Ulysses Huxley, Sunny Shore, Noam Dixon, and Eva Wainwright. Or I used to."

"Used to?" She arched an eyebrow.

"Before I detail everyone's motives, let me lay out something else first. Ever since I left Crystal Cove Inn this morning, I've been working through a timeline in my head." Making timelines were an organized way for me to put my thoughts together. "At six thirty Wednesday night, the reception started at Intime. At seven thirty, after the glass-shattering incident, Wesley left. Sunny followed shortly after. Around eight, everyone departed."

"When did Noam leave?" Rhett asked.

"I can't remember, but he wasn't here when I was heading out. According to Ginny, Sunny had a fight with Wesley in the inn's lobby around eight fifteen. She threw wine in his face and drove off in her rental car at a clip. She returned later calm and collected. Then, around nine, Martha, a puzzler — I don't know her last name; she spoke to Tito — saw Ulysses lurking outside Wesley's room. Around nine fifteen, Lois . . ." I paused and, for Rhett and Appleby's benefit, recapped what I'd learned from Lois Lichtenstein.

"After talking to Lois, she had the car accident," my aunt inserted. "Jenna, you said you saw Sunny and Eva at the inn."

"Yes, and Noam. The accident might not be related."

"But it might," she stressed.

Rhett brushed my hand with a fingertip. "Go on. Around nine fifteen . . ."

"Lois saw Ulysses hiding. Now, he cops to being out of sight, and he claims to have heard Wesley and Noam arguing. Martha heard them, too. Ulysses said he then went to get the salmon from Pepito's. On the way back, he saw Wesley entering Eva's room. He decided to stick around a little bit longer so he could talk to Wesley. But when Wesley left angry, Ulysses determined it wasn't a good time to approach him and went home to bake. Ulysses didn't see Eva leave. An at-risk youth corroborates Ulysses's whereabouts, if she's to be believed."

"Did Wesley go directly to the trail?" my aunt asked.

"Good question. According to Ulysses, Wesley was dressed in the clothes he was killed in when he'd met Eva, meaning he'd changed out of his cocktail party clothes before entering her room."

"Lois heard the door slam," my aunt continued. "Worried that Eva might have been injured, she asked a housekeeper to check on Eva. She was gone. At around nine forty-five, Flora Fairchild saw Eva hanging outside Say Cheese."

Rhett said, "Why was she there? Was she in a car, ready to tail Wesley?"

"No. We have the skinny on that," I said. "We bumped into Eva at the Pelican Brief earlier. We told her we knew she'd lied to us about her alibi, saying she was in her room reading, and we asked her about her whereabouts following their spat. She confessed, and Aunt Vera and I believe her alibi is credible. She attended a private, all-female poker game."

"Charlene Grater confirmed it," Aunt Vera said. "Well, she didn't *confirm* confirm it. She wasn't there. But she knows who can."

Rhett said, "Who'd have thought there was a private all-female poker game in Crystal Cove?"

"Ahem." I cleared my throat. "Don't be sexist."

"Never." He bussed my cheek. "Back to suspects."

For Appleby's sake, I laid out what we'd gleaned from Ulysses at the gym.

"Baking cat food," he said incredulously.

"Hey, if it gives him a legitimate alibi, he's innocent," Rhett said.

"*If,*" I repeated. "I'm not so sure it's the truth. We found out Wesley poached a second puzzle from Ulysses. Who knows if he stole more? Ulysses wants to be a premier cruciverbalist. What if he offered to coach the girl for free if she'd back him up?"

Appleby considered that.

"I suggested Cinnamon follow up with Ulysses's neighbors." I lifted another brie appetizer and inhaled the fragrant aroma. Definitely nutmeg.

"And the girl," my aunt said.

"Yes." I polished off my tart. "And then there's Noam."

"He didn't kill Wesley," my aunt said. "And his alibi is solid."

"Is it?" I explained how we'd caught him in a passionate embrace with Yvette and pressed him for his alibi and how he'd admitted he met regularly on Zoom AA meetings to deal with his alcoholism. "None of the members in his group knows his real name, for anonymity," I said. "Sounds cagey."

Appleby said, "The police could discreetly observe a session to verify."

"Good idea," my aunt said.

"You know what really bugs me?" I asked.

Rhett placed his napkin on the table and leaned forward on his elbows, all ears.

"Yvette shows up in town right when Noam needs her. Why now, after all these years of being incommunicado? Doesn't it seem strange?"

"He begged for her help," my aunt said.

"Weeks ago."

"She heard about the murder," my aunt reasoned. "She wanted to support him."

"I have to return to my previous theory," I said. "What if she and he planned Wesley's murder?"

"Rubbish." Aunt Vera snorted dismissively.

"What if she flew to town to provide him with an alibi?"

"Except she didn't arrive until Thursday at midnight," Aunt Vera countered. "A flight from the Bahamas takes at least five hours."

Appleby opened an app on his cell phone and tapped a note. "I'll check that out."

"What about Sunny Shore?" Rhett asked. "You said she and Wesley had a quarrel in the lobby at the inn."

"Yes, and Wesley was the bane of her existence. He owed her money. If his lack of payment was the reason she had to declare bankruptcy—"

"Sunny." My aunt shook her head. "She's a darling. I can't imagine her doing anything criminal, let alone stabbing someone."

"Sweetheart," Appleby said, "if you rule out everyone, we have no suspects."

She glowered at him.

"When Sunny and I chatted the other day," I said, "she got really hot under the collar, going on about how badly Wesley treated her and how he gave her no credit for helping write all the foodie-themed puzzles for this week's event." I shared how disparagingly she'd spoken of him, saying he didn't have enough zest in his brain to add zing to a puzzle and how he wouldn't know the difference between yellow pudding and lemon mousse.

My aunt *tsk*ed. "That doesn't make her a killer. Heavens, I wouldn't be able to come up with enough clues and answers for five straight puzzles, either. Didn't you tell me she has an alibi?"

"She was on the phone to her girls for hours, but if asked, they might lie to protect her."

"However, if it is true, then given the coroner's time of death, she couldn't have followed Wesley on his jaunt and killed him," my aunt said.

Our dinners came, and we all tucked in, tabling any further discussion.

• • •

When my aunt and I returned to the Center—she'd guessed right, Appleby had business to attend to, and sadly, Rhett couldn't take the rest of the night off as he'd planned because a sous chef had called in ill—the preview of the new musical *Cross Words* was about to begin. Some audience members were seated; others were milling about. I saw Eva Wainwright hanging with Charlene by the water station at the rear of the hall. Had they gone to the precinct to clear Eva of murder? Had Charlene accompanied Eva to the event to fend off questions that might arise? Ulysses approached them. He'd changed from his athletic coach's gear into a nice shirt, slacks, and blazer. He said something to Eva, but she clearly brushed him off. Head hanging, he shuffled away.

Noam, who had switched into pressed clothes Yvette had

brought him, was chatting with her by the far wall. A woman approached them. She handed Noam an event program. He pulled his pen from his pocket, signed it, and returned it to her. When the woman departed, Yvette kissed Noam's cheek pristinely.

My aunt and I lingered by the entrance and watched the entire *Cross Words* movie trailer. It was filled with arguments acted out by performers about puzzles related to disputes. Ten minutes later, when it ended, the audience broke into wild applause.

On the stage, Z.Z. said, "Phew!" into the microphone while wiping her brow. "All that hostility got my blood boiling. How about yours? I'm going to have to see that when it comes out. Who knew crossword addicts could be so—" She stopped short. Had she been about to say *murderous*? "Moving on. It's time for me to announce the winners for all the categories. First and foremost, I want to thank each of you for attending and participating. Despite the sadness that has occurred, this is the best attended Crossword Puzzle Tournament our town has ever sponsored. Also, judging by your submissions, I'm guessing some of you have been spending the other fifty-one weeks this past year boning up."

That elicited laughter.

With flawless efficiency, Z.Z. awarded the honors. First, she announced the winners of the anagrams and Split Decisions, which turned out not to be Flora or Faith—both looked disappointed. She allowed the winners their thirty seconds to thank friends and family. Then she revealed the winners of all the puzzles. As noted yesterday, Noam had swept puzzles one, two, and three. Sunny had mastered puzzle four today, Ulysses had scored the fifth puzzle, and Noam had nailed the sixth.

"And, now, before we move on to honor my good friend Vera Hart," Z.Z. said, "I want to congratulate the Rookie Division Winner. Drum roll, please."

Obediently, the audience members thumped the backs of chairs and tables, making quite a racket.

"Martha Millhouse, please come to the stage."

Martha *eek*ed and set her water glass on her chair. As she strode to the stage, she placed a hand dramatically on her chest, as if she couldn't believe she'd won. A few attendees congratulated her. She smiled and thanked each. Then she took the steps to the stage, the tight skirt of her cocktail dress prohibiting long strides, and collapsed.

Everyone gasped.

Z.Z. dropped the mic on the lectern and rushed to her. She felt Martha's wrist for a pulse. "Martha? Martha?" To the audience, she shouted, "Someone call nine-one-one!"

I yanked my cell phone from my purse and stabbed in the numbers. The responder answered. As I was giving details, a woman who announced she was a doctor rushed onto the stage while pulling a stethoscope from her tote. My aunt followed her. The doctor listened to Martha's heart and started applying CPR, beginning with chest compressions. Before she moved to check Martha's air passage, a siren wailed outside.

Bucky and his associate sprinted into the hall and ordered the folks who were eager for a close-up view to clear a path. Z.Z. and my aunt remained onstage. The doctor opted to stand by, if needed.

Out of the corner of my eye, I saw Ulysses slipping out one of the side doors. A curious thought flew into my mind. Had he put something into Martha's water glass so she wouldn't be able to back up what she'd told Tito about seeing him outside Wesley's room?

Chapter 28

Password: keyword, secret code, open sesame

Martha roused and said, "Where am I?"

Bucky said, "You're in the convention hall. You fainted."

"I . . . I need to sit up."

He propped her into position. "Here you go."

The onlookers applauded her recovery.

Martha caught sight of her wide-opened legs and moaned. Quickly, she pressed her thighs together and tugged at the hem of her dress.

Bucky checked her eyes with his flashlight. "What did you eat for dinner, ma'am?"

"Dinner? I skipped it. I . . ." Her cheeks tinged pink. "Could you help me stand, please? I'm fine."

Bucky braced her shoulders and gingerly lifted her. "You need fluids, ma'am. And some food."

I rushed into the vestibule and collected a selection of mini sandwiches from a vendor and hurried back. *"Psst!* Aunt Vera. Here." I gave her the food, and she offered it to Martha.

"No, please, I'm not hungry. Really." Martha's shoulders sagged. "I'm sorry to have stolen your thunder, Vera."

"Heavens. Forget about it." My aunt flapped a hand. "I've received plenty of accolades in my lifetime. I can wait a few more minutes. You're what's important."

Faith and Flora came to the foot of the stage and offered to assist Martha down the stairs and into a chair.

Z.Z. then said into the microphone, "All right, crisis averted. Let's give a warm thanks to our EMTs and doctor."

The audience obeyed, and Bucky and his partner left the building.

The rest of the evening went off without a hitch. My aunt gracefully accepted her award, and then Z.Z. listed the twenty-five finalists—alphabetically—and reminded everyone to return to the Center bright and early for the toughest crossword puzzle of all, which would determine the overall winner. The twenty-five were ecstatic to have made the cut; of course, there were a few deflated faces in the crowd. Z.Z. added that in the afternoon the tournament would feature the cruciverbalist showdown, following which there would be a memorial for Wesley Preston.

As attendees filed out of the hall, my aunt drew alongside me. She and Z.Z. were going out for a glass of wine. She invited me to join them. I declined, saying I had to get home to the animals. Rook needed a walk, and I was certain Tigger was going stir-crazy after being dropped off by Bailey.

Lights flickered in the hall, signifying a half hour to closing.

My aunt and I kissed good night, and I followed her toward the exit. I paused when I realized Ulysses had reappeared and was talking to Sunny. The coincidental timing of him leaving the room when Martha fainted must have been nothing more than him needing to relieve himself. He and Sunny were standing in a cluster of disarranged chairs that needed to be repositioned. I wondered what they were discussing. After being rejected by Eva, was he setting his sights on Sunny? Had he learned she was estranged from her husband? Were they becoming fast friends and possibly lovers? Were they telling each other lifelong secrets? I laughed to myself. No one told the complete truth about themselves. When you first got to know someone, you scratched the surface. Rhett and I had met a few years ago, but I still felt there was a wealth of information I didn't know about him and was eager to learn.

Sunny turned her cell phone so Ulysses could view the screen. She was probably showing him pix of her daughters. Proud mama. Then she stowed the phone back in her bag.

"C'mon, my fellow ice cream fiend," I heard him say as I drew near. "Let me buy you a congratulatory scoop. My treat."

"But—" She turned to reach for her tote.

"Leave it. No one will steal anything. Plus, you told me your puzzle ideas for tomorrow's competition are locked safely in your hotel room. C'mon. The Taste of Heaven food cart is in the plaza. It'll just take a few minutes." He tugged her out of the hall.

I started toward her tote so I could take it to her. If she was anything like me, she would hate leaving her purse unsupervised, particularly if she'd been robbed when she first arrived in town. In fact, if I'd been fleeced, there was no way I'd let my bag out of my sight, ice cream fiend or no ice cream fiend.

That gave me pause. If the robbery was a lie, what else was? I thought about the timeline of Wednesday according to Ginny. Sunny and Wesley fought. Sunny drove off in a huff and came back an hour later. Did Ginny catch sight of her after that? Did Martha or Lois or a housekeeper see her? On impulse, I pulled my phone from my purse, dialed Crystal Cove Inn, and asked for Ginny.

She answered with her typically breezy, "Concierge, how may I help you?"

"Ginny, it's me." I explained what I wanted.

"*Hmm*, that's a good question. As I was getting off my shift, I did spy her climbing back into her car. She didn't turn it on. Maybe she left something in it."

"What time was that?"

"Around nine forty-five."

I thanked her and glimpsed the clock above the stage—ten p.m., straight up. The time jolted me as I remembered Sunny saying she'd phoned her daughters at that exact time on Wednesday night. She said they'd spoken for nearly two hours. From her car? From her room? It didn't matter where she'd made the call. What mattered was whether her call was as long as she'd claimed. When I was a teenager, the last person I wanted to talk to at ten at night was my mother. I adored her, but I could have a chat with her any time of the day. At ten, with a midnight curfew, I typically finished my homework and got on the telephone to gab to Bailey or Katie or a few of my other friends. If Sunny had lied and the call had only lasted a few minutes, she wouldn't have a verifiable alibi.

Checking again to make sure I was alone, I snagged Sunny's cell phone from her tote to see if I could verify her call history. Sure, I could touch base with Cinnamon and ask her to pull up the records, but I didn't want to reach out *half-cocked*, as she'd chided. I wanted to offer her something concrete.

I stared at Sunny's screen. It required either a password or a face ID. I didn't resemble her in the least, so the latter wouldn't work. What would she have used as a password? It dawned on me that when I'd purchased my phone, it had required a six-digit code. Knowing I'd forget a six-digit numerical code, I'd created a custom code using numbers to spell the password *Tigger*. Had Sunny done something similar?

I recalled our conversation at the inn. She had two daughters. Both girls. Skylar and Sloane. Both of those names were six letters, if I was spelling them correctly. I typed in *Skylar* first. That didn't unlock the phone. Next, I tried *Sloane*. No luck.

I typed in a combo of Skylar and Sloane, *Skyslo*. No go. *Skyane*. Not a chance. *Slolar*. That was a bust, too. I doubted Sunny would have used her husband's name, Samuel, due to their prickly history. I didn't know whether she had pets. That hadn't come up in our conversations or in the deep dive I'd done on her. Out of the blue, something she'd said about her girls during our conversation at the inn came to me. She'd referred to them as her sweet angels. Was it possible?

Giving it one more try, I typed in *angels*. My breath snagged in my chest as Sunny's screen came into view. As expected, she had all the regular apps: photos, camera, maps, clock. I clicked on the telephone icon, which was clustered at the bottom of the screen with the messages, Internet, and email icons, and tapped on *Recents*.

A list appeared that included Skylar Shore, Samuel Shore, Crystal Cove Inn, and Wesley Preston, the most recent call being to Skylar. I selected the icon to the right of the call to Skylar and pulled up the contact information. At the top, there was the date of a call today, and the time of the call—4:02; the call I'd overheard after she'd shown Flora and Faith her boxed-set puzzle; the call I suspected her husband had ended abruptly, which made her moan with frustration.

I returned to *Recents* and viewed the details of the call to the inn. It had lasted nineteen seconds.

Next, I pressed the icon beside Samuel Shore's name. His information tab opened and detailed that Sunny had dialed him Friday morning, at the approximate time I'd run into her at the inn—9:15 a.m. The call had taken ten seconds. I recalled how upset she'd been, most likely because he'd refused to let her speak to her daughters at that time, too.

The call to Skylar Shore on Wednesday night was the vital one. It did, indeed, occur at ten p.m., as Sunny had said, but as I'd guessed, it hadn't lasted long—three minutes. I imagined Skylar rushing through the events of the day so she could ditch her mother and reach out to her friends. I also envisioned another scenario, of Samuel finding Skylar on the phone and ordering her to terminate the call.

Whatever the reason, Sunny had lied about her alibi.

Knowing time was precious and Ulysses and Sunny could return any time, I bent to replace Sunny's cell phone when I glimpsed a file folder poking from the mouth of the tote. Tossing the purse on the chair must have dislodged the contents. The folder was marked *Sunny's Crossword Puzzles*, the words contained in a hand-drawn grid, the letters intersecting through the *u* in Puzzle and the possessive *s* in the word *Sunny's*, but a paper jutting from the folder wasn't a puzzle or event program. It was a legal document with the header *Recording Requested By*.

Quickly, I scanned the hall. A few participants had returned to the room and were standing by the water station. No one was looking in my direction. I noticed folks mingling in the vestibule outside the hall, but none were Ulysses or Sunny.

Using a fingertip, I slid the paper out a tad and realized it was a petition for bankruptcy, confirming what Cinnamon had revealed to me the other day. Something was clipped to it. I dared to pull out the petition, which made a couple of newspaper articles flutter to the floor. I would retrieve them in a second and flipped to the document beneath the bankruptcy filing. It was a denial from Crystal Cove Bank for a temporary loan of twenty thousand dollars. I gawped. I couldn't imagine why Sunny would need that much money. Had the bankruptcy forced a foreclosure on her home? Had she needed the cash to kick-start her inventions? I tried to return the file folder to the tote, but it met with resistance. To make room, I peeked inside and spied a flashlight and a pair of Channellock pliers. I knew what kind of pliers they were because I owned a set. They were useful for plumbing repairs. In addition, I'd seen EMTs use them to force their way into a vehicle at a crash site. Had Sunny been mugged at one time, like Noam? Was this her defense weapon of choice?

Get going, Jenna. Enough snooping.

I scrambled to pick up the articles that had fallen to the floor and gasped. The first was an account of the elevator accident her husband had sustained. The second was a picture of her husband being sworn in as councilman. A thick red X marred his face.

Suddenly, all the details I'd learned about Sunny started populating an imaginary crossword grid in my mind. *Lies*, about the duration of the phone call to her daughters. *Hedged*, the way Sunny had dodged questions about her husband. *Estrangement*—she'd sidestepped that topic, too. *No shoes*, the quick aside about how her children wouldn't have any if Wesley didn't pay up.

Mentally, the words *Inventions* crossed *Bankruptcy* at the *t* and the fact that she'd desperately needed *money* intersected at the *y*.

I flashed on the truncated phone call to her girls on Wednesday night. That must have made her angry. Did that fury foment into holding Wesley responsible for all of the problems in her life—the broken marriage, the custody battle, the lack of success in her business? Had that rage caused her to lash out and kill him? As for the Channellock pliers, carrying them in her purse made sense. After I'd chatted with her at the inn, she must have seen me as a threat, fetched them from her car, and cut my brake line, hoping I'd die, taking any suspicions I had to the grave.

Eager to put as much distance as I could between the tote and me, I raced toward the exit. At the same time, Sunny and Ulysses were reentering the hall. My shoulder brushed hers as I passed. The contact made me shiver.

"No ice cream?" I asked, hoping my voice wasn't shaking as much as my insides were.

"No," she said. "They were all out by the time we made it to the front of the line."

"I bet you could order some from room service."

"Good idea."

"Have a restful night."

"You, too."

I darted into the vestibule and veered right into the hallway of lockers. In the shadows, I dialed Cinnamon. A locker was ajar. Inside, I made out a writing tablet, a couple of pencils, and a set of keys hooked to a lanyard. I eased the door shut, hoping the owner of the keys wouldn't return during my conversation. Cinnamon's number rang once. Twice.

The hall's lights flickered. A voice over a loudspeaker announced it was time to exit the building. I heard a litany of "Good night" and "See you tomorrow" from people in the vestibule. The doors leading to the plaza opened and shut. Opened and shut.

Finally, I reached Cinnamon's voicemail.

Chapter 29

Cleverness: cunning, ingenuity, shrewdness

In speedy fashion, I conveyed what I'd found out about Sunny—the official bankruptcy document, the article with the X-mark on her husband's face, the denial for a loan, the duration of her call to her daughter on the night of the murder, and the deep-seated bitterness she'd harbored for Wesley. I explained that Sunny was at the Center, but I didn't know how long she'd be here because the building was closing up for the night.

All of a sudden, the lights went out completely. A woman cried out. A man assured her everything was fine. More exit doors opened and swung shut.

I turned to leave, fumbling with my cell phone to swipe the flashlight app, when a figure rounded the corner. It was Sunny. Without Ulysses.

"There you are," she said.

It was dark, but there was enough ambient light to make out her features.

I pressed a hand to my chest. "Oh, you startled me."

"Why are you here?" Her voice held an edge. "I thought you'd have left."

"I put a couple of things in a locker for safekeeping." I patted my purse. "Why are you walking around in the dark?"

She cocked her head. "I like the dark. You?"

"I couldn't get the darned flashlight app on my cell phone to turn on." I raised my cell phone and laughed, but I sounded tense. "I swiped and swiped." I demonstrated, and this time the beam illuminated. I aimed it at Sunny's face. She looked ghoulish, her mouth grim and gaze fierce.

"Why did you stick around so long tonight, Jenna?" she asked. "Your aunt left with Mayor Zeller."

"I thought"—I groped for an answer—"someone might need help cleaning up."

"Try again. There's a maintenance crew to see to that."

My cell phone buzzed. Rhett had sent me a text: *Where are you?*

"I've got to go, Sunny." I displayed the text. "My husband is a worrywart."

I tried to move past her, but she blocked me, and I caught the glint of something in her hand. A silver ballpoint pen. "Getting ready to create a new puzzle?" I asked, doing my best to make my voice sound light and friendly. "Hey, I know, you could create another foodie puzzle about techniques, with words like *emulsify*, *cream, combine,* and *shaken but not stirred.*"

She sniffed. "I don't like you, Jenna."

"I'm sorry to hear that. I like you."

"You researched me."

"No."

"Yes. I saw your musings on Cookbook Nook notepaper. I was particularly interested in your thoughts about me."

Shoot. She'd found the notes I thought I'd lost.

"And just now," she went on, "you peeked at the stuff in my tote, didn't you?"

I widened my eyes.

"Admit it. The documents I'd stored in here"—she patted the bag—"were in disarray when I returned, and my cell phone was open to Contacts. My daughter's contact, to be exact. I know I didn't click on it recently, so it must have been you."

"You called her earlier," I said. "I'd wager you didn't close the app."

"What do you think you discovered?" Her gaze turned feral.

"I don't know what you're talking about." I raised my cell phone again. "And I really do have to go."

"Don't move!" Sunny yanked off the top of the pen to reveal a knife similar to the one Noam kept in his jacket pocket, but hers looked sharper and much more lethal.

I gasped and accidentally dropped my cell phone on the floor. I bent to reach for it.

"Uh-uh." She kicked it to one side. It slammed into the base of a locker. "Stand up."

I didn't have anything in my purse to defend myself, and even if I did, I couldn't have retrieved it. The strap was bracing the purse tightly to my chest. I saw my cell phone light up. Rhett had sent another text message. Would he be concerned when I didn't respond? Would he call 911? Would he ping my location? We'd both uploaded *find my spouse's phone* apps.

"I repeat, Jenna, what do you think you learned?"

"About?"

"About me. About my kids. About my life."

I heard someone locking an exterior door. Then a code pinged. Was it the night watchman setting the security alarm? If only he'd come back inside. Didn't he realize I was being held against my will?

"Talk, Jenna."

There was no sense toying with her. She appeared resolute. "You and Wesley argued Wednesday night about him paying you," I said. "He put you off again. That made you angry."

"So angry I decided to take a walk. Create some puzzles. Do some research. Anything to occupy my mind. Go on."

"You tried calling your daughters, but your husband—your ex-husband . . ." I paused. "I saw an article about your divorce. I'm guessing he ended the call to your daughters prematurely, and that irritated you."

She grumbled. "He's a jerk."

"I think you saw Wesley on the inn's grounds, outfitted for his nocturnal birding adventure, and something inside you snapped. *He* was the cause of the downturn in your life. *He* was the reason you had to declare bankruptcy. *He* was why your husband didn't respect you any longer, and why you lost custody of your kids."

"Wesley deserved to die." The venom in her tone rattled me.

"You followed him to the trail that night to have it out with him."

"I went to beg him for the money I was due so I could get my kids back. But you know what he said when I caught up to him on the trail? Not a chance, Baby cakes! *Baby cakes!* What kind of troglodyte was he?" She thrust the knife at me.

I reeled backward and slammed into a locker. The metallic sound was deafening.

She stepped toward me. "He was so cruel. He said I didn't have an ounce of talent. He said I should go back to solving computer equations. The world of crosswords was dead to me. He . . ." The hand holding the knife started to tremble.

"Sunny, I'm sure if you tell the police how cruel he was and that you struck him in self-defense—"

"It wasn't self-defense. He didn't try to hurt me with anything other than his words. He . . ." She growled. "He thought he was the mighty be-all and end-all of crosswords, of cleverness, of wit. *Wit* . . ." She repeated, dragging the word out and dentalizing the *t*. "Poor Ulysses, handing over puzzle after puzzle, not realizing how wicked Wesley was. No one mattered to him. Not your aunt. Not Noam or his publisher. He loathed everyone.

"I sprinted ahead on the trail, knowing how he'd descend. He was so predictable, always choosing a full loop and never doubling back, saying that way he could see every bird that was out there. What a bunch of malarky. I ran ahead and lay in wait. When he drew near, I leaped out and slit his throat with this." She hoisted the knife triumphantly. "'Ah, yes, dear Wesley,' I said as he dropped to the ground, 'the pen is mightier than the sword.'"

"How did you cover up the evidence like your shoe prints and your DNA?" I glanced past her wondering if Cinnamon had received my message. If she showed up, would she think, with the lights off, that Sunny had returned to the inn?

"That was a touch of brilliance on my part," Sunny said. "When Wesley fell, I spotted his Swiss Army knife jutting from his pocket. I used it to cut a branch—mine wouldn't do the trick; it's lethal but not sturdy—and then I swept the area all the way up and down the trail. Wind was kicking up debris everywhere, too, which helped. When I got to the trailhead, I cleaned myself up. I carry wipes in my tote."

"So you said at Latte Luck when we ran into each other. And hand sanitizer and tissues."

"Aren't you the ace student?" Her lips drew thin. "Then you'll remember I also carry a change of clothes—"

"Because you never know when you'll have a job interview."

"I changed and drove to the north end of town. I threw my bloody clothes and Wesley's knife into a construction workers' garbage bin, and then I sped back to the inn, and made sure staff and guests saw me hanging around in case someone, like you, put two and two together and wanted to question my alibi. It was brilliant. *I* was brilliant."

She was right. Ginny's account of seeing her sitting in her car, engine off, would not prove she'd gone anywhere. I said, "Let's call the police and explain that you were crazed. You'll get a light sentence. I'll vouch—"

"No!" She gazed at me like a bird inspecting a pitiful worm. "I can't go to jail. My girls need me. Their father can't raise them. He's as bad as Wesley. No, he's worse."

"Is that why you marked his face with a red X? Is he your next victim?"

She cackled, and I realized she was teetering on the brink of insanity. "When I get back to Santa Barbara, I have plans."

"You'll stage another elevator accident?"

"I never did that. He lied!" She lunged at me.

I dodged left.

She swaggered toward me, brandishing the penknife. "One slice, Jenna. That's all it takes. A horizontal slit across the throat will not only sever the jugular vein but will also cut the trachea and ligaments that control the movement of your head."

Bile rose up my throat. My neck muscles tensed. My knees wobbled. My sore leg ached with a vengeance. But I refused to buckle.

She grinned. "I researched the technique. I'm an ace researcher."

Think, Jenna. I peeked right, searching for something I could use to fend off her attack. Would any of the items in the locker that I'd closed be of use? Which locker was it? The third or the second?

"Sunny, tell me about your girls," I said, hoping to stall her. "What does Sloane like to do?"

"You want to chat? Honestly?" A small titter escaped her lips. "You know what? I do like you, Jenna. You're curious, like me. And intelligent, also like me. But you're not as clever. Don't get me wrong. That's not to say you aren't sharp. I've seen you with customers. You're quick on your feet. And you listen."

"I'm listening now, Sunny. I hear you. I'll help you with your defense. I know what Wesley did to you. My aunt will back you up, too. She and Wesley had a lifelong feud going. She told me it was all in fun, but given what you've told me, I can see now that he was a vile man."

The corners of her mouth twitched. "What's a ten-letter word for vile? *Despicable.* What's a nine-letter word? *Abhorrent, abominable, loathsome.*"

"He didn't deserve someone like you helping him." The locker had to be the closer one, I decided. I inched in that direction. "He was ungrateful."

"Thankless, churlish, coarse." For each word, she ticked the air with the tip of her knife. "Ill-bred, crass, boorish."

Now! I tugged the locker handle. The door opened. I reached inside, clasped the set of keys hooked to the lanyard, and whipped the lanyard like a lasso at the knife. The keys whacked the knife's blade. Sunny lost her grip. The knife flew to the ground. I sprang for it, wincing from the pain that shot through my leg.

Sunny dove for the knife, too, and landed on my back. From behind, she scratched and clawed my face. She poked my eyes. She screamed obscenities. I yowled but persisted and grabbed hold of the knife. With a buck worthy of a bronco, I hurled her off of me and whirled around, knife aimed. "Don't move."

Sunny gasped and sank to the floor, her back sliding down the lockers. She pulled her knees to her chest. "Don't hurt me, please."

"I won't, but stay put."

"I can't go to jail, Jenna." She lowered her head and spoke into her knees. "Please don't make me. My daughters need me." Her shoulders heaved as she cried.

Keeping the knife trained on her, I retrieved my cell phone and dialed 911, quickly telling the responder the situation and our location.

In less than a minute, I heard the Center's alarm system deactivate and the slapping of footsteps on the marble floor. Cinnamon and Appleby raced into the hallway followed by a security guard.

Cinnamon pried the knife from my hand as Appleby helped Sunny to a stand.

"Are you okay, Jenna?" Cinnamon asked.

"I didn't go off half-cocked."

"But you didn't go prepared, either, did you?"

"I'm not going to pack heat, if that's what you mean."

She smirked and slung an arm around me. "Good to know."

Chapter 30

Solution: (noun) key, explanation, resolution; (noun) mixture, liquid, cocktail

Cinnamon applied salve to my face wounds and studied my eyes, saying she couldn't detect any scratches on the iris. I told her about the clothing and other evidence that Sunny had dumped in a construction garbage bin, and she assured me her team would search for it. After debriefing me and declaring me healthy, she asked if I needed a lift home. I said I was fine to drive and happy to be alive.

Rook and Tigger charged me as I entered the house, Tigger batting me with his tail and Rook nudging me with his nose. I petted both animals and stood to face Rhett, who drew me into a long embrace. He stroked my hair and cooed sweet words. How I treasured listening to the steady beat of his heart. After a long moment, I broke free, and he guided me to the kitchen, where he had a glass of brandy waiting.

"Something to settle your nerves," he said.

I sat on the stool at the island, sipped the drink, and pushed it away.

"Want me to dress those scratches?" he asked.

"No. I'm okay. Really."

"What were you thinking?"

"Don't go all Cinnamon-like on me. I was being careful." At least I'd thought I was at the time.

He perched on the other stool and ran a finger gently down my arm. "Why didn't you go outside where there were lots of people?"

"I wanted to have privacy when speaking to Cinnamon."

"Why didn't you call me when she didn't answer?"

"Because I'd expected her to drop everything and magically appear. I . . ." I swung my knees around to face him and cupped his face with my hands.

"When you didn't text me back—"

"I'm sorry I worried you. I couldn't reply. I was at Sunny's mercy. She was pointing a knife at me." A sob escaped my lips.

He petted my hair. "How did you figure out the solution?"

"I thought about the timeline we put together during dinner and Sunny's call to her girls. She'd been shut down by her husband a couple of times. I thought, what if he'd curtailed the call Wednesday night, too? If so, she didn't have an alibi. Then, as I discovered clues in her tote, everything started to fit together like a puzzle. Her motive. Her opportunity."

The doorbell rang.

"That'll be my aunt," I said.

Rhett answered and led her into the kitchen.

"Oh, dear." Aunt Vera swept me into a hug. "It's all my fault. If only . . ."

I wriggled from her grasp. "It's not your fault."

"Wesley was my friend. I invited him here. I brought all the angst and animosity of those in his orbit to our beautiful town. I had no idea he was such a despicable man."

"It's not like you followed his every move these past forty years," I said.

"And Sunny."

"As for her," I said, "you couldn't possibly have known how much she hated him. She was a fragile being, and he pushed her over the edge."

Rhett made us all a cup of tea, and we sat at the kitchen table nursing them until my aunt couldn't stifle her yawns.

"Go home," I coaxed. "I'm fine."

"You don't have to come to the shop in the morning."

"Yes, I do. Work will be my sanity. See you then." I bussed her cheek and saw her to the door.

Rhett drew me into another embrace and guided me to the bedroom. "Take a shower. When you come out, I'll read you a bedtime story."

I pecked his cheek. "How did I get so lucky?"

"Fate."

• • •

In the morning, I felt better. After a barefoot walk on the sand with Rook on a leash and Tigger in his carry sack, I threw on a white sweater, mocha-colored capris, and sandals, and ate the parmesan cheese omelet Rhett had prepared.

"Will I see you later at the cruciverbalist competition?" I asked my sweet husband as I headed to the door with Tigger.

"I wouldn't miss it."

Bailey arrived at the shop before me. So did Gran. My aunt had alerted them about last night's encounter. Both wanted details.

Katie breezed in a half hour later with a tray filled with chocolate banana brownies. "The scoop," she said. "The whole story. I have time. Reynaldo is holding down the fort at the café." She carried the tray to the children's table and plopped onto a stool.

How could I refuse such an invitation? I ate a brownie as I related the story.

When my father and Lola marched into the shop, I knew I'd get an earful, but I didn't care. Their concern made me feel loved and appreciated.

As the eleven o'clock church bells were chiming outside—I'd propped the door open to let in the delicious breeze—attendees for the tournament trooped into the shop. Each seemed eager to pick up a memento. I wasn't sure if they were making purchases because I'd survived Sunny's assault or because a crossword-themed apron, cookie jar, or salt shaker would remind them of a most unusual week. Whatever the reason, Bailey was continually crooning *Cha-ching*.

At one p.m., I headed to the Center with my aunt. Rhett planned to meet me there later on.

Appleby was waiting in the plaza. Casual in jeans and a polo shirt, he greeted me and took hold of my aunt's arm. "Sorry I got in so late last night," he murmured.

She smiled. "With good reason."

Cinnamon had cleared him to rejoin the investigation.

"Let me buy you a fresh-squeezed lemonade," he said to my aunt.

They sauntered away, and I strolled inside. The vestibule was packed with excited attendees. The convention hall was equally as busy. The noise was deafening.

Ulysses met me near the water station. "I heard what happened," he said. "I'm so sorry I left without checking on you."

"How would you have known?" I smiled. "I feel badly for

Sunny." And I did. She'd terrorized me, but because of Wesley Preston, she'd suffered.

"By the way," Ulysses went on, "I hold no grudge against you for telling the police you weren't sure about me or my alibi."

I winced, wishing I didn't have a tendency to suspect good people of horrible crimes. My one solace was I was certain Cinnamon made the same mistake . . . occasionally.

"In fact, I should thank you. See, I met some terrific individuals at the precinct, officers as well as do-gooder citizens who want to help me with the at-risk kids. Plus, one guy's wife is a baker and cat lover and wants to partner with me in my new business venture."

"Gee, that's great. Good luck with this afternoon's event."

"Thanks."

He moseyed off to meet Eva Wainwright, who'd dressed in a stunning black-and-white dress and two-toned heels. When she kissed Ulysses warmly on each cheek, I wondered if, now that Wesley was dead and Ulysses was exonerated, she might woo him to be her prized cruciverbalist, and, if Ulysses got his wish, love might blossom after all.

"Ladies and gentlemen." Z.Z. stood center stage, speaking into the microphone. She thanked everyone for attending, and then without further ado, announced the overall winner. "Noam Dixon, please come up and receive your trophy and reward."

He was standing with Yvette at the rear of the room, his outfit clean and pressed, his eyes bright. Yvette, in another stylish getup, seemed completely in her element, her hair loose around her shoulders, a professional camera hanging on a strap around her neck.

"C'mon, Noam, don't be shy," Z.Z. said.

Noam scuffed a foot, pecked Yvette on the cheek, and moseyed to the stage. A professor by trade, I was surprised by how stilted his acceptance speech was, as if he hadn't believed he'd win and, therefore, hadn't prepared anything. He held the trophy overhead — it was a beautiful silver bowl affixed to a burlwood box with silver plaque — and cheers erupted from the crowd.

As he left the stage, Z.Z. said, "Okay, let's get to the grand finale. The cruciverbalist competition will start in thirty minutes. Yes, you may use puzzles you've previously created, though I doubt you've been able to properly practice for this theme. When I start the clock, each of the twenty-five competitors . . . twenty-four," she revised — murmurs of Sunny's name filtered through the room — "will have one hour to complete an original crossword puzzle. The puzzles must have at least a fifteen-by-fifteen grid, and must utilize the theme . . . wait for it" — she held up a palm — "fruits and vegetables."

Noam looked stunned. Ulysses, too.

Flora and Faith whizzed past me, Flora dressed in a white dress with black bolero jacket and Faith making a statement in sparkly black leggings, snug white top, crossword-themed sport jacket, and checkered Keds. Each was reciting a list of fruits and vegetables.

"Sweet potatoes, cantaloupes, peaches," Flora said.

"Apples, bananas, artichokes, rutabaga," Faith replied.

My mind was drumming up other words, like *produce, harvest, crops.* I suppose that went along with what I did for a living. I was regularly considering yields and bottom lines.

I glanced again at Noam and Yvette. She was taking pictures of the tournament attendees. He was saying something that was making her grin from ear to ear. On the way over, my aunt had commented that she'd always hoped Noam and Yvette would reunite. She couldn't imagine what had provoked Wesley to steal Yvette's heart years ago and then dump her like trash, but she decided to let the past and sad memories fade away.

Twenty-five minutes later, when the cruciverbalists sat at their tables and the audience took their seats, the room grew quiet. Some observers impatiently tapped their toes. Others checked their watches repeatedly. The jingle from *Jeopardy!* — a musical metaphor for the ticking of a clock — cycled silently through my mind.

An hour later, Z.Z. said, "Time's up. Put your pencils down. Jenna and Jake, if you'd collect the puzzles."

Her husband and I moved from one puzzler to the next collecting worksheets. Jake handed his stack to me, and I carried them to the stage, where my aunt, Z.Z., and Eva were sitting at the judging table.

Music piped through the speaker as we waited for the decision. Rhett arrived during that time and gave me a hug. Sotto voce, he asked what had occurred, and I filled him in.

Forty-five minutes later, the winning puzzle was chosen, created by, of all people, Flora. She was invited to the stage to enlighten the audience about her work.

Using the microphone, she said she'd designed a puzzle around salad greens, the anchor clues being *Babyarugala*, *Tendercress*, and *Bladderwrack*.

"Bladderwrack," Rhett chuckled. "What the heck is that?"

"Got me."

We weren't the only ones in the crowd who didn't know the word.

When asked, Flora explained that it was a brown seaweed that grew in the Baltic Sea, contained alginic acid, and was a kind of dietary fiber.

"I bet dimes to donuts she didn't share those words with her sister," I said to Rhett.

He snorted.

Flora went on to add that she planned to donate half of the ten-thousand-dollar prize to a local charity that helped women and children of domestic abuse. That earned her respectable applause from the attendees.

At four forty-five, Z.Z. dismissed the crowd for a short break.

At five, we reassembled, and my aunt welcomed everyone to Wesley's memorial. How could they not go through with it, she'd said to me privately, once they'd put it on the schedule?

On the screen above the stage, Z.Z. clicked through many of Wesley's unique puzzles. Eva made a speech, as did my aunt, each honoring Wesley for the enduring cleverness of his puzzles and the inspiration he provided to cruciverbalists around the globe.

The memorial was touching. A few attendees cried.

Those in the know—me, Rhett, my aunt, Appleby, Ulysses, Noam, Yvette, and Eva—remained dry-eyed.

Recipes

Banana-Date Coffee Cake + Gluten-free Version
Caramel Pumpkin Muffins with Caramel Sauce + Gluten-free
Version
Choco-Monkey Brownies + Gluten-free Version
Coffee Crunch Cookies + Gluten-free Version
Brie-Leek Appetizers
Crispy Salmon Appetizers
Lobster Bisque
Mini Spinach Quiches
Mum's the Word's Mini Chicken Pot Pies
Pumpkin Cardamom Tart
Zucchini Patties with Dill Sauce

Banana-Date Coffee Cake
(Yield: 9–12 slices)

From Katie:

This cake is a hit with all of the kitchen staff. Reynaldo even asked how something so simple could taste so scrumptious. Be sure to soak the dates. That makes all the difference. If you're not a date person, try raisins. Enjoy!

For the cake:
⅔ cup butter, melted
1 cup white sugar
1 teaspoon vanilla
2 large eggs
1 cup cream cheese
1 teaspoon cider vinegar
2 cups flour
1 teaspoon baking powder
1 teaspoon baking soda
½ teaspoon salt

For the filling:
½ cup chopped dates, pre-soaked
¼ cup cacao nibs, if desired
½ cup brown sugar
1 teaspoon cinnamon
2 bananas, peeled and sliced

For the topping:
¼ cup brown sugar
1 teaspoon cinnamon

Preheat oven to 350 degrees. Grease a 9x9 pan or line with parchment paper.

Meanwhile, soak the chopped dates for the filling in ½ cup hot water and set aside.

For the cake batter: In a large bowl, mix melted butter, sugar, and vanilla. Add eggs and beat on low. Continuing to beat on low, add cream cheese and vinegar. Then add the flour, baking powder, baking soda, and salt, and stir until thoroughly mixed. Don't overmix.

For the filling: drain the dates. In a small bowl, mix dates, cacao nibs (if desired), brown sugar, and cinnamon. Slice the bananas.

Spoon half of the batter into prepared pan. Pat down with your fingers. Layer the bananas on top of the batter and sprinkle all of the date-sugar filling on top of the bananas. Spread the rest of the batter over the filling. Again, pat down with your fingers.

Mix the topping ingredients and sprinkle topping all over the coffee cake.

Bake for 30–35 minutes, until nicely browned.

Let cool for 20 minutes and remove from the pan. Serve warm or room temperature.

Banana-Date Coffee Cake
Gluten-free version
(Yield: 9–12 slices)

For the cake:
⅔ cup butter, melted
1 cup white sugar
1 teaspoon vanilla
2 large eggs
1 cup cream cheese
1 teaspoon cider vinegar
2 cups gluten-free flour
2 tablespoons whey powder
2 teaspoons baking powder
1 teaspoon baking soda
½ teaspoon salt
½ teaspoon xanthan gum

For the filling:
½ cup chopped dates, pre-soaked
¼ cup cacao nibs, if desired
½ cup brown sugar
1 teaspoon cinnamon
2 bananas, peeled and sliced

For the topping:
¼ cup brown sugar
1 teaspoon cinnamon

Preheat oven to 350 degrees. Grease a 9x9 pan or line with parchment paper.

Meanwhile, soak the chopped dates for the filling in ½ cup hot water and set aside.

For the cake batter: In a large bowl, mix melted butter, sugar, and vanilla. Add eggs and beat on low. Continuing to beat on low, add cream cheese and vinegar. Then add the gluten-free flour, whey powder, baking powder, baking soda, salt, and xanthan gum, and stir until thoroughly mixed.

For the filling: drain the dates. In a small bowl, mix dates, cacao nibs (if desired), brown sugar, and cinnamon. Slice the bananas.

Spoon half of the batter into prepared pan. Pat down with your fingers. Layer all of the bananas on top of the batter and sprinkle the date-sugar mixture on top of the bananas. Spread the rest of the batter over the filling. Again, pat down with your fingers.

Mix the topping ingredients and sprinkle topping all over the coffee cake.

Bake for 30–35 minutes, until nicely browned.

Let cool for 20 minutes and remove from the pan. Serve warm or room temperature.

Caramel Pumpkin Muffins
(Yield: 12–16 cupcakes)

From Jenna:

After inhaling the aroma of these muffins at Latte Luck, I knew I had to try my hand at them. I went in and begged for the recipe. It didn't hurt that I'd brought two of Katie's recipe cards in exchange. We swapped cards, and I'm so happy we did. I love the caramel brushed on top of these little goodies. BTW, you can make your own caramel sauce, see recipe below – so easy – but a store-bought sauce is fine. However, make sure you don't get caramel "sundae" syrup. It's a different consistency.

2 cups flour
½ cup sugar
1 teaspoon baking powder
½ teaspoon salt
¼ teaspoon baking soda
2 large eggs
¼ cup caramel sauce
½ cup pumpkin puree
½ cup sour cream
1 stick melted butter
¼ cup light brown sugar
more caramel for brushing on top of the muffins, about 2 tablespoons, plus water, if necessary

Preheat oven to 350 degrees F. Set 12–16 cupcake liners in cupcake pan.

In a small bowl, mix the flour, sugar, baking powder, salt, and baking soda.

In the mixing bowl of a standing mixer, mix the eggs, caramel sauce, pumpkin puree, sour cream, melted butter, and brown sugar.

Add in the dry ingredients and mix well.

Pour the mixture into 12–16 cupcake liners, about ⅔ full. Bake for 24–27 minutes.

Remove from oven and brush with more caramel sauce. If the sauce looks too thick, add a tablespoon of water, stir, and then brush

Caramel Pumpkin Muffins
Gluten-free version
(Yield: 12–16 cupcakes)

2 cups gluten-free flour (I prefer a mixture of sweet rice flour and tapioca flour)
1 tablespoon whey powder
½ teaspoon xanthan gum
½ cup sugar
1 teaspoon baking powder
½ teaspoon salt
¼ teaspoon baking soda
2 large eggs
¼ cup caramel sauce
½ cup pumpkin puree
½ cup sour cream
1 stick melted butter
¼ cup light brown sugar
more caramel for brushing on top of the muffins, about 2 tablespoons, plus water, if necessary

Preheat oven to 350 degrees F. Set 12–16 cupcake liners in cupcake pan.

In a small bowl, mix the gluten-free flour, whey powder, xanthan gum, sugar, baking powder, salt, and baking soda.

In the mixing bowl of a standing mixer, mix the eggs, caramel sauce, pumpkin puree, sour cream, melted butter, and brown sugar.

Add in the dry ingredients and mix well.

Pour the mixture into 12–16 cupcake liners, about ⅔ full. Bake for 24–27 minutes.

Remove from oven and brush with more caramel sauce. If the sauce looks too thick, add a tablespoon of water, stir, and then brush

Caramel Sauce
From scratch
(Yield: 1 cup)

1 cup brown sugar
½ cup half-and-half
4 tablespoons butter
Pinch of salt
1 tablespoon vanilla extract

Mix the brown sugar, half-and-half, butter and salt in a saucepan over medium-low heat. Cook while whisking gently for 5–7 minutes. Add the vanilla and cook another minute to thicken.

Turn off the heat, cool slightly, and pour the sauce into a jar with a tight lid. Refrigerate until cold.

Choco-Monkey Brownies
Gluten-free version; see below for regular flour version note
(Yield: 9–16 brownies)

From Katie:

There's nothing like a moist brownie to bring a smile to someone's face. In particular, Jenna's. She hasn't met a brownie she doesn't like. I continue to test out recipes to keep her on her toes. I remember when we were kids how much she'd liked frozen chocolate bananas, so I created this recipe as a tribute to those days.

1¾ cup milk chocolate *or* dark chocolate morsels, divided
1 cup gluten-free flour
¾ teaspoon baking powder
¼ teaspoon xanthan gum
1½ teaspoons whey powder
½ teaspoon salt
1 cup light brown sugar, packed
½ stick unsalted butter, softened
2 large eggs
1 teaspoon vanilla extract
2 medium-sized ripe bananas, quartered lengthwise and chopped

Preheat oven to 350 degrees F. Grease or use parchment paper in a 9-inch-square baking pan.

In a small bowl, microwave 1 cup of the chocolate morsels on medium for about 45 seconds. Stir. If necessary, zap again 10–15 seconds, stirring until smooth. If using dark chocolate, you might need to add a teaspoon or two of water. Cool to room temperature.

In a small bowl, combine gluten-free flour, baking powder, xanthan gum, whey powder, and salt.

In a medium bowl, beat the light brown sugar, butter, eggs, and vanilla extract until creamy. Beat in the melted chocolate. Gradually beat in the gluten-free flour mixture. Stir in the bananas and remaining ¾ cup morsels. Spread mixture into the prepared baking pan.

Bake for 40–45 minutes until a toothpick inserted comes out clean. Cool completely on a wire rack. Cut into 9–16 squares. Store in an airtight container. I like to wrap the individual squares in plastic wrap so that they stay moister. Wrapping individually really helps with gluten-free baked goods.

If you'd like to make this using regular flour, substitute flour for the gluten-free flour and omit the xanthan gum and whey powder.

Coffee Crunch Cookies
(Yield: 24–30 cookies)

From Jenna:

I received this recipe from Latte Luck Café when I finished the crossword puzzle of the day and was treated with the cookies as my reward. They are delicious, and the recipe is so easy. Okay, it's not five ingredients, but it is two six-ingredient recipes merged into one, if you look at the butter to vanilla extract ingredients as one "recipe," and the flour to baking powder ingredients as the other. Easy-peasy. I love the flavor of coffee in this. If you want a deeper flavor, use espresso beans.

⅓ cup butter, room temperature
½ cup sugar
½ cup light brown sugar
1 large egg
1 tablespoon milk
1 teaspoon vanilla extract
1½ cups flour
2 tablespoons ground coffee
¼ teaspoon cinnamon
¼ teaspoon salt
¼ teaspoon baking soda
¼ teaspoon baking powder

Preheat oven to 400 degrees F. Line a baking sheet with parchment paper.

In a large bowl, cream together butter, sugar, and light brown sugar. Beat in egg, milk, and vanilla.

In a small bowl, whisk together flour, ground coffee, cinnamon, salt, baking soda, and baking powder. Stir the flour mixture into the butter mixture.

Drop dough by rounded, walnut-sized spoonfuls on the baking sheet. These do spread so don't put them too close, about 12 cookies per baking sheet.*

Bake until cookies are golden at the edges, about 8–10 minutes.

Cool on baking sheet for 5 minutes and then transfer to a wire rack to cool completely.

*Use a new piece of parchment paper for each batch, if necessary.

Coffee Crunch Cookies
Gluten-free version
(Yield: 24–30 cookies)

⅓ cup butter, room temperature
½ cup sugar
½ cup light brown sugar
1 large egg
1 tablespoon milk
1 teaspoon vanilla extract
1½ cups gluten-free flour (I like a mixture of sweet rice flour and tapioca starch)
¼ teaspoon xanthan gum
2 tablespoons ground coffee
¼ teaspoon cinnamon
¼ teaspoon salt
¼ teaspoon baking soda
¼ teaspoon baking powder

Preheat oven to 400 degrees F. Line a baking sheet with parchment paper.

In a large bowl, cream together butter, sugar, and light brown sugar. Beat in egg, milk, and vanilla.

In a small bowl, whisk together gluten-free flour, xanthan gum, ground coffee, cinnamon, salt, baking soda, and baking powder. Stir the flour mixture into the butter mixture.

Drop dough by rounded, walnut-sized spoonfuls on the baking sheet. These do spread so don't put them too close, about 12 cookies per baking sheet.*

Bake until cookies are golden at the edges, about 8–10 minutes.

Cool on baking sheet for 5 minutes and then transfer to a wire rack to cool completely.

*Use a new piece of parchment paper for each batch, if necessary.x

Brie-Leek Appetizers
(Yield: 12 portions)

From Rhett:

These are zesty appetizers that go down in one easy, mouthwatering bite. They are sure to be a hit at any party. By the way, Jenna guessed right. The secret ingredient is nutmeg.

1 medium leek, whites only, finely chopped
3 tablespoons butter
1 garlic clove, minced
½ cup heavy whipping cream
¼ teaspoon salt
¼ teaspoon pepper
dash of nutmeg
1 package miniature phyllo tart shells or pie shells, regular or gluten-free
2 ounces Brie, rind removed
parsley for garnish, if desired

Heat oven to 350 degrees F. Line a baking sheet with parchment paper.

In a small skillet, sauté the chopped leek in butter about 1 minute. Add the garlic and cook 1 more minute. Stir in the cream, salt, pepper, and nutmeg. Cook about 2 minutes.

Place tart shells or pie shells on the baking sheet. Slice the brie cheese into 12 pieces, placing 1 piece in each tart shell. Top each with 1½ teaspoons of the leek mixture.

Bake for 6–8 minutes. Remove from oven and top with parsley for garnish, if desired.

Crispy Salmon Appetizers
(Yield: 12–16 appetizers)

From Katie:

I adore these appetizers. They are one of my all-time favorites. One of the challenges of cooking with oil or butter is that it splatters when it reaches a certain temperature, and that temperature is hot! So wear potholders and stand back when flipping these morsels of deliciousness. Also, I love the flavor of prosciutto, and when it's wrapped around a good-sized chunk of salmon and sautéed, it's exquisite, but be careful when seasoning with salt. The prosciutto is already salty. If desired, omit the salt from the recipe and add later, if you think you need it. This recipe would also work nicely as a side dish, serving the salmon bites on a piece of butter lettuce.

1 pound salmon filets, no skin
¼ pound prosciutto
3 tablespoons butter
4 ounces cream cheese
1 tablespoon sour cream
3 tablespoons fresh chives, chopped finely
½ teaspoon garlic powder
⅛ teaspoon salt
¼ teaspoon ground pepper

Slice the salmon into 1x1-inch or 1x2-inch cubes and wrap with prosciutto.

Heat a large sauté pan over medium-low heat and add the butter. Place the wrapped salmon cubes in the butter. Cook for 2 minutes on one side, then flip (turn) and cook for another 2 minutes. If you want them really crispy and cooked through, cook another 2 minutes.

While the salmon is cooking, in a small bowl combine the cream cheese, sour cream, chives, garlic powder, salt, and ground pepper.

When the salmon is cooked, remove from pan and drain on paper towels. Let cool for 3 minutes. When plating, add a dollop of the cream cheese–chives mixture on top of the appetizers.

Lobster Bisque
(serves 6)

From Rhett:

This lobster bisque recipe is my mother's recipe, tweaked from her mother's recipe, which Grandmother tweaked from her mother's recipe. I love how traditions pass from one generation to the next. My mother says the balance of vegetables and garlic to tomatoes and paprika is key. Finely diced vegetables matter, too. Enjoy.

1 cup onions, finely diced
½ cup carrots, finely diced
½ cup celery, finely diced
2 garlic cloves, diced
4 cups water
2 cups dry white wine
2 cups chicken broth (use gluten-free, if necessary)
2 lobster tails
½ cup butter
¼ cup brandy
½ cup flour (*use gluten-free flour, if necessary)
1½ cups canned diced tomatoes, liquid strained
1 teaspoon paprika
1 teaspoon thyme
1 tablespoon salt
2 cups heavy cream

Finely chop the onions, carrots, celery, and garlic cloves, and set aside.

Put water, wine, and chicken broth in a deep pot and bring to a boil. Place lobster tails in the broth. Reduce heat to medium and cook uncovered for 6 minutes. Remove lobster from broth and set to the side. When cool, remove the back shell and dice the lobster meat into tiny cubes.

Meanwhile, strain broth through a sieve into a bowl and set aside.

Return pot to the stove and add the butter. Melt. Add the chopped onions, carrots, celery, and garlic. Heat for 3 minutes on medium. Stir. Add the brandy. Stir. Add the flour (or gluten-free flour). Stir until all the flour is incorporated.

Add the diced tomatoes, paprika, thyme and salt. Stir well. Add the reserved broth. Stir and bring to a boil. Cook for 25–30 minutes on medium low heat.

Remove from the heat and puree the mixture in small batches. Return to the pot. Add the lobster and cream. Heat about 3–5 minutes and serve.

Mini Spinach Quiche
(Yield: 24–30)

From Rhett:

I think quiche is the quintessential French dish. It can be made with vegetables, seafood, or meat and served warm or cold. These mouth-sized bites are perfect for entertaining. You can prepare ahead and bake right when your guests arrive. Note: these quiches will pop up during baking, but they will shrink back as they cool.

3 cups spinach, packed
1 tablespoon butter
3 eggs
¾ cup heavy whipping cream
½ cup finely shredded cheddar cheese
½ teaspoon black pepper
1 pie crust, in roll form (store-bought or homemade)

Preheat the oven to 375 degrees F. Place a mini muffin pan on top of a cookie sheet with a lip.

On a cutting board, chop the spinach into little pieces. Melt butter in a saucepan on low heat and sauté the spinach until it is soft, about 1 minute. Set aside.

In a medium-sized bowl, mix the eggs, cream, shredded cheese, and pepper. Whisk until smooth.

Unroll the pie crust on parchment paper. If it feels too thick, feel free to roll it into a thinner rectangle. Using a 2- to 2.5-inch cookie cutter, or the mouth of a small glass, cut out small circles from the dough. Keep the scraps so you can reroll them to make more circles.

Place the circles into the mini muffin pan. You can press it up the sides with your fingers.

Put a half tablespoon of spinach in each muffin cup. Pour the egg mixture into the muffin cups on top of the spinach.

Bake for 20 minutes, or until the crust is lightly brown. Remove from oven and let cool about 20 minutes before serving.

Mum's the Word Mini Chicken Pot Pies
(Yield: 12–16)

From Mum's the Word Chef:

This is perhaps the most scrumptious potpie I've ever made. The dough is flaky and buttery. The stew inside is savory and hearty. If you want to make these in advance, assemble them, cover with foil, refrigerate, and wait to bake.

1 pound skinless chicken breasts, precooked and shredded
4 cups chicken broth (gluten-free, if necessary)
½ cup butter (one stick)
1 onion, chopped
2 large carrots, peeled and cut into thin rounds
1 celery stalk, diced
1 tablespoon dried parsley
½ teaspoon dried sage
1 clove garlic, chopped fine (if desired)
1 teaspoon salt
1 teaspoon freshly ground black pepper
¼ cup cornstarch
¼ cup heavy cream
3 tablespoons white wine
1 cup frozen peas
1 recipe pastry dough (see below for regular and gluten-free dough recipes)

Precook your chicken breasts. To cook chicken breasts, wrap them in foil and pop them in the oven at 300 degrees F for 35–40 minutes. Remove from oven and let cool.

While the chicken is cooking, make pastry dough (see below) and refrigerate.

Preheat your oven to 375 degrees F.

In a 6-quart saucepan, heat the chicken broth over medium heat for 2 minutes.

Meanwhile, in a large stockpot, melt butter over medium heat. Add onions, carrots, celery, parsley, sage, and garlic. Sauté until tender, about 10 minutes. Add salt and pepper. Stir.

To the hot broth, add the cornstarch and whisk together until it thickens, about 5 minutes. Add the mixture to the vegetables. Stir in the heavy cream, white wine, chicken, and frozen peas. Bring to a boil then reduce to a simmer for 5 minutes.

With a ladle, fill 4–6 ovenproof ramekins or bowls with the filling. Place the ramekins on a baking sheet.

For the crust, you can use store-bought pastry dough, or you can make it from scratch using this recipe. The key is the butter must be as cold as possible. Note, there is a gluten-free pastry dough recipe accompanying the pumpkin cardamom tart, below, if you prefer.

Pastry Dough
(Yield: one single-pie crust)

1¼ cups sifted flour
1 teaspoon salt
6 tablespoons really cold butter
2–3 tablespoons water
1 egg beaten with 1 tablespoon water, for egg wash on pastry (see below)
kosher salt

Put flour and salt into food processor fitted with a blade. Cut in 3 tablespoons of really cold butter and pulse for 30 seconds. Cut in another 3 tablespoons of butter. Pulse again for 30 seconds. Sprinkle with 2 to 3 tablespoons water and pulse a third time, for 30 seconds.

Remove the dough from the food processor and form into a ball. Wrap with wax paper or plastic wrap. Chill the dough for 30 minutes.

Place a large piece of parchment paper on the countertop or board. Sprinkle with flour. Remove the dough from the refrigerator and remove the covering. Place the dough on top of the sprinkled flour. If desired, cover the dough with another large piece of parchment paper. This prevents the dough from sticking to the rolling pin. Roll out dough so it is ¼ inch thick.

To construct the ramekins:

Using a biscuit round or mold (or be daring and go freehand), cut out dough large enough to cover the tops of the ovenproof ramekins, leaving about ½ inch hangover.

Place each round on top of the individual bowls filled with pot pie mixture, and crimp the dough over the edge. Brush with the egg wash and, *important*, make 4 small slits on the top of each to let out steam. Sprinkle with kosher salt. Place the baking sheet with ramekins in the preheated oven. Bake for 15–20 minutes. Remove from the oven and serve hot.

Pumpkin Cardamom Tart
(Yield: 6–8 slices)

From Katie:

I love the flavor of cardamom. It adds a nice touch, sweeter than cumin and more citrusy than fennel, giving this tart an autumn twist. You may use a store-bought pie crust or homemade crust. I'm providing a terrific gluten-free pie dough recipe. Making a crust with gluten-free ingredients can be tricky. The key is using parchment paper or plastic wrap and chilling the dough. This recipe provides a large amount of dough so you will have enough to decorate with pastry leaves and such, too. For the recipe for regular pie dough, see the Mum's the Word's Mini Chicken Pot Pies recipe, above. If you use that recipe, you might want to make 1½ recipes so you'll have enough for the leaf decorations – see the leaf decoration instructions below.

For the tart:

2 cups pumpkin
¾ cup brown sugar
⅔ cup heavy cream
3 large eggs
1 teaspoon ground cardamom
1 teaspoon ground ginger
½ teaspoon ground nutmeg
¼ teaspoon salt

For the pastry dough:
(Gluten-free version)

3¾ tablespoons ice water
2¼ tablespoons sour cream
2¼ teaspoons rice vinegar
1 cup sweet rice flour
1 cup tapioca starch
1 tablespoon whey powder
½ teaspoon xanthan gum

2¼ teaspoons sugar
¾ teaspoon salt
12 tablespoons unsalted butter, cut into small pieces and frozen for
10 minutes

Make the pie crust or tart crust first.

Preheat the oven to 350 degrees F.

In a small bowl, combine the ice water, sour cream, and vinegar. Set
aside.

In a food processor, blend the sweet rice flour, tapioca starch, whey
powder, xanthan gum, sugar, and salt. Add the butter and pulse
until the mixture looks like cornmeal, about 10 pulses.

Pour half of the sour cream mixture into the flour mixture and pulse
about 3 times. Pour the remaining sour cream mixture over the flour
mixture and pulse until dough comes together, about 6–10 times.

Because gluten-free pie dough is soft, it requires patience. You can't
just pick it up and fit it into the pie plate or tart pan. It works best if
you chill the dough for about thirty minutes.

After chilling, roll the dough between two pieces of parchment
paper or plastic wrap. Remove the top sheet and put the pie plate or
tart plate upside down on the dough. Gripping the parchment paper
or plastic wrap, flip the plate over and now ease the dough into the
plate by working around the edge. Trim as you would a regular pie
dough, leaving a slight overhang, if using a pie plate, or a smooth
edge, if using a tart pan. Crimp as desired.

If you need to prebake the shell, as you do for this recipe, set pie
plate in oven and bake the crust for 15 minutes until a light golden
brown.

For a fully baked pie shell, bake 15–20 minutes.

For the pie filling:

Pour pumpkin, brown sugar, heavy cream, eggs, cardamom, ginger, nutmeg, and salt into the bowl of a stand mixer and mix until smooth. Pour the mixture into the prebaked pie crust or tart shell.

Bake for 40–45 minutes, until center barely jiggles. Remove from oven and let cool.

For the leaf decorations:

Meanwhile, bake the leaves for decoration, if desired. With remaining pie dough scraps, roll out on parchment paper or plastic wrap, and, if you have them, use leaf-shaped cookie cutters to make 8–10 leaves for decoration. Place on a baking sheet, brush with egg white, and bake at 350 degrees F for 15 minutes, until golden brown. Remove from oven and cool. Add to the pie when the pie has cooled.

Zucchini Patties with Dill Dip
(Yield: 20–24)

From Jenna:

I mastered these in a matter of minutes. The trick was to make sure the oil was hot enough to cook them fast. They turn a lovely brown on both sides. Remember to let them cool slightly; otherwise, you could scorch your mouth. Another tip: if for some reason you don't have seasoned panko, then add an extra teaspoon of the seafood seasoning to regular panko. Katie turned me on to Old Bay Seasoning, a delicious blend of eighteen spices.

2 tablespoons minced fresh dill, more for adorning
1 teaspoon lemon juice
¼ teaspoon pepper
¼ teaspoon salt
½ cup sour cream
2½ cups shredded zucchini
¼ cup finely chopped onion
1 cup seasoned panko (you may use gluten-free panko)
1 teaspoon seafood seasoning
¼ teaspoon garlic powder
1 large egg, lightly beaten
2 tablespoons butter, melted
¼ cup all-purpose flour (you may use gluten-free flour)
½ cup canola oil

For the dip:

In a small bowl, combine the minced dill, lemon juice, pepper, salt, and sour cream. Cover with plastic wrap and refrigerate until serving.

For the patties:

Place zucchini in food processor with the onion and pulse about 10 times to shred. Put the vegetables in a colander to drain; squeeze using a spatula to remove excess liquid. Pat dry with paper towels; set aside.

In a large bowl, combine the panko (gluten-free panko is fine), seafood seasoning, and garlic powder. Stir in the egg and melted butter. Add the zucchini and onion.

Place flour (or gluten-free flour) on parchment paper or in a pie tin. Shape zucchini mixture into 24 small patties and dredge with flour.

In a large skillet, heat oil over medium heat. Make sure it's hot. Now, fry patties, a few at a time, about 6–8 in the pan, until lightly browned, which takes about 3–4 minutes per side. Drain on paper towels. Let cool slightly.

Serve with the dill dip.

About the Author

Agatha Award–winning, nationally bestselling author Daryl Wood Gerber writes suspense novels as well as cozy mysteries. She is best known for her Cookbook Nook Mysteries, featuring an admitted foodie and owner of a cookbook store in Crystal Cove, California, and her Fairy Garden Mysteries, featuring a fairy garden shop owner in Carmel, California. She also writes the French Bistro Mysteries, featuring a bistro owner in Napa Valley. Under the pen name Avery Aames, Daryl writes the Cheese Shop Mysteries, featuring a cheese shop owner in Providence, Ohio. Her suspense novels, including the Aspen Adams novels, *Girl on the Run,* and *Day of Secrets* have garnered solid reviews.

As a girl, Daryl considered becoming a writer, but she was dissuaded by a seventh-grade teacher. It wasn't until she was in her twenties that she had the temerity to try her hand at writing again . . . for TV and screen. Why? Because she was an actress in Hollywood. A fun tidbit for mystery buffs: Daryl co-starred on *Murder, She Wrote* as well as other TV shows. As a writer, she created the format for the popular sitcom *Out of This World.* When she moved across the country with her husband, she returned to writing what she loved to read: mysteries and suspense.

Daryl is originally from the Bay Area and graduated from Stanford University. She loves to cook, read, golf, swim, and garden. She also likes adventure and has been known to jump out of a perfectly good airplane. She adores Lake Tahoe, and she has a frisky Goldendoodle named Sparky who keeps her in line.

Visit Daryl at www.darylwoodgerber.com, and follow her on Bookbub at http://bookbub.com/authors/daryl-wood-gerber, on Goodreads at http://goodreads.com/darylwoodgerber, and on Amazon at http://bit.ly/Daryl_Wood_Gerber_page.

Ingram Content Group UK Ltd.
Milton Keynes UK
UKHW040757250423
420747UK00004B/240